>Dear Stranger,
Dearest Friend

G·K
Hall
&Co.

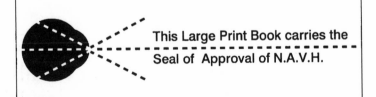

This Large Print Book carries the
Seal of Approval of N.A.V.H.

>Dear Stranger,
Dearest Friend

LANEY KATZ BECKER

G.K. Hall & Co. • Thorndike, Maine

Published in 2001 by arrangement with William Morrow,
an imprint of HarperCollins Publishers, Inc.

G.K. Hall Large Print Inspirational Series.

The text of this Large Print edition is unabridged.
Other aspects of the book may vary from the original edition.

Set in 16 pt. Plantin by Susan Guthrie.

Printed in the United States on permanent paper.

Library of Congress Cataloging-in-Publication Data

Becker, Laney Katz.
    Dear stranger, dearest friend / Laney Katz Becker.
        p.   cm.
    ISBN 0-7838-9403-1 (lg. print : hc : alk. paper)
    1. Female friendship — Fiction.   2. Breast — Cancer — Patients
— Fiction.   3. Electronic mail messages — Fiction.   4. Women —
United States — Fiction.   5. New York (N.Y.) — Fiction.
6. Middle West — Fiction.   7. Large type books.   I. Title.
PS3552.E25616 D43 2001
813'.6—dc21   00-143886

Dedicated to my children,
Whitney and Mitchell.
I am twice blessed, to be sure.

Subj: Help, please
Date: 09-14
From: cre8f1@mindspring.com
To: www.bcancer.org/support/L.board/html

I hope I'm in the right place. Actually that's not true. I hope I'm *not* in the right place at all. See, it's like this: I found a lump in my left breast this morning, and basically, I'm a wreck. I can't focus. I can barely even function. So far I've managed to burn my hand on the coffeemaker, finish a load of laundry (only to realize sometime during the spin cycle that I never added the detergent), and most recently, on one of my seemingly endless trips to the bathroom, I noticed that I put on my underwear inside out. Under normal circumstances I might find all of this funny. But these aren't normal circumstances and I'm not laughing. Trust me.

I've already made an appointment to see my gynecologist — only it's not for another two weeks. I don't know how I'll make it till then. I'm trying not to, but I keep imagining the worst — which is probably why I'm posting this message on your bulletin board for *breast cancer*. I know that it looks like I'm jumping the gun, but what I'm really looking for are some reassurances that it's *not* cancer — and that I don't belong here. Is there someone out there who can tell me something that will make me feel better? Anyone? Anything? I'd really appreciate it.

Subj: re: Help, please
Date: 09-14
From: no1mom@netscape.com
To: cre8f1@mindspring.com
message ID: 199&920.001@bcancer.org

Dear cre8f1:
    I'm keeping my fingers crossed that you are indeed in the wrong place. Statistically, the odds are that you're perfectly fine, since most lumps turn out to be completely benign. Still, you're smart to check it out, just in case. In the meantime, I know it's hard, but try not to think about it for the next two weeks. There's nothing you can do, anyway. Keep us posted.
    Margie

Subj: re: Help, please
Date: 09-14
From: Susan_P@aol.com
To: cre8f1@mindspring.com
message ID: 199%9220.01.9@bcancer.org

On 09-14 cre8f1@mindspring.com wrote:
>*I don't know how I'll make it till then.*

Oh, you'll make it. Your fingers may be burned to a crisp, and you may be wearing dirty laundry, but you'll make it.

Obviously, I just finished reading your post. Don't be mad, but you made me laugh. It reminded me of how I felt when I found my lump. My mouth went dry, my hands started shaking, and my heart was pounding so fiercely that I don't know if I was more afraid of having breast cancer or of having a heart attack. (20/20 hindsight leaves me wishing it was a heart attack. Kind of.) Anyway, that was two years ago. Obviously, my lump turned out to be cancer. (Why else would I be reading the BC bulletin board two years later?) I wound up having a lumpectomy, chemo and radiation. I am happy to report that since then, I've been completely healthy. (Feel free to get up from your computer, find something made of wood and give it a good hard knock for me.)

So you — who wears her underpants inside out — do you have a name? I'm Sue. And the best advice I can give you is to see your gyno sooner. Waiting two weeks will only make it worse. Call your doctor's nurse, tell her you're a mess, and beg her to squeeze you in. Fake-cry if you have to. It worked for me. :-)

Subj: re: Help, please
Date: 09-14
From: PanOtchr@mindspring.com
To: cre8f1@mindspring.com
messageID:199%432.0%#00.091@bcancer.org

9

Hi. Welcome to the club. I hope you're right and yours is a mistaken membership. If not, remember these things:

1. Early detection is everything.
2. There are a lot of women out here to give you support.
3. Positive thoughts really do make a difference.
I will pray for you.
Daniella

Subj: Thanks
Date: 09-15
From: cre8f1@mindspring.com
To: www.bcancer.org
message ID: 199%90.0&34.500@bcancer.org

Thank you, ladies, for all of your responses. You've helped me calm down (a bit), and I truly appreciate your kind words. I promise to let you know what happens. Be well.

Subj: Do You Mind?
Date: 09-15
From: cre8f1@mindspring.com
To: Susan_P@aol.com

Dear Sue,
Thank you for responding to my message on the breast cancer bulletin board. I'm writing to

you directly — I hope you don't mind. But the truth is, I really don't feel comfortable posting my life on the Internet for the entire world to see. Maybe that's why I (subconsciously) neglected to give my name. Or maybe it's because by being anonymous this whole thing is somehow not as real. Weird, I know, but this whole thing is weird.

Three women (including you) responded to my letter about my lump. In spite of my somewhat hysterical state, your message made me laugh, especially when you wrote that I should call my gyno and fake-cry to get an earlier appointment. That sounds like the same kind of good, solid advice I would give to someone in my predicament — if only I could think straight.

Anyway, you sound like someone I can talk to, and that's really what I need right now. That, and some information from someone who's been through what I'm going through. (I know what you mean about the heart pounding. If I didn't know better, I'd swear that I could actually hear mine beating.) I'm trying really hard to remain calm, but I'm not having much success — otherwise I would not have just banished my 11-year-old daughter to her bedroom for the next 11 years.

Do you mind if I pick your brain a bit?

Over the years I've read countless magazine articles about breast cancer. In fact, if I could remember a fraction of what I've read, I think I'd be in pretty good shape. But my brain feels fuzzy, and I'm having trouble separating what I *think* is true from what I *want* to be true. Here's what I mean:

First, I'm only 38. (I'll be 39 next month.) Doesn't breast cancer happen to women who are older? Second, there is no history of breast cancer in my family. None. And third, my lump does not hurt *at all*. I mean, if it's cancer, it should cause me *some* kind of discomfort, even just a little twinge, shouldn't it? I'm thinking these are all good things, right?

I appreciate your taking the time to answer my questions. And by the way, I'm Lara. (Rhymes with Sarah.)

Subj: re: Do You Mind?
Date: 09-15
From: Susan_P@aol.com
To: cre8f1@mindspring.com

Hi, Lara.

It's nice to meet you (even though we haven't really met). Ah, the magic of the Internet.

Allow me to be the first to wish you a happy early birthday — and many more. And no, I don't mind if you write directly to me at all. In fact, it's probably better. Some of the postings on the breast cancer board are pretty tragic, and you don't need to read those right now. You're already nervous enough. :-)

Hopefully, all your worries will prove to be nothing. That's usually the case. In fact, 80% of the time breast lumps turn out to be benign. (That means not cancer.) The point I'm making here is that the odds are definitely on your side. So expect the best, not the worst. In the meantime, you need to slow down. Take a breath. Now take another breath. Good. (Don't you feel better already?) Seriously though, before I answer your questions, you've got to answer mine: Did you call your gyno's office and ask for an earlier appointment? And did you have to fake-cry to get one?

Sue

Subj: Breathing
Date: 09-16
From: cre8f1@mindspring.com
To: Susan_P@aol.com

Dear Sue,

I've been breathing. In fact, I feel like I've just completed a Lamaze class, and I still feel like shit. (Sorry, but sometimes the four-letter words really *are* more expressive.)

I did not call my gynecologist for an earlier appointment. Here's why:

- I'm supposed to get my period next week. I know that women sometimes develop cysts in their breasts that go away after their periods.

I'm hoping that will be the case with me, and that after next week my lump will disappear as suddenly as it popped up. Besides, if I wait until after I finish my period, I figure my doctor will get a "better feel."

- I do monthly breast self-exams. All right, I do them *most* of the time. When I don't forget. But I've been doing them since I turned thirty-five. I always do them after I *finish* my period — never the week before. In other words: For all I know, I always have a lump in my left breast the week before my period . . . capiche? (sp?) The only reason I even noticed the lump is because I was standing naked in front of the mirror, blow-drying my hair. I *saw* the darn thing sticking out. That makes it sound large, but it's not. It's teeny-tiny — pea-size, in fact. I still can't believe that I even noticed it.

- I'm due for a Pap test. My doctor won't do it until after I finish my period. I figure that I may as well get my Pap *and* check out my lump in the same appointment. (Please Note: While I admit to being hysterical, I remain efficient in the use of my time.)

There you have it, three reasons I'm determined to wait to see my gynecologist.

Subj: Efficiency
Date: 09-18
From: Susan_P@aol.com
To: cre8f1@mindspring.com

Hi there.

See, Lara, you *can* think clearly when you try. And you're right. You should wait to see your gyno. That way he'll be able to give you a better exam and you'll be able to give him more accurate information about how your breast feels compared to "the usual." So it's decided: You'll wait until your period's done. But you must PROMISE ME that even if the lump disappears after your period you will still go in to discuss this entire episode with your doc. (You said that you need a Pap anyway, so don't forget to mention that you had this suspicious area/lump thing, OK?) You're right about another thing, too. The fact that you're expecting your period is probably why you have the lump in the first place. In fact, back in the olden days when I still got my period (pre-chemo), I sometimes got cysts, too. But your other facts are incorrect. Allow me:

— Most women who get breast cancer are over 60, but not all.
— More than 85% of the time there is *no family history* when women develop breast cancer.
— Lumps don't have to hurt to be cancerous; in fact, they *usually* don't.

15

I'm just a regular walking encyclopedia, aren't I? Actually, I have to be informed — I run a breast cancer support group in Canton, Ohio, which is where I live. (I'll spare you the flip through your atlas. It's outside of Akron, which is outside of Cleveland, which should be a name you recognize, and Stop Laughing!) I just started the support group a few months ago but already have a lot of women attending. (Should I be glad it's a success or sad that so many women have BC?) Anyway, I'm sure that you're fine, and once your period is over, all of your concerns about your lump will be a thing of the past. Be well.

Susan

Subj: My reality. Sort of.
Date: 09-20
From: cre8f1@mindspring.com
To: Susan_P@aol.com

Dear Sue — or do you prefer Susan? (You introduced yourself in your first e-mail as Sue, but I notice your screen name is Susan_P, and you also signed your last letter Susan. I'm confused!)

I'm getting used to the waiting (sort of) and feeling a bit calmer (sort of, again). Still, the other night I had a weak moment and broke down and told my husband (sort of). The truth is, I showed him. (FYI: His name is Michael.) I wasn't planning on mentioning any of this to him because I didn't want him to worry. I'm the tough one in our family, and I figured I was already stressed out enough for the both of us. Also, I think that I felt like as long as I didn't *say* anything to him, the lump wouldn't be real. (Telling the world on the Internet doesn't count because I just *wrote* about my worst fears, I didn't have to say anything *out loud*.) As I try to explain all of this to you now it sounds pretty screwy, but since finding the lump I've been acting pretty screwy: I'm in the shower and I linger over my left breast, feeling for any changes (or disappearing lumps). I'm in my car and suddenly I'm aware that my left breast is being groped, only *I'm* the one doing the groping. I'm in the supermarket and slip my hand inside my rain slicker pretending to scratch an itch, but really I'm checking just one more time, hoping that *poof!* it's gone.

I guess I just couldn't hold in my fears any longer, because the other night I slipped off the straps of my nightgown and asked Michael to feel my breast. He made some crack about how it would be his pleasure. I told him this wasn't a joking matter, grabbed his hand and put it right on the lump, which I had no problem locating since, as I've just explained, I'm checking out the darn thing at least twenty times a day! Anyway, I push Michael's fingertips into my breast and say, "Do you feel that?" Looking pretty pale, he just nods. I ask him if "that bump" has always been there. He says he doesn't know and tells me I should go to the doctor. *No shit, Sherlock.* He starts with questions about when I found it, when I'm seeing the doctor, and get this: What do I think it is? I immediately have second thoughts about telling/showing him the lump because this is exactly what I *didn't* want. I spend the next twenty minutes fielding questions and trying my best to reassure *him.* I'm angry with him, and I don't even know why. Yes I do. He was supposed to tell me that "the bump" in my left breast has always been there, that he noticed it the first time he ever touched me, in fact he always thought it was sort of a cute little defect. All right. Maybe I didn't expect him to go that far, but I could have used some reassurances, you know? But instead, what did I get? Concern, worry, fear. And why? Because he loves me. The nerve of this man! (I told you I was screwy.)

Anyway, Sue/Susan — Thanks for *your* words of encouragement. They definitely helped. (Nothing sort-of about it!) And most definitely yes, I promise — I will keep the appointment with my gynecologist.

FYI again: I got my period today. Right on schedule, too. If I really had cancer, I think I would know — my body wouldn't be operating like clockwork. At least that's what I've managed to convince myself. (Sort of.)

I feel so guilty. I've been so obsessed with my lump that I haven't asked you anything about yourself. All I know is that you found a lump two years ago, had a lumpectomy, chemotherapy and radiation, and that you run a support group in Canton, Ohio (hee-hee). Just kidding. Seriously, though, you are obviously very knowledgeable and are a very kind and special person to have taken the time to help ease a total stranger's fears. But tell me more. Do you have a job (besides the support group)? Are you married? Kids? How old are you? (Or is that a no-no?) And how's your health now?

Lara

Subj: My Life
Date: 09-22
From: Susan_P@aol.com
To: cre8f1@mindspring.com

Dear Lara,

You make me blush. Me, *kind?* My 13-year-old (Gabby) might disagree. In fact, you gave me a good chuckle when you told me about banishing your 11-year-old to her room for the next 11 years. I've been known to extend my daughter's punishment to her *afterlife!* I love her dearly. It's her fresh mouth I could live without. (Do you think that by naming her "Gabby" I showed clairvoyance, or did I create my own destiny by naming her "Gabby" in the first place? Inquisitive minds want to know.)

Gabby was 11 when I discovered my cancer. (I know, the same age that your daughter is now — but you do *not* have cancer. Repeat that three times. Then click your heels, just for good measure.) Anyway, Gabby's an only child. Artie (my hubby) and I wanted to have more kids — and tried — but had second-child infertility. (That's when you've been pregnant once and can't get preggers again and the docs don't know why but feel compelled to give you a diagnosis — hence: Second Child Infertility.) I'm 42 years old. I'll save you the complex math — I was 40 when my cancer appeared. I didn't feel a lump, but it showed up on my mammogram. I won't bore you with the nitty-gritties, but I had chemo, which made me lose all of my hair (including eyebrows). It's grown back curly. (No! Not the eyebrows, silly.) I look like Annie, only my hair's very dark brown, not red. No freckles either. I also had 6 weeks of daily radiation. I now glow. (Kidding, of course.)

My hubby also put me through the Q&A about my lump, but he's an attorney, so I figured that was just him. However, my experience in the support group has led me to conclude that it's universal: Men expect women to know what's happening to their bodies, why and what it all means. Michael sounds like a normal, concerned husband who just doesn't understand about cysts or lumps or periods (and if he's at all like Artie, he probably never wanted to know either). So try to be patient and remember — you're Michael's only source of info (unless you want to give him my e-mail address), so it's up to you to calm his fears while you nurse your own. Sorry, Lara, but no one said that being a wife was easy. :-)

All right, you asked about my work: In addition to running the support group, I have a part-time job as a computer programmer at a tire factory. (Bet you didn't know that Akron is the rubber capital of the world, did you?) Oops, I'd love to complete my bio, but I have to go pick up my daughter from field-hockey practice. So ask me again, if you really want to know.

Sue or Susan. (I use both and don't have a preference.)

Subj: What?
Date: 09-23
From: cre8f1@mindspring.com
To: Susan_P@aol.com

Dear Sue,
On 09-22 Susan_P@aol.com wrote:
>*I'd love to complete my bio, but I have to go pick up*
>*my daughter from field-hockey practice. So ask me*
>*again, if you really want to know.*

What does *that* mean? Of course I want to know. Otherwise, why would I ask?
L.

Subj: Explanation
Date: 09-24
From: Susan_P@aol.com
To: cre8f1@mindspring.com

Dear Lara,

I didn't mean to be rude. I just meant that when you see your gyno and he tells you that you're fine, we won't have the need to correspond. You wanted information — I provided it. You needed someone to calm your fears — I'm happy to have done so. The rest . . . well, does it really matter? I don't mean to be . . . well, *mean,* but think about it: Breast cancer has united us, however briefly, and when it's no longer a concern of yours, you will move on and so will I. I'll start another correspondence with another woman who won't be as lucky as you. It's OK. We women are supposed to help each other out. In the meantime, if you'd like, I'm happy to hold your hand until you get the all-clear.

Sue

P.S. Speaking of hand-holding . . . Is Michael going with you to the gyno's?

Subj: Hand-holding
Date: 09-26
From: cre8f1@mindspring.com
To: Susan_P@aol.com

Dear Sue,

You're right. I have a full life, and I don't need to write letters to a faceless person who lives halfway across the country which, by the way, you do. I live in Armonk, New York. It's a suburb about 45 minutes north of Manhattan. Armonk (which is in Westchester County) is basically a small, rural town, where the deer (but no antelope) roam and have us all in a panic about being infected with Lyme disease!

I guess that by asking you all about yourself I was trying to make you more than a stranger who lives in the Midwest. I'm not sure why, exactly. But I do know that I'd like to take you up on your offer to hold my hand a while longer, if that's OK. For some reason it helps just knowing you're there, and . . . well, I don't know — I'm having trouble expressing what I want to say. That's unusual; I'm usually a very clear thinker. At least I used to be. These days I'm not sure of anything much. About the only thing I do know is that my doctor's appointment is tomorrow at 10:00 A.M., and no, I'm not allowing Michael to accompany me. He wanted to, but the truth is, whatever the news, I want Michael to hear it (prescreened?) from me, not my doctor. I will let you know when I'm given my clean bill of health. (Just so you know: I typed that last sentence with my legs firmly crossed.)

Lara

P.S. A computer programmer, huh? Maybe I *do*

need to write letters to a faceless stranger halfway across the country. When I get over this lump scare, will you help me with a computer problem I'm having? My computer seems to have developed a mind of its own and periodically just freezes. Problem is that "periodically" is happening more and more frequently :- (

Subj: Computers Rule
Date: 09-26
From: Susan_P@aol.com
To: cre8f1@mindspring.com

Hi, Lara.

Welcome to the computer age. Didn't you know? All 'puters have minds of their own.

According to my calculations, you should be at the doc's right now. I'm sending a bunch of good thoughts your way. Let me know how you make out.

Susan

Subj: My Appointment
Date: 09-27
From: cre8f1@mindspring.com
To: Susan_P@aol.com

Dear Sue,

I just returned from the gynecologist's and feel like a new woman. He didn't even *feel* the lump when he did my breast exam. (Although I didn't mention anything about it until *after* he'd examined my breasts. Pretty tricky, huh?) Once he finished, though, I told him about the lump and showed him the spot. Even still, it took him *forever* to feel it. (I *told* you it was teeny-tiny.) Anyway, my doctor's convinced that it's only a fluid-filled cyst. He wants me to have an ultrasound and have it aspirated, whatever that means. I called Michael from the car with my good news. He screams "Great!" into my ear and then confesses that *while he didn't want me to know* he'd been really worried. *Oh, really? Who would have guessed?* He tells me that he slept in the guest room last night, not because he had to get up really early for a morning meeting (as he told me and I believed) but because he knew he'd be too nervous to sleep and didn't want to toss and turn and keep me up all night. He's such a sweetheart.

Since I had a baseline mammogram done at 35 (and I'm not due for another until the big 4-0, a full year away), my doctor says that there's no need for another mammogram. (Yes!) Before I left his office, he gave me the name of a place that does ultrasounds. It's only five minutes from my house. (Yes! again.) The good doctor says there's no hurry, but once I send this off to you, I'm booking it — just so I can stop thinking about it. Later.

Lara

Subj: Hip-Hip-Hooray
Date: 09-27
From: Susan_P@aol.com
To: cre8f1@mindspring.com

Dear Lara,

I told you it was probably nothing. Forgive the gloating, but when it means that someone *doesn't* have cancer, I just love being right. When's your ultrasound? And just so you know, "aspirating a cyst" simply means that they'll put a tiny needle into it so the liquid drains out and the cyst collapses. No biggie, trust me.

Subj: Thanks
Date: 09-28
From: cre8f1@mindspring.com
To: Susan_P@aol.com

As long as it's only a cyst, you can gloat about being right all you like. My appointment to have it aspirated is Oct. 1. I hope you're right and it's painless. I *hate* needles.

Subj: Eruptions
Date: 09-29
From: Susan_P@aol.com
To: cre8f1@mindspring.com

Dear Lara,

Is there smoke coming out of your computer? I'm burning mad at this end, and I was just wondering if you can see the steam seeping through on your end. I am so angry with my darling daughter. I swear, I think she's becoming more trouble than she's worth. OK, not really. But that doesn't mean that I'm any less angry.

Let me share:

An hour ago I walked into Gabby's room with a pile of her clean clothes. She's finishing up a phone conversation by saying, "Don't worry. I told you that I'll get out of it, and I will."

ME: What was that all about? What are you going to get out of, Gabby?

GABBY: Baby-sitting this weekend for the Stanfords. (She says this very matter-of-factly.)

ME: What do you mean?

GABBY: Well, I told the Stanfords that I'd baby-sit. But I just found out that Katie's having a slumber party the same night. Everyone can go. Rebecca, Anne, Mary . . . (she names all of her closest friends). So I told Katie that I'd cancel on the Stanfords and go to her party instead.

ME: You told her *what?*

I'm in a state of disbelief. She's really acting like this whole thing is no big deal. So I start talking about responsibility and commitment. I'm talking logically and calmly, trying to make Gabby understand why 1) this *is* a big deal and 2) she can't just cancel on the Stanfords because something better comes along.

Gabby switches into active volcano mode and starts screaming that she's not the *only* baby-sitter in the world and that I don't understand. She further informs me that I don't understand *anything*.

I make it very clear that I *do* understand. I understand being irresponsible, and I understand being unreliable. I tell her that I also understand about honoring commitments and that I thought we'd raised her to know better. She starts complaining about guilt trips and making mountains out of molehills. And then she zings me with "Mom, get a life."

Usually after one of our arguments I send her (and her fresh mouth) to her bedroom. That's where she is now. But this time it's her choice. She pushed me out of her room, then slammed and locked the door behind me. This, however, is not necessarily a bad thing. I could use the time to cool down.

What? Still no steam on your end?

Susan

Subj: Yikes
Date: 09-29
From: cre8f1@mindspring.com
To: Susan_P@aol.com

Dear Susan,

That's it. After reading your letter, I told Wendy that she's not allowed to grow up and how does she feel about remaining 11 forever? Of course, she had absolutely no idea what I was talking about. She just gave me a strange look and said, "Sure, Mom, whatever you say." I'm counting my blessings. She may be forgetful, but at least she's still agreeable.

Lara

Subj: Preteens
Date: 09-30
From: Susan_P@aol.com
To: cre8f1@mindspring.com

On 09-29 cre8f1@mindspring.com wrote:
>*but at least she's still agreeable.*

Oh, yeah? Just wait. :- 0

Subj: Wrong Place
Date: 10-01
From: cre8f1@mindspring.com
To: Susan_P@aol.com

Dear Sue,

Apologies in advance for my shitty mood. I just got back from the ultrasound place. Before she took me into the exam room, the receptionist asked why I was there. I told her about the cyst and needing it aspirated. Turns out they do ultrasounds, *but they don't aspirate cysts.* I should have known that anyplace a mere five minutes from my house was too good to be true. Anyway, I called my doctor (from the ultrasound place) and asked him what he wanted me to do. He apologized, said, "They *used* to aspirate cysts" and told me not to go through with the appointment. He gave me the name of another place that he's absolutely certain can do both the ultrasound *and* the aspiration. Naturally, it's not nearly as convenient. (It's still in Westchester, but a 30-minute drive from my house.) They're gonna see me in a week. I'm getting better at this waiting thing. How are things in Canton? Have you and Gabby made up? And how's field hockey?

Subj: Crazed
Date: 10-07
From: Susan_P@aol.com
To: cre8f1@mindspring.com

Dear Lara,

Now it's my turn to apologize to you. Sorry it's taken so long to get back to you, but things in Canton have been hectic. Yes, Gabby and I are back on speaking terms, but that could change at any minute. (That's just how things are these days.) As for field hockey — we've moved on, thank you very much. The season is winding down, and just my luck, basketball begins today. And not just basketball, *traveling* basketball. She tried out for the team, made it and has *25* games. If only they gave frequent-flier miles for driving! My butt is sore just thinking about it. (Once they put toilets in minivans, I will never again have a good reason to get out of my car.) But I'm happy for her. The accomplishment is even more meaningful because Gabby tried out for the team last year and didn't make it.

Have you gone for your second attempt at an ultrasound/aspiration yet? Did it hurt? Write back soon, and I promise I'll be more prompt with my responses.

Susan

Subj: BC Awareness Month
Date: 10-14
From: cre8f1@mindspring.com
To: Susan_P@aol.com

Dear Susan,

I go for my ultrasound tomorrow. As usual, Michael volunteered to take off from work and go with me. As usual, I declined. Both you and my gyno say that it's a simple procedure, so I can handle it. Hey, I can handle just about anything now that I know it's only a cyst!

All righty, my dear . . . I've got a riddle for you:

Q. When is National Breast Cancer Awareness Month NOT a good thing?

A. When you're still just a wee bit panicky because you've recently had a breast cancer scare and since it's October, every newsmagazine show you watch, every magazine article you read and every other radio commerical is reminding you to have your breasts examined every year by a physician, perform your own breast exams every month, have regular mammograms and oh, yes, remember that *all women are at risk.* Yikes!

My girlfriend (Amy) participates in one of the breast cancer walks every October. She says it's her way of honoring her aunt, who passed away from breast cancer six years ago. Anyway, for the last five years I've sponsored Amy by writing out a check. This year I doubled the amount. It's like I'm trying to buy myself a little extra insurance or something. "Maybe if I'm *really* generous . . ." How sick is that? I can't wait 'til tomorrow when (hopefully) this whole thing will be over.

Subj: HELP
Date: 10-15
From: cre8f1@mindspring.com
To: Susan_P@aol.com

Dear Susan,

I'm really scared. I just got home from my ultrasound. I was at the place for four hours! The bottom line: There's something on my mammogram called "microcalcifications," and they want me to see a breast surgeon. I'm freaking out!

Subj: What's going on?
Date: 10-16
From: Susan_P@aol.com
To: cre8f1@mindspring.com

Dear Lara,

Slow down. What *mammogram?* I thought you were having an *ultrasound.* Please, please, tell me everything. I want to know what's going on. Maybe I can help. I'm off to work right now, but will check my e-mail during lunch. If there's nothing from you then, I'll check again when I get home. I need to hear from you. S.

Subj: Well?
Date: 10-16
From: Susan_P@aol.com
To: cre8f1@mindspring.com

Lara, dear, I'm getting nervous. Please write.

Subj: It's Late
Date: 10-18
From: cre8f1@mindspring.com
To: Susan_P@aol.com

Dear Susan,

It's 2 A.M., and I can't sleep. (Wonder why?) Anyway, I have nothing but time, so I'll give you the details, and hopefully you can give me some encouragement.

I go for my ultrasound. I tell the technician that my gynecologist wants them to find my cyst and aspirate it. I am wearing an examining gown and absolutely freezing. (And this is *before* she puts a ton of cold goop on my left breast.) I am shaking, and she tells me to try to relax. I tell her that I'm just cold. (Lie #1: I'm cold *and* nervous.) She says they have to keep the room cold for the equipment. She seems pleasant enough and asks me to show her the lump, which I have no trouble doing, since I'm still touching it (hoping it's miraculously disappeared) about a million times a day. The technician feels the lump with her fingers, then tries to find it with the ultrasound. She can't. She tries again and again, but it's obvious that she's having no luck. She smiles at me and says, "Don't worry." I tell her I'm fine. (Lie #2.) She finally gives up, leaves and comes back with the doctor (a radiologist). She too (lots of women in this place) can't get my lump to appear on the ultrasound and says that maybe it would show on a mammogram. She suggests I *schedule an appointment!* I get slightly pushy and beg them to do the mammo immediately. (This has already dragged out long enough, don't you think?) Anyway, I'm in the middle of my menstrual cycle, which they inform me is not when they like to do mammograms (since the radiation can harm a growing fetus). I assure them I am not pregnant. (Lie #3: I am *probably* not pregnant, but my husband has not had the big V, as I claim.) They make me sign a waiver absolving them of any responsibility in the event that I turn out to be pregnant. Man!

Since I thought I was only having an ultrasound, I put on my deodorant that morning. They make a big deal over the fact that I need to wash off all of the deodorant really well, otherwise it will show up as flecks and interfere with their ability to read the mammogram films. They give me an extra dressing gown to use as a washcloth and send me into the bathroom. I take them literally and scrub my underarms until they are bright red. They give me my mammogram. I wait 20 minutes. The doctor reappears and tells me to wash off again. "Really well this time." By this point I am even more nervous, because I have already washed myself raw. I'm sweating to death, have no deodorant on, and just to make matters worse and even more embarrassing — I *smell* like I'm not wearing any deodorant!

Anyway, the technician repeats the mammogram. I wait another half hour. Then the tech comes back and tells me that the doctor is out to lunch and not to think that it means anything because it's taking so long. (Somehow that does precious little to calm my nerves.) Another 20+ minutes pass. I've read every magazine in the place before the technician finally resurfaces and says the doctor wants certain positions of my left breast retaken — only this time with magnification. I lose track of how many more X-rays are taken, but I'm sure that it's more than enough to kill the fetus I am not carrying. (By the time she's done, I'm amazed that my breast hasn't fallen off.) I get dressed and wait some more. The technician finally returns and escorts me to a huge, brightly lit room with a telephone. She tells me that in a moment the phone will ring and I should answer it. She closes the door on her way out and leaves me sitting there staring at the damn phone. Finally it rings, and it's my *gynecologist.* He explains that he's just had a conversation with the radiologist. My gyno says there are some suspicious areas on my mammogram called microcalcifications. He asks if I'm OK. (Lie #4: Sure, I'm swell.) He then says that the microcalcifications may or may not be related to my lump — they can't tell from the mammogram. Then something about needing to see a breast surgeon for more information. I don't remember much else, except somehow the radiologist reappeared and basically repeated everything the gynecologist had just said. She gave me the name of the breast surgeon my gynecologist mentioned and told me that she refers many patients to this surgeon and he's very nice. And that was it. I paid my bill and left. I don't even remember driving home.

It must have been 10 P.M. before I got up enough nerve to tell Michael what happened. He completely fell apart and started to cry. (Have I told you that both of his parents died from cancer?) I told him that I'm scared enough already and it's all I can do to keep myself together — I can't worry about him right now. Then I went upstairs and locked myself in our bedroom for the rest of the night. (How's *that* for mature?)

I've got an appointment to see the breast surgeon in 1 ½ weeks. I thought I was scared when I found my lump. That's nothing compared to how I'm feeling now. Michael keeps looking at me with basset-hound eyes like I'm going to die. It's awful. But I keep trying to tell myself that they really don't know anything yet, right? Right?

I'm rambling, it's late, and I'm exhausted, even though I can't sleep. I'm sorry to dump all this on you, but I obviously can't talk to Michael, and I don't know anyone else who would understand. Thanks for listening.

Lara

Subj: Breathe
Date: 10-19
From: Susan_P@aol.com
To: cre8f1@mindspring.com

Dear Lara,

Dump on me all you want. Let's go back to that take-a-breath idea, remember? You're jumping the gun — way bad, as Gabby would say. Remember: Most lumps (80%) turn out to be perfectly harmless. But doctors need to be careful and make sure that they really *are* per-

fectly harmless. Breast surgeons deal with this stuff all the time. I know it's hard, but try not to panic. Wait until you see the breast surgeon and see what (s)he has to say. In the meantime, keep breathing, girlie, and think positive thoughts. (I don't know if that really helps, but it sure can't hurt.) {{{ }}}
Susan

P.S. What is the exact date of your appointment with the surgeon? And please tell me that Michael is going with you.

Subj: Going Solo
Date: 10-19
From: cre8f1@mindspring.com
To: Susan_P@aol.com

Dear Susan,

My appointment with the breast surgeon is on the 27th, which just happens to be my birthday. No, Michael's not coming with. He wanted to, of course, but I said no (also, of course). I just don't want him there. If something is really wrong, I want to feel free to ask the doctor questions without worrying about how Michael is doing (which, believe me, won't be well). If I get the (bad) news first, I can filter how Michael gets the information. You just have to trust me on this one, Sue. I know my husband, and it really is better this way. Besides, as I explained to Michael, the appointment with the surgeon isn't worth missing work. It's only an exam and a talk. How much will we really even know at that point? And if I *do* need some sort of surgery, then I really will need Michael to take off some time from the office. (He's a CPA at a midsize accounting firm in the city. He's a partner, which gives him some flexibility, but also means a lot of responsibility. In other words, he just can't take off for every little thing. I know, I know, this isn't just "every little thing," but until I know otherwise, I'm trying to get him to look at it that way.) Anyway, I don't need Michael wasting vacation and/or personal days to sit and talk to a doctor, something I'm completely capable of doing myself. I hope that makes sense without making me sound like a control freak who's married to a wimpy husband, because that's not the case at all. At least the part about the husband isn't true. ;-)

That's it. Except for one question. What's with the {{{ }}} ?

Subj: Hugs
Date: 10-21
From: Susan_P@aol.com
To: cre8f1@mindspring.com

Dear Lara,
{{{ }}} Those are hugs. Cute, huh? Stick with me kid, I'll teach you all kinds of neat Netspeak. That's what we programmers do when we're

bored . . . which I'm not. Always lots of activity in the Peterson house. (BTW, [that's **By The Way**], what's your last name?)

Gabby jammed her finger at b'ball practice and will most likely miss her first game. Poor kid, it's like her world has come to an end. It's sad watching kids live through disappointments, but hey, that's life and that's how they learn, right? I really do feel sorry for her, though — she's already been through so much. Watching me go through my treatments was not easy on her. She never said anything, but I could tell that there were times she was really scared that I was going to die. Yes, I'd definitely say she's had more than her share. The ironic part of all of this is that now, when she gets really angry with me and says she hates me, you can tell that she really means it (at least at that moment). I can tell by her eyes that there are times she wishes I really had died. And then she feels guilty for feeling that way and showers me with kisses. I guess it's all part of being a teenage girl. Who knows? Did you ever wish your mom dead when you were growing up? (Inquisitive minds want to know.)

So how are things going with Michael? Don't worry about sounding like a controlling bitch. (Oops, you called yourself a control *freak,* and I've gone and elevated you to bitch status. Sorry.) But seriously, Lara, try to remember, it's tough on the guys, too. I mean, think about it: If they make a big deal about it, they're obsessed with breasts. Which they are. :-) And if they don't make a big deal about it, we accuse them of not understanding how scared we are of losing a body part associated with our sexuality. Poor guys, they really *are* in a no-win situation.

I know that you've got to do what's best for you, and like you said, you know your husband, but sharing this kind of adversity can actually be good for a marriage. That came out wrong. I don't mean *good* good, I mean that it can make a marriage stronger. I never loved Artie more than the day we learned that I was going to need the chemo. We got home from the oncologist's office and Artie disappeared. I was pretty annoyed, thinking, "Where did he run off to hide?" But a few minutes later I hear Artie's footsteps. He's walking toward me with a cup of herbal tea. (I always drink tea when I need to think, and I guess he knew I had some serious thinking to do.) Anyway, his hand is shaking and the cup is making a clinking noise against the saucer. Now, you don't know him, but shaking hands and clinking saucers are not Artie. He's of the Mr. Cool variety. Anyway, he put the tea down on a table and pulled over a chair so he could sit facing me. Without saying a word, he took my hand between both of his. I must have dropped my head, because I distinctly remember that he put his finger under my chin and lifted it so he could look me right in the eye. He just looked at me and then after what seemed like five minutes, but was probably really only five seconds, Artie said, "Susan, just tell me what you need. What can I do for you?"

My big chance to get 24-hour-a-day maid service, daily foot massages, a new car every year and a full-time cook, and what do I say? Not a word. I was too busy crying over Artie's shaky hands. The point of this little story, dear Lara, is not that I blew my shot at a pampered life (which I did!) but that I was lucky to have a husband who, in spite of his own fears, was in my corner and willing to step up to the plate and do whatever I needed. It sounds to me like you are fortunate to have an equally supportive spouse. Michael is only knocking. Don't be afraid to let him in.

All right, enough about that . . .

We had our support group meeting last night. A breast surgeon came to speak. She was great. I want you to know, she repeated that 80% of the time lumps that are biopsied turn out to be benign. So let's just pray that you're part of that majority. But in case you're not, remember this: Having breast cancer does not mean you're going to die. In fact, the surgeon said that today the survival rate for breast cancer found in its early stages is more than 90%. Let's see, 80% and 90% — they sound like good odds to me!

I know the 27th must seem like a million years away. How are you holding up?

Sue

Subj: Stats
Date: 10-23
From: cre8f1@mindspring.com
To: Susan_P@aol.com

Dear Sue,
On 10-21 Susan_P@aol.com wrote:
>*she repeated that 80% of the time lumps that are*
>*biopsied turn out to be benign.*

I know you're trying to be encouraging when you quote such statistics, but it's not working. If the statistics were coming from someone else, maybe I'd find them reassuring. But they're coming from *you* — someone who didn't beat the odds!
　Lara

Subj: Numbers
Date: 10-25
From: Susan_P@aol.com
To: cre8f1@mindspring.com

Dear Lara,
　You're right. Forgive me if I'm being insensitive by quoting numbers over such an emotional issue. And you're right, I didn't beat the percentages regarding my lump. *But I'm part of the 90% who survive!* (And I didn't even find my breast cancer early. My tumor was already slightly more than 2 centimeters.)
　Keeping a level (and statistical) head helps many women handle their sense of panic. I know, that's easy for me to say now that I've been through it. But remember, I was pretty crazed when I first found out, too. In fact, I'd

forgotten all about this, but it's true-confession time:

When I first found my lump, I used to toss dice. I played this little game with myself. "What are the odds of throwing two numbers that add up to five in fewer than six rolls of the dice?" And then I'd sit there and roll the dice. I was trying to prove to myself how much the odds were in my favor. Goofy stuff, I know, but what can I say? Cancer is scary, and I — who didn't beat the odds — am quoting numbers to you. Pretty stupid, huh? I'm sorry. Don't be mad.

Sue

Subj: Never mad
Date: 10-26
From: cre8f1@mindspring.com
To: Susan_P@aol.com

Oh, Sue, how could I be mad at you? You were only trying to help, with all of your numbers, percentages and odds. (Have you and Artie ever considered relocating to Las Vegas?) Sorry that I overreacted. Wish me luck tomorrow.

Lara

Subj: Odds 'n' Ends
Date: 10-26
From: Susan_P@aol.com
To: cre8f1@mindspring.com

44

I accept your apology. Whew! We've survived our first fight. :-)

Good luck tomorrow. Write me ASAP. And oh, yeah, I've been meaning to ask, What does "cre8f1" mean?

Subj: Wasted Day
Date: 10-26
From: cre8f1@mindspring.com
To: Susan_P@aol.com

Hi Susan,

Contrary to the way it appears, I do have a life. And in spite of the fact that this is the second letter I've sent to you today, I also have a career. I'm a freelance copywriter (cre8f1 is "creative one." Get it?). These days I write mostly brochures, which aren't nearly as interesting or exciting as the commercials and radio spots I used to write (when I worked on staff at various ad agencies in the city). I stopped commuting and started freelancing around ten years ago. It pays well, and I can work from home, which means that I can be here for the kiddos, which is sort of the whole point. Wendy is my 11-year-old (who has been banished to her room for the next 11 years, remember?), and Gregory is my delicious little kindergartner, who still can't remember to get off the school bus unless he sees me standing at the bus stop. BTW, our last name is Cohen, although for work purposes I still use my maiden name, Feldman. (In case you couldn't tell from my last name[s] that practically scream it, we're Jewish.) That brings me to my other job. I also write all the press releases for our temple, although those assignments fall under the heading of Volunteer Work. (Translation: I do them as freebies.)

Right now I'm supposed to be working on a series of brochures for a dentist. One of the pamphlets is going to be about (yawn, yawn) bonding teeth. (I can hear you laughing all the way through my computer. Stop That This Instant!)

Technically it's up to my clients to supply me with all the info I need to write their brochures. But I've never had a single client who was either articulate enough or organized enough to do a thorough job, so I rely a lot on the Internet for my background research. But today I couldn't keep my mind on the job at hand. (Wonder why?) I started my Web search, and instead of typing in "tooth bonding" or "bonding of teeth," I wasn't thinking and just entered "bonding." My search came back with nothing about dentistry, but let me tell you, there are a helluva lot of sites out there featuring pornography and S&M! I got disgusted and signed off. That was a couple hours ago. I decided to try my search again, and that's when I discovered your prompt response to the letter I sent this morning. So now I'm answering that. I'm sorry. I'm rambling. Think I'm a little nervous about tomorrow? Well maybe just a bit. Wish me luck.

Lara :- D

Subj: Happy Birthday
Date: 10-27
From: Susan_P@aol.com
To: cre8f1@mindspring.com

Happy birthday to you.
Happy birthday to you.
Happy birthday, dear Lara.
Happy birthday to you.

I sent you a virtual hot-fudge sundae over the Net. Did you get it yet? You're probably at the doctor's right now. Hopefully you're getting a great birthday present from him, too. (But what could possibly be better than an ice-cream sundae with NO calories?) And one more thing: I've been writing to you for how long now, and all of a sudden there's a *Gregory?* Any other kids you just happened to forget to mention? :-)

Subj: re: Happy Birthday
Date: 10-27
From: cre8f1@mindspring.com
To: Susan_P@aol.com

Hi Sue,
Thanks for the birthday greetings. No, I didn't get the sundae yet. And no, no other kids. And no, it's not cancer. (You like how I just slipped that in there, like it's just another fact?) The doctor says that I'm perfectly FINE.

47

I'll give you the details tomorrow. Right now Michael and I are going out for a celebration dinner — birthday *and* good checkup. Yippeeeeee.

2

Subj: I'm Back
Date: 10-28
From: cre8f1@mindspring.com
To: Susan_P@aol.com

Hi Susan,

Sorry I was so rushed yesterday. Let me give you all of the good news:

Saw the breast surgeon. Dr. Crumb. (Poor guy, must be tough being a doctor with a name like that.) Anyway, he says that the lump and the microcalcifications are separate things. First the lump. He could tell by feeling it that it was fine. He says that the microcalcifications are also probably nothing but that I should have another mammogram in 6 months just to be sure that there are no changes. Isn't that great? I'm so thrilled. I'm going to post a note on the breast cancer bulletin board (where we met) and let everyone know how things turned out. I promised to let them know what happened, and I *always* keep my promises. But before I go . . .

Thank you, thank you for helping me get through the last month. You've been a godsend. I'd love to send you a little something to express my thanks. Do the Petersons have a snail-mail address?

Love, Lara

Subj: Don't Hate Me
Date: 10-30
From: Susan_P@aol.com
To: cre8f1@mindspring.com

Lara,

You're not going to want to hear this, but I couldn't live with myself if I remained silent. You need to see another breast surgeon. Dr. Crumb may be absolutely correct that you are perfectly fine (in fact, I'm sure that you are), but you *cannot tell* from feeling a lump that it's harmless. You can have a pretty good *hunch* that everything's OK, but you can't be sure without doing some sort of biopsy. That's why they do biopsies — because you can't tell just from feeling. Like I said, I'm sure you're fine, but you simply must get another opinion. Besides, what have you got to lose? This way you can have two different doctors tell you you're fine and you can feel doubly better. Please, please, get a second opinion. You asked me for my address so you could send me a thank-you gift for helping you through this. But the best thank-you that you could give me would be to see another breast surgeon. Humor me. Please.
  Susan

Subj: Trick or Treat
Date: 10-31
From: Susan_P@aol.com
To: cre8f1@mindspring.com

Hi, Lara,

Happy Halloween. You haven't responded to my request that you get a second opinion. Are you annoyed with me? I know, I may have come on a little heavy-handed, but I really feel strongly about this. I've seen too many women in my support group who've seen too many doctors who said, "Let's wait." Sometimes it's the right thing to do, but sometimes it's not. I just want to make sure that you're being properly cared for. And this business about being able to tell that your lump is fine simply by feeling it makes me nervous. It's contrary to everything I've ever heard or read about this, and you know I hear and read plenty. I'm bugging, I know, but if it is BC, it deserves attention. If it's not, well, your insurance company will have an additional bill. (You do have insurance, don't you?)

On a lighter note — are Wendy and Gregory going out for Halloween? Gabby has a bunch of kids over here right now for a costume party. She's Gumby. (Brings back memories, no?) Thirteen is such an odd age: They're too old to go out trick-or-treating but still young enough to get into the spirit (pun intended) of the whole thing. So she and her friends decided to have this party, and who knows what they're doing. Hopefully they didn't sneak out and toilet-paper anyone's house or egg any mailboxes. (Actually, Gabby and her friends are basically good kids, so I don't have to worry about them doing such dastardly deeds. At least I hope not.) :- o

51

I'm waiting to hear from you. This time it's your turn to send *me* some positive thoughts. I get my yearly mammogram tomorrow. I still get nervous whenever I have to go. Gee, I wonder why?

Subj: Are You There?
Date: 11-03
From: Susan_P@aol.com
To: cre8f1@mindspring.com

You *are* angry with me, aren't you? At least write back and let me know that you're OK and nothing bad has happened to you. It's not like you to be so silent.
    Sue

Subj: re: Are You There?
Date: 11-04
From: cre8f1@mindspring.com
To: Susan_P@aol.com

Dear Sue,
    Please forgive me for taking so long to write back. I'm sorry if you were worried; it's just that I've been swamped with work. With all my doctors' appointments (and all the time I lost because I was searching the Net and dragging up porn sites or too paralyzed with worry to work at all), I'd fallen far behind and deadlines were closing in.

But fear not. As of yesterday the dentist has his brochure copy (complete with anything and everything you ever wanted to know about bonding, bleaching and braces), and Almost-Elementary, a local preschool, now has literature about their newest after-school enrichment program. You may not sleep easier tonight, but I sure will.

With everything that was due finally cleared off of my desk, I was able to hit the bookstore this morning. I picked up a couple of books about breast cancer. You're right. Everything I've skimmed and/or read so far says that a lump should be investigated (as one book put it) and even says that a doctor's hunch isn't enough to go on (as another book put it). That, coupled with the fact that I'm still groping myself dozens of times each day (a sure sign of anxiety, no?), has made me decide to get a second opinion. The only trouble is that I'm driving 50 million carpools a day, have more deadlines lurking right around the corner and haven't been to the gym in more than a week — but, hey, surely finding a few hours for yet another appointment is possible. (Yeah, right.) Still, I'm going to do it. Like you said, it couldn't hurt to have two doctors tell me I'm fine. And we do have insurance (through Michael's firm), so this is all very doable. All I need is time . . . which I'm running out of right now. Gregory's due home from school any moment, and he still needs me standing outside as his visual cue to get off the darn bus. (Hey, he's making progress. Two weeks ago I had to get *on* the bus and tell him it was time to get off! Now at least he knows to look out the window for me.)

Later, Lara

P.S. Oops, almost forgot . . . how'd your mammogram go? I assume fine or you would have said something — or is that "typed" something?

Subj: My Mammogram
Date: 11-06
From: Susan_P@aol.com
To: cre8f1@mindspring.com

Lara,

It was good to hear from you. I'm glad it was simply work that kept you from reading/responding to my e-mail and it wasn't my harping on you about that second opinion. I'm so glad you're getting one. How are you going about choosing another breast surgeon? Want some advice? Good. Get the phone number of a local breast cancer support group. (There must be tons of them in NY.) Ask them who they'd recommend. Women who've "been there" are the best resources for finding great doctors. (Un)fortunately, they also know which doctors to avoid. So make a phone call and see what they have to say. Onward —

It's probably a good thing that we weren't in touch for a while. For a few days there I was a mess. The radiologist saw something on my mammogram, and I was convinced I was having a recurrence. They did something called a "core needle biopsy." Numbed the area, inserted a needle and sucked out some cells, which — thank you, God — turned out to be just fine. But let me tell you, I was a terror to live with until the pathology report came back three days later. On day two of waiting I even called Artie at work, told him I was losing it and warned him that I might do bodily harm to his daughter if he didn't come home early. (I hadn't done that since my diagnosis, two years earlier, so he knew I meant business.) He was home by seven (which is early according to Artie standards). He rubbed my feet for a half hour and kept cooing re-assurances but was realistic enough to pepper them with the statement ". . . and even if it turns out to be something, it'll still be okay. We've crossed that bridge before." I sometimes wonder if I'll ever get used to this. Actually, I don't mean to pat myself on the back too hard, but I think I deal with the stresses that go along with being a sur-vivor pretty well . . . and then I get close to another doctor's appointment (you know, just for a checkup) and realize I'm not nearly as together as I think I am. Stop me, I'm whining. Oh, oh, I can't believe I forgot! I must share this with you. My sis-ter-in-law e-mailed me this joke the day before I went for my mammogram. I guess she figured I could use some comic relief. (She figured right.) Anyway, here it is:

"Many women are afraid of getting their first mammograms. But really, there's absolutely no need to be scared — as long as you're prepared. By simply taking a few minutes every day to do these practice exercises (starting a week before your exam), you'll be completely ready for your test. Best of all, every one of the exercises can be done from the comfort and privacy of your very own home.

Exercise One: Open your refrigerator door and insert one breast between the door and the main box. Have one of your strongest friends slam the door shut as hard as possible and lean on the door for good measure. Hold that position for five seconds. Repeat again, just in case the first time wasn't effective.

Exercise Two: Visit your garage at 3 A.M., when the temperature of the cement floor will be absolutely perfect. Take off all your clothes and lie comfortably on the floor with one breast wedged under the rear tire of the car. Ask a friend to slowly back up the car until your breast is sufficiently flattened and chilled. Turn over and repeat for the other breast.

Exercise Three: Freeze two metal bookends overnight. Strip to the waist. Invite a stranger into the room. Hold one bookend against each side of your breast. Ask the stranger to smash the bookends together as hard as she can. Set up an appointment with the stranger to meet her next year to do it again.

Congrats! You are now properly prepared for your mammogram."

Bye, Susan

Subj: Ha-Ha
Date: 11-08
From: cre8f1@mindspring.com
To: Susan_P@aol.com

Dear Sue,

That mammogram joke was a riot. I actually laughed out loud. Michael wanted to know why I was sitting in front of the computer snickering. I shared. He says to tell you that he thought your joke was cute, but I don't care what he says: If you've never had a mammogram, you can't truly appreciate how hysterically funny it really is. Thanks for the smile.

I feel absolutely awful that you had that mammogram scare and I was nowhere to be found. Some friend. And after you've been there for me. I feel like a total shit. I just wish I'd known. What kind of friendship is this anyway, if you're there to help me through the nervous times and I can't do the same for you?

I'm humoring you and getting my second opinion (the 11th). By the time I got your e-mail suggesting I ask someone from a support group to recommend a breast surgeon, I had already scheduled an appointment with another surgeon that my gyno recommended. (And the appointment is set in stone, since it works with my complicated schedule.)

Anyway, now it's your turn to make me a promise. Promise me that in the future you will write to me when (bad) stuff happens in your life. I don't want to hear that you waited to tell me a blessed thing. Is that understood, young lady? (That's my impression of me talking to Wendy!)

Thinking of you, L.

Subj: Promises, Promises
Date: 11-10
From: Susan_P@aol.com
To: cre8f1@mindspring.com

Dear Lara,

You're right. I promise, no more secrets in the future, *MOM*. Thanks for caring.

Sue

Subj: Second Opinion
Date: 11-11
From: Susan_P@aol.com
To: cre8f1@mindspring.com

Hi, Lara.

Well, kiddo, today's the day. I know better than to even *ask* if you're allowing Michael to accompany you for the second opinion, you stubborn girl, you. I'm keepin' my fingers crossed that I was simply being a Nervous Nellie and that you're A-OK. Let me know when you know something. I'm anxiously waiting for that sexy male voice to utter the words we've all grown to love (and some of us even live for): "You've got mail."

Subj: Nothin' Good
Date: 11-11
From: cre8f1@mindspring.com
To: Susan_P@aol.com

SHIT! I just got home from the breast surgeon's office. You're right. So are all the books I read. The doctor said that he can't tell what's with the lump without a biopsy. (His name is Walker, and he's so young he doesn't even look old enough to vote!) You know how desperate I must be, because I asked him if I could have the kind of biopsy you described. You know, with the needle? (And you know how I *hate* needles.) But he said that because the lump may *or may not* be related to the microcalcifications he needs to do a *surgical biopsy*. He says that's the only way to know if the two issues are related or separate. And if they are separate issues, he wants to make sure that both of them are fine. The intelligent part of my brain knows what he says makes sense, but the scared part of my brain keeps asking why I didn't leave well enough alone. Tell me again how lumps almost always turn out to be nothing.

Michael is gonna freak. He didn't even know I was getting a second opinion. I didn't want him to worry.

Subj: I'm sorry
Date: 11-12
From: Susan_P@aol.com
To: cre8f1@mindspring.com

Lara, I am so, so sorry that you have to go through this, but it's the only way to find out — for sure — what's going on. If it's cancer, you need to know so you can deal with it — early — when it's most treatable and *curable*. If it's not cancer . . . well, you'll be so relieved that you won't be upset to have been put through all of this. Please, please, let me know if there's anything I can do to help.

You've already read some books, so you probably understand what's going on. Did the surgeon say whether or not you need to have a needle localization? If so, I recommend you take a pain pill of some kind about an hour beforehand. Even if you didn't hate needles, I would make the same recommendation, since needle loc's can be painful and the medication will help take the edge off. Ask your doctor to write you a prescription. Oh, I feel just horrible . . . but it's really better to know, even though you may not see it that way right now.

Hang in there, Sue

Subj: Surgery
Date: 11-13
From: cre8f1@mindspring.com
To: Susan_P@aol.com

I'm having the surgery (biopsy) on the 19th. I have to be at the radiology place at 8 A.M. Snafu: Gregory doesn't get on the school bus until 8:45, and I don't want the kids to know what's going on. Solution: I'm having one of my girlfriends pick me up at home and drop me off at the radiologist's on her way to work. Michael will head down to meet me (at the radiologist's) immediately after putting Gregory on the bus. Then he'll drive me to the hospital, where Dr. Walker will meet us and do the biopsy. I should be home before the kids come back from school. (Please Note: My organizational skills remain intact in spite of my nervous disposition.)

I called Walker's office and said that a friend of mine (you) suggested I get a prescription for pain medication to take before the needle localization. The nurse said it shouldn't hurt that much — the radiologist is supposed to be very good — but phoned something in to the pharmacy for me anyway. Thanks for the heads-up. As far as I'm concerned, even if it doesn't hurt, *it's a needle*. Besides, I'll probably be so scared that being a little light-headed from a pain pill could only help. And there are no extra points given for bravery here, are there?

OK, now explain this needle localization procedure. I looked it up in one of my books, but I want the scoop from you. Also, do you speak from firsthand experience or didn't you have one?

Me

Subj: Needle Localization
Date: 11-13
From: Susan_P@aol.com
To: cre8f1@mindspring.com

A needle localization, huh? No, I didn't have one, but many women in my support group have. I'll be straight with you: Some say it's no worse than having a mammogram, and others say it's excruciating. But if you take something beforehand, you're covered either way, right?

Radiologists do needle localizations when the area the surgeon needs to biopsy is small. The only way the surgeon can be sure he's removing the right sample is to have it marked beforehand. They mark you with a needle, hence the name. (I knew you'd appreciate that, being a writer.)

Anyway, first they give you (another!) mammogram so they can see the suspicious area. Then, while your breast is still in the mammogram "vise," they insert a needle into that spot. (Now you know why I recommended the painkillers. Even if it doesn't hurt, it sounds terrible, even to me, and I don't have a problem with needles.) Depending on the radiologist who does the procedure, they sometimes also inject dye through the needle to (double) mark the spot. Just think of a needle localization as the radiologist's version of Hansel and Gretel's bread crumbs.

Sue

P.S. You never mentioned — How'd Michael take the news about the biopsy?

Subj: Blunt, but clear
Date: 11-14
From: cre8f1@mindspring.com
To: Susan_P@aol.com

On 11-13 Susan_P@aol.com wrote:
> *Just think of a needle localization as the radiologists'*
>*version of Hansel and Gretel's bread crumbs.*

Susan, I'd prefer it if they really did use bread crumbs!

I know that I asked for the details, but did you have to make it sound so bad? Actually, I appreciate your honesty. Believe it or not, I'm the kind of person who does better with more information, not less (however brutal it may be).

As for Michael . . . let's just say that I do believe I missed my calling in life. I should have been a damage-control specialist. I really did an outstanding job (if I do say so myself) of positioning the whole biopsy as little more than a fact-finding procedure. "The doctor thinks I'm fine, but there's only one way to be absolutely certain and that's to go in there and take a sample." Thanks to my boiled-down explanation, Michael seemed to have little trouble understanding what's going on, why it's necessary and most important, why there's nothing to be really concerned about — at least not yet. (And if he didn't buy into my practically pooh-poohing the whole thing, then he did a such a great job of fooling me that he deserves the Oscar for Best Actor.)

Last night Michael and I went out to dinner with another couple that we've been friends with for 10 years. I was telling them what was going on with me. Needless to say I told them all about you and how wonderful you've been. (I mean that, Susan. You've been such a tremendous help through all of this. You wouldn't believe how much it means to me just knowing that you're out there for me.) Anyway, my friends found it incredible that you and I haven't just picked up the phone. They kept asking me why. I tried to explain, but I must have sounded like an idiot. Is it just me, or do you also feel that there's something special in our relationship because we *don't* just pick up the phone?

Subj: It's Not You
Date: 11-15
From: Susan_P@aol.com
To: cre8f1@mindspring.com

Lara, I vote against the phone. No pictures either. I already have an idea of how you look and sound — and can think of no reason to let reality correct my impressions of you — or yours of me. I mean, what if you sounded like Minnie Mouse? :-)

Besides, I look forward to getting your letters.

I think we'd stop writing if we started talking.
Don't you?

Sue

Subj: No calls. No pics.
Date: 11-16
From: cre8f1@mindspring.com
To: Susan_P@aol.com

I do *not* sound like Minnie Mouse. I sound like *Mickey*. :- O

Actually, I agree with everything you said. It reminds me of blind dates. (Michael and I have been married for so long — 18 years — that I sometimes have trouble remembering what single life was like. But blind dates? *Those* I recall.) Over the phone the guy always sounded sexy, intelligent and humorous. Over the phone we always found plenty to talk about. But face-to-face he never looked anything like I imagined. And face-to-face we never had *anything* to talk about. Yes, blind dates were always awful. So yes, I definitely vote to keep our relationship the way it is. We can always change our minds later anyway. Right?

OK, let's move on. I'm trying not to dwell on my upcoming biopsy and trying instead to focus on a job that's due tomorrow. ("Trying" is the operative word.) It's for a local bank. I'm supposed to be writing a statement stuffer. That's one of those things that's sent along in the same envelope with your bank statement. Anyway, the bank is pushing their free-checking-with-interest accounts. (Free toaster, anyone?) But there is an upside to such bo-ring work: I did the whole job from home, including choosing a layout (via fax) from the graphic designer. In fact, with e-mail, fax machines and express mail I rarely need to meet *anyone* face to face anymore. (Gee, I wonder if this is a pattern I've failed to recognize in myself until now — communicating via technology versus up-close-and-personal!) Actually, I am very much a people person; I just find it more enjoyable to work from the privacy of my house, in my sweats, minus the time sheets and bosses.

Listen, you, I've got some wordsmithing to do before zapping the bank, so I'd better skedaddle. I also have to write a press release (for our temple's upcoming interfaith Thanksgiving service) if I want it to make the papers before turkey day. (I do.) So it's time to stop procrastinating. See ya. (Not really.)

Me

Subj: Luck
Date: 11-17
From: Susan_P@aol.com
To: cre8f1@mindspring.com

Hey, Lara. You're sounding mighty chipper. Good for you! Just wanted to wish you luck on

Friday and let you know that I'll be thinking of you. Need to fly. I just got home from a hectic day at work, and Gabby's screaming that her wrist is killing her. She's been complaining for days, and I told her to ice it and take Advil, figuring it would be fine. I guess I figured wrong. Fortunately the pediatrician's office could squeeze us in before they close, *if we leave right away.* Gabby's yelling at me to shut down the computer, NOW. What a mouth!

Subj: Well?
Date: 11-20
From: Susan_P@aol.com
To: cre8f1@mindspring.com

Hi, doll. I'm still waiting for news about your biopsy. How'd everything go?

Subj: Waiting
Date: 11-21
From: cre8f1@mindspring.com
To: Susan_P@aol.com

Dear Sue,
Sorry to keep you waiting. The anesthesia wiped me out, and I spent most of yesterday sleeping. Or maybe it was the stress of the last few weeks (months!) catching up with me. Either way, I was exhausted. Still am.

The doctor said that everything looked fine, but he won't have the complete pathology report until after the weekend. I'm to call him at his office on Tuesday (the 23rd), after 3:00 P.M. How's that for specific? But that's what he said. Look for an e-mail from me that day, starting at 3:01! (Joking. Sort of.) I hope you don't mind, but it really hurts, so I've got to cut this short.

L.

Subj: No pressure
Date: 11-21
From: Susan_P@aol.com
To: cre8f1@mindspring.com

Hi, Lara.

Thanks for writing. It was good to hear from you, although I'm sorry you're in pain. You'll feel better over the weekend. I know it's hard, but try not to worry too much. When you feel up to it, let me know how the biopsy went (particularly the needle loc). But please, don't feel any pressure to spend more time typing than feels comfortable.

Work's been a zoo. Got a new supervisor. It's too soon to tell whether that's good news or bad news. She's female. You know, sometimes I think we're harder on our own kind. When I told her that I had to leave a half hour early to take Gabby to the hand specialist, she gave me that raised eyebrow, like I need to get my priorities straight. I got the distinct impression she disapproved and was asking, "Are you a professional or are you a mom?" (Mind you, I got all that from a single raised eyebrow! Think I'm a little paranoid?)

Well, dolly, feel good. I can't wait to hear from you.

Susan

Subj: Question
Date: 11-22
From: cre8f1@mindspring.com
To: Susan_P@aol.com

I thought this was supposed to be a simple surgery. It still really hurts. A lot. I was hoping to hide all of this from the kids, but it's not possible. I had to be able to explain my pain, so I told them that I had a mole removed. Of course, Wendy wanted to know why. (I said that it bothered me when my bra rubbed against it.) Gregory isn't even allowed to hug me (my rule), since any pressure or arm movements just kill. (And that's *really* killing me, because I could sure use one of Gregory's hugs right about now.)

Q. Is it supposed to hurt so much?

Speaking of hurting, the needle localization wasn't so bad. And that's without pain medication. (I was so nervous that morning I forgot to even take the pill!) My girlfriend dropped me off at the radiology place as planned. The tech put my breast in the vise, squished it and took some pictures. I had to wait (breast in vise) until she developed the pics to be sure the microcalcifications showed up. Then the radiologist came in and inserted a needle into my breast. (Ouch, but not a huge ouch.) Then they took more pics to make sure that the needle was actually hitting the right spot. All in all, my breast was in the vise for entirely too long. It was no picnic. But like I said, it was doable. By the time they'd finished with me, Michael had arrived. They taped the end of the needle (it's flexible) that was sticking out of my breast onto my skin and sent me off to the hospital with Michael, my designated driver. He barely spoke to me on the drive over, and at the hospital he seemed more interested in the newspaper than in me. But I'm not complaining. At least he wasn't falling apart. In fact, if I could choose between seeing his face buried in a newspaper or dripping with tears, the *New York Times* gets my vote every time. But I do feel sorry for him. In spite of the fact that he's playing it cool, he's obviously *very* scared. But good for him. He knows that right now I can't handle him talking about his fears. I've got too many of my own to deal with. I sometimes ask myself if it's possible that this is more difficult for him than it is for me. But I'm sure it's not. (See. I'm multitalented. I not only ask myself questions, I answer them, too.)

Anyway, everyone at the hospital was really nice. A definite upside to being able to have the surgery in Westchester, as opposed to the city. No one treated me like I was simply one of the masses.

Well, that's really it. Except for the fact that the place where Walker cut me is still killing me.

Lara

P.S. I know that I'm somewhat brain-dead, but did I *know* Gabby was seeing a hand specialist? I don't recall. Is she OK? I'm off to take a nap. Later.

Subj: Gabby
Date: 11-21
From: Susan_P@aol.com
To: cre8f1@mindspring.com

Hi, Lara.

Gabby's wrist is fine. The pediatrician wanted her to see a specialist just to be safe. It's some sort of soft-tissue irritation. He wrote out a prescription for an antiinflammatory. Doctor says that if she feels like it she can go back to basketball next week. I am always amazed at how quickly kids are able to bounce back and how easily they heal, while us old bags take forever. Which brings me to you. (Notice that I have lumped you with me in the "old bag" category?) All joking aside, I'm sorry that you're still hurting. Really. I *am* surprised that you're not feeling better and don't know why you'd still be in pain. If you're not better when you call Dr. Walker for your results on the 23rd, mention it to him.

Susan

Subj: Clock-watching
Date: 11-23
From: cre8f1@mindspring.com
To: Susan_P@aol.com

It's 1:00. I can't believe I have to wait for *two more hours* to call Dr. Walker. I hate this.

Lara

Subj: Still Clock-watching
Date: 11-23
From: cre8f1@mindspring.com
To: Susan_P@aol.com

OK, now it's 2:00. T minus one hour — and counting. (How do you like my impression of John Glenn?)

L.

Subj: re: Still Clock-watching
Date: 11-23
From: Susan_P@aol.com
To: cre8f1@mindspring.com

Lara, it's 3:05. I logged on hoping for news

but so far have only received your updates of 1:00 and 2:00. I'll try again at 3:30. Hope to find new mail from you then. Everything's crossed and I've said a prayer. (I'm Catholic. I figure if we both pray, one of us is bound to get through. What are the odds that we both have the wrong connection?) Only joking. Oops, I've just violated that rule about not discussing religion or politics with those you care about. Ah well, I think you're tough enough to take it.

Speaking of politics, you do know that between space outings John Glenn was a senator from this great state of Ohio, do you not?

Subj: Benign!
Date: 11-23
From: cre8f1@mindspring.com
To: Susan_P@aol.com

Hallelujah! It's 4:00 and everything's BENIGN. I'm sorry it took so long, but good news is worth waiting for. When I called Walker's office at 3:00, his nurse said, "He'll have to call you back. Are you at home Mrs. Cohen?" I was sure it was bad news, just from the way she said it. It was the worst half-hour wait of my life. But I'm fine. I was so relieved when he said, "Everything came back benign," that I forgot to ask him about the pain that I'm still having. But I have to see him on Friday for a follow-up appointment to the surgery (and to

73

have my stitches removed?), so I'll ask him then. I must go. I haven't even called Michael yet.

Subj: Yes!
Date: 11-23
From: Susan_P@aol.com
To: cre8f1@mindspring.com

Congratulations, kiddo. That's great, great news! And you deserve it. It hasn't been easy, and you certainly took the long road to get there, but you did it! *You really are fine.* I can't imagine how relieved you must feel. Strike that. Yes I can! When I signed on at 3:30 and there was still no word from you, I was really getting concerned. I must admit, I was starting to second-guess our decision not to exchange phone numbers. Then I realized, I know your name, your husband's name, the town you live in . . . I could just call directory assistance. But I forced myself to wait for your e-mail. I don't know, maybe it's the dramatic part of me coming out, but it seems to be such a fitting end to this whole nightmare — knowing that the two of us were both sweating it out and waiting for the news *together.*
Congrats again, Susan

Subj: My friend
Date: 11-25
From: cre8f1@mindspring.com
To: Susan_P@aol.com

Dear Susan,

Happy Thanksgiving. This year I feel like I have so many things to give thanks for, and you, my friend, are at the top of that list. You have become such a wonderful friend. I don't know if I could have made it through all of this without you. The truth is, I do know. I would have; that's just the kind of person I am. But I also know that you made it easier for me. Much easier. You helped me manage my fears and keep my anxiety in check. You have been a gift to me. I know that a million years ago I asked for your snail-mail address so I could send you a thank-you gift. But now I know you better and have come up with a more appropriate way to let you know how much I've grown to admire and appreciate you. When I feel better, I am going to go back to the breast cancer bulletin board where we met. I'm going to keep reading it until I find a woman I can relate to and I think I can help. And then I'm going to answer her letter. I'm going to tell her that while I am not a breast cancer survivor myself, I owe a great deal to an extraordinary woman who is very much a survivor and will always have a special place in my heart.

Susan, as a tribute to you, I promise that I will find one woman, every year, to befriend in this way. (And you know that I *always* keep my promises.) Giving back in this manner seems the most appropriate way to thank a woman who has given so much. Hey, who knows, maybe I'll even meet another great lady who lives in a cornfield in the middle of nowhere. But no matter how many women I meet in cyberspace, none will ever take your place in my heart. Not ever.

With love, Lara

Subj: Your letter
Date: 11-26
From: Susan_P@aol.com
To: cre8f1@mindspring.com

Wow! Thank you for that lovely letter, Lara. But who are you implying lives in a cornfield in the middle of nowhere? *I* live in a well developed city, thank you very much. Seems to me that *you're* the one who described Armonk as a sleepy, deer-infested town in the middle of nowhere!

To tell you the truth, Armonk sounds delightful right now. I'm having job stress. My gut was right about the new supervisor. She's a bitch. Artie is also stressed, but for him that's more the norm. He's got a small practice (only one other partner), and he's always working long hours. Lately, though, it's been especially bad. (I'm talking 10 P.M. or later.) That's because he's in the midst of a trial. To hear Artie tell it, his day is "wasted" in the courtroom, so once the court day is over, he has to go back to the office if he wants to get any "work" done. For the past two weeks he's been working weekends, too. (He's a medical-malpractice attorney. Do you think that makes *my* doctors at all nervous?) Anyway, this case has been especially bad, since it involves a 10-year-old girl. (Cases with kids are always [emotionally] difficult.) But the point I was going to make is that Gabby's furious with Artie because he hasn't made it to any of her basketball games yet. I don't blame her for being angry. But on the rare occasions when he *is* home, the two of them are engaged in WWIII right under my nose. And get this: They don't even look at each other for the "reaction shots" after Gabby sends a zinger (à la: "Obviously you *don't* care.") Instead they both look at *me!* I'm trying my best to stay out of it. Lord knows, Gabby and I have enough opportunities of our own for conflict; I don't need to steal any of the thunder (anger?) directed at Artie.

I printed out that lovely letter you sent me, and I intend to reread it when I need a reminder that, contrary to Gabby's belief, I am not a bad person. I can practically hear you tittering at your keyboard. But just you wait. Soon Wendy — sweet little 11-year-old Wendy — will turn into a 13-year-old. Out of your darling little treasure a new Wendy will emerge. She will be a living, breathing mouth-with-attitude. Her pet name for you will be "Bitch" (uttered under her breath, never in full voice, and never facing you directly). Her favorite protest will be "You're so unfair," followed closely by "You don't understand," and her favorite pastime will be sleeping. I won't even try to prepare you for what her bedroom will look like. I wouldn't want to spoil the surprise. Besides you don't have heart problems, do you? :- [

Anyway, enough of my ranting for one day. How are you feeling? Better, I hope. I ducked out early today and brought some work home. I'd better go if I want to finish it before anyone arrives.

Susan

3

Subj: Yogi Berra
Date: 11-29
From: cre8f1@mindspring.com
To: Susan_P@aol.com

Susan —

We're all big Yankee fans in this house. And you know Yogi Berra's expression "It ain't over til it's over"? Well, I swear, he could have been talking about me. This is obviously someone's idea of a big joke, only I'm not smiling. And I sure as hell am not laughing.

Let me explain:

I saw Dr. Walker on Friday. I'm complaining about how much it still hurts where he did the biopsy. He has the nerve to ask me if I have a low threshold for pain. That was strike one. (Hey, I've started on this baseball metaphor, I may as well stick with it.) Anyway, I assure him that I'm tough stuff, but the incision really hurts. He cuts me off in midsentence. (Strike Two: I *hate* to be interrupted.) He tells me to get dressed and meet him in his office, where we can talk. (As quickly as I called it, I revoke strike two, figuring he's right — we should talk when I'm clothed and therefore in a less vulnerable position.) In his office I remind him that before the biopsy he told me that I'd be back to playing tennis in 3 to

5 days. It's already been a week, and I'm still in too much pain to even think about picking up my racket. He interrupts me again. (Strike Two: And I'm not taking it back this time.) "Let's talk about the surgery," he says. He proceeds to tell me:

1. He was able to remove all of the micro-calcifications, and the pathology report indicates that they were benign.
2. While he was "in there," he was able to feel the lump and also removed that.
3. In about three months I should have another mammogram taken of my left breast. He explained that anytime there's surgery there are changes to the breast, and a new baseline mammo will give him something to compare against (in the event I have any problems with that breast in the future).

So far, so good. Then I ask him about why my breast still hurts. He says he doesn't know why. "It shouldn't hurt anymore. But let's not talk about that right now. We need to talk about your pathology report." He says it just like that. Slips it in like it's nothing. I innocently ask, "What about it?"

WALKER: Well, we need to talk about what it means. They found some atypical cells.

ME: *WHO THE HELL KNOWS WHAT I SAID!* I was in such shock that I practically threw up. I didn't hear most of what he said after that. I mean, we had a whole conversation about "atypical cells." All about what they are and how they mean that I'll need to have breast exams done by doctors more frequently and lots of other stuff. I just don't remember most of it. I know that I asked him some questions, but because I refused to even use the C word, I'm not sure that he even knew what I was asking. Does any of this make any sense? Of course not. And that's how idiotic I sounded in his office, too. I was so stunned that I couldn't put my thoughts together. I mean, I went into his office thinking that everything was normal. Apparently "normal" is not the same as "benign." Benign, I now know, just means "not cancer."

I left his office, and I know that I drove home, because that's where I was when Michael arrived that night. I told Michael what happened, and (after turning pale) he started asking me — you guessed it — questions. But this time his questions were almost the same as mine. (Does this mean I'm going to get cancer? Does it increase the likelihood? Do atypical cells *turn into* cancer? Does this in any way put my sisters at risk for breast cancer?) We agreed that I'd call the doctor the next day to get my/our questions answered.

I didn't sleep all night.

The next morning I call Dr. Walker. I preface the conversation by apologizing. I tell him that I am sure he covered a lot of these things with me in his office the previous day, but I was in such shock after hearing that word "atypical" that I know I missed a lot of what he said. Then I ask him a question about whether or not having atypical cells increases the likelihood that I'll develop breast cancer. He doesn't miss a beat. The asshole tells me that I *obviously* wasn't paying attention because he did, in fact, go over all of that with me already. (STRIKE THREE.) I should hang up on him. But do you know what I, Lara, Wimp of the Year, do instead? I *listen* as he explains that atypical cells are a whole lot of nothing. I uh-huh and yes him as he makes point after condescending point and speaks to me in a tone so childish that even Gregory would find it offensive. I continue to remain on the line as he tells me that I should not worry about this. I listen as he, the expert, instructs me: "You can't push this finding all the way out of your mind, because atypical cells mean that you need to be followed more closely in the future. But this finding shouldn't be in the front of your mind either. Leave this in the middle of your mind — in fact, don't worry about a thing. Just leave everything up to me." This was all delivered in the manner of "Don't worry your pretty little head about this. Just leave everything up to me, the *man*, the *professional*, the *doctor*."

I am so angry with myself. I allowed him to intimidate me — this *experienced* doctor who probably still gets carded every time he orders a beer. I should have just told him to take a hike. But what did I do instead? I remained polite and kept saying "Yes doctor, no doctor" and other stupid stuff. Disgusting, huh? Then I got off the phone and cried my eyes out. (Please, God, help me to raise Wendy to be a more forceful and confident woman and not a dishrag like her mom. Amen.)

A couple of hours later I call my internist in the city. I haven't seen him in years, 'cause I'm never sick. Well, I occasionally get strep throat from Wendy or Gregory. But I've never felt the need (or had the time) to go into the city for a strep test. I usually just see one of our local yokels for a quick Q-tip down the throat, and they write me a prescription. Good-bye and good luck. Anyway, I call Dr. Berns. (He's the internist in Manhattan.) In spite of the fact I have not been to see him in eons, he remembers me. I tell him what's going on and ask if he can answer some questions about atypical cells. He's such a doll and says that while he's happy to answer my questions over the phone, I should make an appointment to see him, since it's been so long anyway. I know he's right and that our conversation won't be as rushed if we meet face-to-face. (And after everything I've been through, I really do want to do this right.) Dr. Berns asks me if I know that he's also an oncologist who specializes in breast cancer. (I didn't know that he had a dual practice. I'd only used him as an internist for a couple of years when Michael and I lived in the city before Wendy was born.) Anyway, Berns tells me to get a copy of my mammogram, pathology report and biopsy tissue slides from the hospital. He says that he's sure everything is fine, but he'll feel better (and so will I) if he sends everything to one of his colleagues who's a pathologist and an expert in analyzing breast tissue. He calls this guy a "guru" in the field. That's good enough for me.

I call Walker's office to get copies of everything I need. The nurse asks why I need this stuff. I tell her that my internist is also a specialist in breast cancer and wants to look over everything. Susan, I swear, she practically yells at me through the phone, "But you don't have breast cancer." I tell her I know that, but my doctor wants to see everything anyway. She tells me she'll fax me a copy of my pathology report, but I need to call the hospital to get everything else and NO, she doesn't have the name or number of anyone at the hospital who can help me locate my mammogram or the slides. BITCH!

After four phone calls I find the right person/department and make arrangements for the hospital to assemble my stuff. (They won't send it. I have to pick it up and sign it out.) My appointment with Dr. Berns is Dec. 2. Oh, geez — I thought I'd given myself enough time to write this letter in great detail, but I must have gotten carried away, 'cause it's getting late. The bottom line: If I leave now, I'll be able to get to the hospital and back before W & G come home from school. Bye.

Lara

Subj: Whoa
Date: 11-30
From: Susan_P@aol.com
To: cre8f1@mindspring.com

On 11-29 cre8f1@mindspring.com wrote:
>*(Please, God, help me to raise Wendy to be a more*
>*forceful and confident woman and not a dishrag like*
>*her mom. Amen.)*

Now cut that out. You are not a dishrag. A dishrag would not have immediately called her internist for more information. You took action and are to be commended. Do you know how many women would have heard that they were fine and that would have been the end of it? Do you know how many women would have been content not to worry their pretty little heads over the matter. BTW, are you? Pretty, I mean? Also, you never mentioned that you play tennis. Me, too. I play on a USTA team (rated 2.5), which as you probably know is not very good. Artie calls it Helen Keller tennis. But it's good exercise and I enjoy it, so he can joke all he likes.

OK, let's get serious. You're very brave, Lara, and you've done the right thing. You told me a while ago that you're the kind of person who does better with more information, not less. Now you'll get it. Dr. Berns thinks that you're fine, too, but is obviously the kind of doctor every woman deserves: one who wants to double-check, *just to be sure.* I'm sure you'll feel better after seeing him anyway. Please don't be so hard on yourself. When you talked to Dr. Walker, you were in an extremely vulnerable state, not to mention that you were blindsided. I'd say you did very well, and under less than stellar circumstances, too. But may I make a suggestion? If you insist on seeing these doctors by yourself, at least take a tape recorder with you. That way if you have questions about what's been said, you can always play back the tape. Better yet, stop trying so hard to protect Michael and have him come with you to some of these doctors. Taking Michael would also make your ride home from your appointments less dangerous. This is the second time you've written to me telling me that you don't remember driving home. If you insist on driving around in such a state, sooner or later you're gonna hit some poor innocent bystander. (And you think you feel lousy *now?*) Seriously, Lara, stop trying to go through this all by yourself. I'm there for you, but I can't literally be *there* for you. Get Michael or one of your friends or family members (you mentioned sisters, where are they?) to be with you. You lose no points for leaning on others. Swear.

Susan

Subj: Someone
Date: 12-01
From: cre8f1@mindspring.com
To: Susan_P@aol.com

Dear Susan,

I'm really warped. As I read over your last letter, I kept hearing "Someone to Watch Over Me" playing in my head. At least I'm starting to regain my sense of humor. Sort of.

Your point about having someone come with me to my doctors' appointments is well taken. But I really thought I was going to Dr. Walker's simply to get my stitches out. And I did have someone with me. Gregory had a play date, so Wendy tagged along. She saw "breast surgeon" on Walker's door and wanted to know why I was seeing *him*. (She doesn't miss a trick.) I told her that since the mole was near my breast, that's the kind of doctor I needed to see. She accepted that. She sat in the waiting room while Walker examined me and delivered his news about atypical cells.

I know that Wendy doesn't count as having someone with me, though. It's just that I didn't think it was necessary to ask Michael to miss work over a few stitches being removed. And I'm taking the train into the city tomorrow to see Dr. Berns, so you don't have to worry about me driving around in an altered state and killing any innocents. But I'm not concerned about leaving his office in a daze. This appointment really and truly is just a checkup and an information-gathering thing anyway.

Lara

P.S. Helen Keller tennis, huh? I'd whip your butt. Artie sounds like he has a great sense of humor

87

(just like his wife). I'm a pretty good player. Better at singles than doubles. I play in a league once a week, and Wendy and I share a one-hour lesson every Friday. She takes the first half hour, I take the second. It's a nice way for us to spend some time together. Besides, I love my lessons (my instructor's a doll), and it's great to have something at the end of the week that I can look forward to. It's really the only true thing I do for *me*.

P.P.S. I have two younger sisters. Both live outside of Chicago, which is where I'm from. So they are clearly not going to be attending any doctors' appointments with me anytime in the near future. ;-)

Subj: Hometowns
Date: 12-02
From: Susan_P@aol.com
To: cre8f1@mindspring.com

Lara, Lara. You've been holding back on me. Midwestern roots, huh? No wonder we get along so well. When you say you grew up outside of Chicago, where exactly? i.e., How *hick* is it? (And you tease *me* about living in a cornfield in the middle of nowhere. How dare you?)

Subj: Dr. Berns
Date: 12-02
From: cre8f1@mindspring.com
To: Susan_P@aol.com

I don't know why, but taking the train to the city really makes me tired. Poor Michael has to do it every day. I guess you just get used to it. Anyway, I'm home. Dr. Berns assures me that there's nothing to worry about. (But he didn't do it in a condescending way.) He explained that atypical cells are not cancerous, nor will they necessarily become cancer, nor do they mean that I will ever develop cancer in my whole, entire life, which he expects to be very long. But he says since atypical cells are not entirely normal, I need to be followed and watched a bit more carefully. I can live with that. That means continuing to do monthly breast self-exams (only now I'll *really* do them every month), seeing a doctor twice a year for "professional" breast exams and having a mammogram every year. See, like I said, it's all very doable.

Dr. Berns seemed to think that a lymph node under my arm was inflamed. He said that sometimes happens after a biopsy but told me to keep an eye on it, just in case it stays that way. (He showed me how he wants me to check it.) He also told me that he was sending my biopsy slides to some pathologist who is one of the country's experts in breast tissue. This is where it pays to live so close to the city, where the best and brightest are (supposedly) drawn. (BTW, I grew up in Winnetka, Illinois, a North Shore suburb of Chicago — which is about as far from being in a cornfield as you can get!)

Anyway, Berns said that it would be a week

before he knew anything and to give him a call then. That's it. Then I got on the train and finished rereading *To Kill a Mockingbird*. I never get tired of that book. I'm leaving it lying around, hoping Wendy will pick it up. She's a real bookworm who reads everything she can get her hands on. Lately, however, she's not very eager to accept my book suggestions. I think adolescence is beginning.

Later. Lara

Subj: Hi
Date: 12-03
From: Susan_P@aol.com
To: cre8f1@mindspring.com

I'm glad your appointment with Dr. Berns went well. He sounds like a good guy. I'm LOL over Wendy rejecting your recommended reading. Just wait. It gets better.

Me

Subj: Translation, please
Date: 12-05
From: cre8f1@mindspring.com
To: Susan_P@aol.com

Susan. Allow me to display my ignorance. What's LOL?

Subj: This 'n' that
Date: 12-08
From: Susan_P@aol.com
To: cre8f1@mindspring.com

LOL is Laughing Out Loud. Which, BTW, I'm not doing much of these days. I hate my job, all thanks to this truly despicable new supervisor. In fact, I think I'm going to resign. That's one of the good things about my breast cancer experience — it taught me that life is too short to spend day after day being miserable. Artie makes a good living (he'd better, for all the hours he puts in!), so I don't really need to work for financial reasons. But I've always enjoyed the emotional fulfillment. However, lately the only emotions I've been feeling are anger and resentment. I'm going to stay until after the holidays, though. I may not depend on the financial aspects of working, but I'm not stupid either. I'll resign *after* getting my Christmas bonus, thank you very much.

I've already put my résumé together. I'm good at what I do. Toot! Toot! (Hear that? That's the sound of me blowing my own horn.) But really, I *am* a good programmer and can't imagine that I'd have any trouble finding a job if I were willing to work full-time. That's the problem, though. I'm not. I will only consider part-time. Even though Gabby begins high school next year, I still like to be here for her. She's been acting out a lot more lately.

Something's going on with her. She's not talking about it, but hopefully, when she decides to let it out, I'll be here for her. I think she's still sorting through some of the issues of my cancer. In fact, I know it. One of her good friends' moms was just diagnosed, and it seems to have awakened a lot of Gabby's old fears. She left a poem she wrote for English class on the kitchen table (where she is in the habit of doing her homework, despite my protests).

I REMEMBER

I remember when I was young
and shouts of laughter filled the house,
not worrying if I was too loud
or if I was giving Mom a headache.

I remember when my dad
wasn't so high-tempered.
He didn't yell at me
if I didn't listen the first time.
Instead he laughed and said,
Remember,
the next time.

I remember when I was carefree
and never thought about tomorrow.
I remember how life used to be
I remember last September.

Cancer came into our house
uninvited and unwanted.
It stayed long enough to change my entire world,
as I remembered.

Now I have to be quiet,
and listen the first time.
I am no longer carefree.
I remember the way things used to be.
And I remember,

I liked it better.

Subj: Poem
Date: 12-10
From: cre8f1@mindspring.com
To: Susan_P@aol.com

Oh, Susan, that poem made me cry. I can't even imagine how it made you feel. Do you think that she left it on the kitchen table intentionally? I don't know Gabby, just what you tell me, but she's obviously a very caring girl who feels things deeply. It sounds to me like she needs to talk. BTW, on a professional note I feel compelled to add that Gabby is a *very* talented writer. If you decide to tell her that you read her poem, you should tell her to submit it to one of the teen magazines. I'm sure there are a lot of other girls out there who would be greatly moved and able to identify with Gabby's words.

I spoke to Dr. Berns. He tells me that the pathologist looked at my biopsy slides. The pathologist *thinks* he sees something called "lobular carcinoma in situ." Berns says it's a misnomer. Even though the word "carcinoma" is in it, it's not cancer. But apparently these cells act as a tumor marker, warning that cancer *might* happen later. I looked it up in one of the books I have, and again, it's one of those things that simply means I must be watched more carefully. It's not something they even remove with surgery, since it isn't cancer. I feel like I'm in breast cancer purgatory or something. You're fine — no you're not. Well, yes you are, but you may or may not be fine in the future! Anyway, this pathologist (that Dr. Berns sent my stuff to) wants to do a deeper cutting of the tissue removed during the Walker biopsy. That means that I have to go back to the hospital and get the block (apparently, they put the biopsy tissue in paraffin) so this pathologist can look at the cells *beneath* the ones on the slides that I've already given him. I feel like I should open a delivery business and start charging for my schlepping. But they won't send this stuff; I have to personally sign it all out of the hospital. Afraid of lawsuits in case something gets lost, I guess. And it's a good thing, too, since I happen to know a great malpractice attorney. :-)

I guess I'm pretty relaxed about this latest information. Dr. Berns made it quite clear that with lobular carcinoma in situ there's nothing to be done except get my checkups, which of course I'll do.

The good doctor and I are going to talk again after the holidays, which is swell with me. I'd love to forget that I even have breasts for the remainder of the year. Hopefully, I'll start the new year fresh and with better luck.

Subj: Ho-Ho-Ho
Date: 12-13
From: Susan_P@aol.com
To: cre8f1@mindspring.com

On 12-10 cre8f1@mindspring.com wrote:
> *Hopefully, I'll start the new year fresh and with better luck.*

Excuse me, Lara, but exactly what is wrong with the luck you have? OK, you had a breast cancer scare, but you turned out to be fine. Lobular carcinoma in situ sounds like a pretty good place to be when you consider the possible alternatives, no? Count your blessings and enjoy the season.

I'm off to Artie's Christmas party. I'm a lousy corporate wife. I hate these things and have serious trouble remembering anyone's name. He may only have one partner, but there are other attorneys, associates, paralegals and secretaries, *plus* everyone's spouse or significant other. I'm hoping they'll all have enough eggnog and won't notice that I never utter anyone's name. I'll

simply smile and say, "It's great to see you."
Cheers.

Subj: Bah, Humbug
Date: 12-17
From: cre8f1@mindspring.com
To: Susan_P@aol.com

Artie's pretty smart. I noticed that he held his office party on a weeknight. No one can get too drunk or stay too late since there's work the next day. Smart. Michael's firm hasn't learned that lesson yet. His party is tonight. Since it's Friday, everyone will get good and polluted. Joy, oh, joy. I, too, am a pretty sorry excuse for a corporate wife. I also can't remember anyone's name, but I'm even worse than you. This year I'm ducking out of the party completely! Michael is going to tell everyone that I couldn't find a sitter for the kids, which is true. But that's only because I didn't even try. (I told you I was bad.)

Did you ever tell Gabby that you saw her poem? Did you talk about it? Just wondering. If I'm prying, just tell me to back off.

L.

Subj: Oops
Date: 12-20
From: Susan_P@aol.com
To: cre8f1@mindspring.com

Hi, Lara.

It just occurred to me that I missed Hanukkah. I'm sorry. A happy belated season's greetings. I'd like to send you one of our Christmas cards but don't know if that would be appropriate. It's a for-real Christmas card, as opposed to a general, all-purpose, all-religion, "Season's Greetings" card. It's just that when you open it, there's a picture of all of us, and I thought you might like to see what we look like. I'll leave it up to you. If you send me your snail-mail address, I'll send one — if not, I won't.

No, I never got up the guts to tell Gabby that I read her poem. Never the right moment, I guess. We've been getting along pretty well, though. Maybe it's the time of year. Christmas is always such a happy time in our house. We actually had a nice Thanksgiving, too. We always have all of Artie's family over for dinner. This includes his parents, five brothers and sisters and all their kids. It adds up to a grand total of 36! Right before we eat, we have this nice little tradition of going around the table and giving everyone a chance to say what they're grateful for. (With 36 people to get through, I'm always grateful to finally *eat*.) Anyway, this year when we got to Gabby, she said she was grateful that we were all together and that everyone was healthy this year — "especially Mom." Sometimes the nicest things come out of that giant mouth of hers. I bit the insides of my cheeks to keep from crying.

Subj: Can't wait
Date: 12-23
From: cre8f1@mindspring.com
To: Susan_P@aol.com

You can send the Peterson family Christmas card, dripping with all of its holy Christian sentiment to:

The Cohen Family
Ten River Lakes Road
Armonk, NY 10504

I'll look forward to getting it. And don't feel bad about missing Chanukah, I almost missed it myself. It came so darn early this year. We usually send one of those family photo cards, too, only ours doesn't open. (It's just the photograph with the greeting printed along the side.) This year the greeting says "From Our House to Yours." Think that's nondenominational enough? Send me your address and you can see what we all look like, too.

BTW, who does the cooking for 36 people? If you tell me that you do, Betty Crocker, I think I'll croak. I couldn't imagine. I'm a lousy cook, my kids are lousy eaters, and we have no family nearby, so we've got no excuse to have a huge meal. To make the holiday special we eat in the dining room instead of the kitchen. This year I must also confess that dinner consisted of takeout. I am *so* bad.

Subj: Christmas Day
Date: 12-25
From: Susan_P@aol.com
To: cre8f1@mindspring.com

It's Christmas Day, and I didn't want the day to pass without letting you know that I'm thinking of you. I even prayed for you and your continued good health at midnight mass.

Please send the card ASAP. Inquisitive minds are dying for visuals!

The Peterson Family
4267 Northview Circle
Canton, OH 44711
I'll be waiting by my mailbox.
Susan

Subj: Snowstorm
Date: 12-27
From: cre8f1@mindspring.com
To: Susan_P@aol.com

Hi Susan,

Those of us with the dubious distinction of being located "north and west of the city" have been snowed in for two days. One and a half feet. Michael and the kids are outside trying to shovel the snow away from the door so we have an emergency exit, if necessary. This was Michael's great idea. Like, where would we go once we got outside? The roads aren't plowed, and even our mail delivery has been suspended. So much for "Neither rain, nor snow, nor dark of night . . ." Liars. But the worst part is that I just know your Christmas card would have arrived today. I'm dying to see what you look like. I can't believe we waited so long. We could have exchanged photos at any time, yet both of us felt the need to wait for an "occasion" to make it acceptable. The Internet is such an anonymous place that asking people for pictures or addresses is like breaking an unspoken rule, don't you think? Maybe I should write a book about manners and protocol for the Internet. I could include things like how long you need to "know" someone before it's considered appropriate to ask to see what they look like. I could call it . . . well, I don't know what I'd call it, but I'm sure we could put our heads together and come up with something snappy. I'm getting punchy, I know. But give me a break. In addition to a raging case of cabin fever, I've got really bad PMS this month, and just to make matters even more interesting, Michael's been on the warpath. Why? (So glad you asked.)

Around two weeks ago Michael's junior accountant's wife (got that?) went into premature labor and delivered a slightly-more-than-one pound preemie. (Isn't that so sad?) Needless to say, the accountant (Elliot) hasn't been around the office much. That, coupled with the days off thanks to the holidays, coupled with the missed days now, thanks to the snow . . . well, let's just say that Michael's jaw is in a permanent state of clench. You should hear him walking around the house muttering, "The timing on this couldn't be worse. How could this happen to me?" like this snowfall is all part of a giant conspiracy directed against him. I do feel sorry for him, though — he knows that there's going to be a mountain of work when he's finally able to make his way back into the city. Even so, none of this is *my* fault; yet I'm the one he's been so snappy with. (But better me than the kids, right?) And who knows, maybe shoveling the snow is just what he needs to help him release, or at least redirect, some of his frustration/anger. It sure couldn't hurt, and besides, *I'm* sure going to be much more relaxed knowing that we've got a tunnel leading from our house into the street, you know, just in case there's an emergency. :-)

Because I'm all dressed up with nowhere to go (hee, hee) I've been packing up some boxes of clothes the kids have outgrown. I send their old stuff to one of my cousins, who takes all the hand-me-downs she can get. Whenever I pack up clothes, I'm always shocked by how quickly the kids have changed. In Gregory's case the change is physical. All of a sudden he can't get his T-shirts over his head and his pants are flashflooders. But with Wendy the change isn't as dramatic. In fact, everything of Wendy's that I'm giving away still fits her — she just won't wear it. It's all "too bright." No longer wanting to attract attention to herself, she's into neutral colors only. And all of her clothes must be solid. (Anything with a pattern went into the discard pile months ago.) I guess this is her stab at making her own fashion statement — or lack of. Well, I'd better go if I'm ever gonna finish packing those boxes. (One day the snow will disappear, the post office will resume operating, Michael will go back to work [YES!], and I'll be able to get the boxes out of here.)

Lara

P.S. It's 11:15 A.M. The kids are about to come in, track snow everywhere and demand hot chocolate with marshmallows and lots of whipped cream. Is there a rule about sweets before noon, Mrs. Crocker?

Subj: Stormy Weather
Date: 12-28
From: Susan_P@aol.com
To: cre8f1@mindspring.com

Dear Lara,

Really bad PMS *and* snowed in? My condolences to Wendy, Gregory *and* Michael (who I can't believe for one single instant is nearly as crabby as you made him sound — at least not after you've confessed that you're suffering from the agonies of PMS). I'll tell you, Lara, that's something I don't miss *at all*. My chemotherapy put me into immediate menopause, which, trust me, was no picnic. While I'm sure that going through menopause *gradually* is no fun, having your body shut down all at once (which typically happens from chemo) has got to be worse. Between the menopausal symptoms — sleeplessness, mood swings, hot flashes (some nights we must have slept with the air-conditioning set at 50°!) — and all the sickness from the chemo drugs, I was miserable. I made sure that everyone knew it about, too; I complained *incessantly*. Artie was super-understanding, tried really hard to give me slack, but didn't want me to wallow in too much self-pity, which he said couldn't possibly be healthy. (I love it, don't you? I've got cancer, but I shouldn't do anything that's not healthy!)

*Any*way, just to make sure that I didn't sink too low, Artie bought one of those calendars — the kind that's cube-shaped, with a different sarcastic or snide remark printed on each page. Well, I don't know where he stashed the darn thing, but every morning I'd wake up (dripping wet from my night sweats), drag myself into the bathroom, and there, perched against the tube of toothpaste, I'd find one of the pages from his calendar. He'd leave a different page every morning before tiptoeing off to work, and he never left the page that corresponded with the day's true date or even necessarily the actual month. Instead, he'd leave a page that said something that seemed to mirror our situation or my feelings. Like, "Has anyone told you how wonderful you are lately? No? You think maybe you're losing your touch?"

When I write about it now, it sounds almost mean, but those pages nearly always made me smile, and I loved the image of Artie leafing through that calendar, looking for just the right insult. Hey, what can I say, except that love is strange and we all show our feelings in different ways. Take my dear daughter Gabriella, for instance. She and I didn't have a single fight that entire year. (She was also much younger when I was going through my treatments, which may be the real explanation behind our more harmonious relationship.) Having said all of that, I must admit: As awful as it was going through my instant menopause, I just *love* not getting my period every month. See, there really is an upside to developing breast cancer. (My sick sense of humor emerging. Sorry.)

I got your family picture. It reminded me of that song they used to sing on *Sesame Street* about one of the things not belonging, because it didn't look like any of the others. (I don't remember the exact lyrics. It's been a long time, you know?) Anyway, both of your kids look just like Michael. You're definitely the odd man out. Did you have *anything* to do with either one of them?

The kids are adorable, though, which isn't to say there's anything wrong with you, my dear. You're cute. I've never seen so much hair. (I'm insanely jealous.) I also didn't picture you so tiny. Do you eat? Ever?

I think it's a riot that both of your kids wear glasses. They look so intelligent. Gregory is precious. He looks like a little Poindexter. His idea or yours to sport a buzz cut? And Wendy's *very* pretty. (She wears her dad's face well.) I wasn't expecting her to be such a looker. (When you said she was a bookworm, I had "librarian images" in my mind.) Take my advice and just lock her up now.

Anyway, I hope you're out and about. We're having beautiful weather in Canton. (Tee-hee.)

In the event you're still snowed in, why not try *cooking* something? You look like you could use some food! (BTW, hot chocolate doesn't count as cooking, no matter how many marshmallows you add!)

Subj: Happy New Year
Date: 12-31
From: cre8f1@mindspring.com
To: Susan_P@aol.com

Susan,

Are you *sure* you're not Jewish? The way you're harping about food, I don't believe that you're pure Catholic.

Actually, our family picture was taken when I was going through my breast cancer scare, and I'd lost a few pounds. Don't worry, though, *Mom*, I've put them back on. (I've never been big, though. I hover around 103 pounds, which is fine with me.)

You don't look *one bit* like I imagined. First of all, I think your hair is great. You do *not* look like Annie; you've got waves, not curls. As you no doubt noticed, *I've* got curls. Corkscrews, really. I inherited them from my dad's side of the family. *Thank you, Grandma Mollie!* Actually, I used to hate my hair, but after around 30 years of trying (unsuccessfully) to straighten it, I finally threw in the towel. Sure enough, once I struck a truce with my tresses, they started to grow on me. (Pun intended.)

I never imagined that you'd be tall. (I guess I always think that everyone is short like me.) Are you taller than Artie? (BTW, he's *very* good-looking.) Gabby also looks tall, or is that what 13 looks like these days? I think I have to reevaluate all of your complaints about Gabby's mouth. She looks too sweet to be capable of uttering all those "nasties" you accuse her of spewing.

Happy New Year. Are you doing anything special to mark the holiday? We're getting together with three other couples. We've been spending New Year's Eve together for years. We're all going out to dinner then coming back to our house for (store-bought!) desserts and to watch the ball drop. Until next year . . .

Subj: A New Year
Date: 01-02
From: Susan_P@aol.com
To: cre8f1@mindspring.com

Happy New Year to the Cohens. I'm disappointed in you, my friend. You mean you didn't go into the city and watch the ball drop *in person?* Why not?

Did you make any New Year's resolutions this year? I've promised to fight less with Gabby and to get more exercise. How 'bout you?

Subj: Surely You Jest
Date: 01-04
From: cre8f1@mindspring.com
To: Susan_P@aol.com

Dear Susan,

You're nuts. No one who lives here goes into the city to watch the ball drop. At least not if they're at all sane. The mob scene in Times Square is for crazy tourists and fools. I don't qualify either way. :- Ø(That means "shut up." Cute, huh?)

A few years ago, before Gregory was born, we *did* take Wendy to the city to see the Thanksgiving Day parade. Now *that* was neat. (You don't really get a sense of how huge the balloons are when you watch it on TV.) But to get good viewing positions you have to get to the parade early. It's a long time to stand around in the cold. Of course, we were only there for about 10 minutes before I had to go to the bathroom. (I *always* have to pee.) They have Porta Potties set up on every street corner. Let me tell you how much I enjoyed *that* experience. But if we have another mild Thanksgiving, maybe we'll do it again anyway. Gregory would love it, and Wendy doesn't even remember going the first time, so she would probably get a kick out of it, too. (She wouldn't admit it, though. She's cool now that she's in middle school, you know?)

The snow has finally all melted. I hope all of the Christians enjoyed their white Christmas. This Jew found no pleasure in it. I hate the winter. I sometimes wonder why we even live here. Michael hates winter, too. And yesterday when I drove Gregory down the hill to his bus stop, he complained that *he* was cold and wanted to know, "How much longer until it's summer again?" It must be genetic.

Enjoy the day.

Lara

P.S. I made no New Year's resolutions. I'd feel too compelled to keep them. (Me and promises, you know?)

Subj: Update
Date: 01-04
From: cre8f1@mindspring.com
To: Susan_P@aol.com

No sooner did I hit the send button than Dr. Berns called. He talked to the pathologist who did the deeper cuttings. He (Berns) says I'm fine, but the pathologist is fairly certain that it is not just atypical cells that he sees. He's pretty certain that his initial hunch was correct and it is lobular carcinoma in situ. (I didn't know pathology was so inexact. I figured it's one thing or it's not, end of story.) Anyway, Berns says that he wants me to see a breast surgeon that he works with a lot. He says that the surgeon will probably only want to watch me closely, but I should make an appointment anyway. Before I see the breast surgeon, though, Berns wants me to have another mammogram (so I can take the new films with me to the surgeon's office). He gave me the name of the mammogram place he wants me to use (because no, they're not all created equal) and the radiologist (a woman) that he wants me to see. He was very specific. But he assures me that he's sending me to the top places/people in Manhattan. Berns said that I should use his name when I make the appointments and if I have any problems getting in to see anyone, let him know and he'll make the appointments for me. He's such a sweetheart. Anyway, I'd better go. I want to schedule everything before the children invade. (I don't want Wendy to overhear me on the phone.)

Lara

4

Subj: School break
Date: 01-05
From: Susan_P@aol.com
To: cre8f1@mindspring.com

Hi, Lara.

Gabby and her mouth went back to school yesterday. Thank goodness. This winter vacation seemed especially l-o-n-g. (It wasn't. Just seemed that way.)

You're such a lucky lady to be having another mammogram — and so soon. Are you slamming your breasts in the refrigerator door yet to practice for the big event?

I go to my oncologist's for a checkup on the 10th. I'm already getting sweaty palms. I feel perfectly healthy, but I also felt just fine when I was walking around with a cancerous tumor growing in my breast — so what do I know? Anyway, I always get nervous before my checkups. And they're really no big deal. My onco will examine my breasts, along with the rest of my buff bod (yeah, right), draw some blood for tests, and tell me to call him in a few days for the results. But until I get the all-clear (somewhere around the 13th or 14th), I'll be tightly wound. (Or as Gabby puts it, a bitch on wheels.) You'd think that knowing this I'd be able to keep my emotions in check. But no, I just blew up at her, and I'm the first to admit that it was over nothing. Gabby was wrong, mind you, but I definitely overreacted. The whole thing is so incredibly stupid, too.

I walked into the bathroom and discovered that after stinking up the place, Gabby forgot to spray. (Don't ask how someone can forget, she does this at least once a month!) I went ballistic. (Hey, I already admitted that it was stupid *and* that I overreacted.) On the other hand, Gabby's 13 years old; she should be able to remember that "stuff" smells. Even hers.

Subj: Just wondering
Date: 01-10
From: cre8f1@mindspring.com
To: Susan_P@aol.com

Dear Sue,

I have one question for you: Does a child receive punishment for not spraying? I ask because Gabby isn't the only girl who suffers this lapse. (If it makes you feel any better!)

How'd the appointment with your oncologist turn out? I'm having my mammogram on the 12th. However, I did not practice for the special day by shutting my breasts in the refrigerator door. Sorry, we'll just have to wait for some other guinea pig to find out if the technique really works. ;-)

Subj: Potty humor
Date: 01-11
From: Susan_P@aol.com
To: cre8f1@mindspring.com

Dear Lara,

I threatened to make Gabby sit in the smelly bathroom *(with the door shut)* for 10 minutes when she forgot to spray. I didn't make her do it, though. However, I did send her to her room for an hour. But that was more for her sake than mine. I needed time to cool down, and I figured that if she was safely tucked away, I wouldn't inflict any more of my wrath on her. Anyway, I realized it could be worse when I was having coffee at my neighbor's yesterday morning. (See, I need to find another job quickly, before I do nothing but waste mornings "having coffee.") Anyway, I went into her daughter's bedroom to use her bathroom. (Their guest bathroom is being retiled and not available for use.) This woman's daughter not only didn't spray, she didn't *flush*. STOP! I can't even believe we're exchanging letters about such things. *Enough potty talk.* Be sure to put a chapter in your Internet protocol book (which I've decided should be called *Cyber Dos and Don'ts*) about avoiding letters that dwell on bodily functions, OK?

My appointment with the oncologist went fine. He says that I look good and he expects that my blood work will also be fine. I need to call him in a few days, just to be sure, but I'm feeling pretty darn terrific about everything. Including Gabby. Yesterday morning at the neighbor's made me realize that she could be worse. :-)

Happy mammo. Let me know how you do. (I know you will, but I just thought I'd remind you.)

Subj: Work?
Date: 01-12
From: cre8f1@mindspring.com
To: Susan_P@aol.com

On 01-11 Susan_P@aol.com wrote:
>*(See, I need to find another job quickly, before I do*
>*nothing but waste mornings "having coffee.")*

You really quit? You didn't tell me. When? I'm off to the city for my mammogram. Gotta fly or I'll miss my train.
Later. L.

Subj: News
Date: 01-12
From: cre8f1@mindspring.com
To: Susan_P@aol.com

Dear Susan,
I left the house at 10:00 A.M. and I didn't get home from the mammogram place until 6:30 P.M. The bottom line: I need more surgery. And

I know that the doctor who did my ultrasound thinks I've got cancer. He didn't say so, but I could just tell. I'll write tomorrow when I've had time for my head to clear. I've got a massive headache and I'm exhausted. I'm taking a sleeping pill and hoping it lives up to its name and that I will, in fact, sleep.

Subj: The bad news
Date: 01-13
From: cre8f1@mindspring.com
To: Susan_P@aol.com

Dear Susan,

I'm sorry for the cryptic message I sent last night, but I was wiped. Since you haven't written back, I'm going to assume that you haven't read my letter yet, and when you *do* read it, this letter will be waiting for you so you'll get the complete and full story all at once.

I'm tempted to simply skip the details, but I know that you'll write with questions about why and how and when, so I'm going to force myself to slow down, *breathe* and tell you what happened, in the order that it happened. Keep in mind, I *thought* I was going for a simple mammogram. Period. So no, I didn't bring anyone with me, and no, I didn't bring my tape recorder, as you suggested. But why should anyone bring a tape recorder to a simple mammogram? (ANSWER: Because it didn't turn out to be a simple mammogram.)

Oh, Susan, this is like a bad dream. I can't seem to get a definitive "You're fine." I'll tell you, though — I've had it. As far as I'm concerned, someone should just cut off my left breast right now. It's got to be easier than dealing with the stress of this entire, never-ending saga. I'm whining, and I hate it when I whine. But I'm really scared, angry, confused — you name it. I've got so many emotions swirling around in my head (which is still pounding) that I'm ready to rupture. And if one more doctor asks to see my breasts . . .

OK, now that I've gotten that off my chest (no pun intended), here's what happened:

It takes about 40 minutes to get to the city by train. I never eat breakfast, but since my mammogram was scheduled so close to lunchtime (11 A.M.), I grabbed a bagel at Grand Central and figured I'd eat it while I waited for my appointment. But no. I get to the mammo place and discover an engraved sign that says *Absolutely No Food or Drink Is Permitted in the Waiting Area.* Have you ever? I should have known then that luck was not on my side.

I give the receptionist my file (which includes copies of my last mammogram, my Walker pathology report and the two subsequent pathology reports done by Dr. Berns's guru). The receptionist tells me to take a seat — she'll call me. She doesn't tell me the doctors are running *one hour late,* because then I would have left,

115

eaten the bagel and returned at noon.

Anyway, the mammo is incredibly painful. They'd never really bothered me that much before, but my breast is still really sore/tender from my biopsy. In fact, when the tech takes the pictures of my left breast, it hurts so much that I cry. (At one point I think I am actually going to faint, and I make her stop. Not eating probably doesn't help with my light-headedness, but hey, who knew?)

The technician finally gets all the pictures she needs and leaves me sitting in the gown we all know and love, with the slit up the front. Of course, the room is freezing. (The exam room and the mammogram-machine room are one and the same.) I must have waited 20 minutes before the tech comes back and says that the doctor needs more pictures of my left breast. Again I cry as she tries to sit my rather small breast onto the rather large shelf of the machine. She keeps muttering about the doctor needing to see behind my biopsy incision. She takes a few more pictures, leaves and comes back *again*. More pictures. I don't even wait for her to start messing with my breast. I just start the waterworks. (Call me a baby, but it *hurt*. My surgery was only two months ago!)

The technician somehow manages to get another film or two snapped off (before my breast follows suit). She leaves again. Ten minutes later she's replaced by an attractive young woman (with a mane of straight blond hair that hangs down past her butt). Mademoiselle Hair races into my exam room like she's finishing up the 100-yard dash. "You know, you can't walk around like this," she says, gathering all that hair into a handheld ponytail before letting it fall loose again. "You need more surgery."

Susan, I swear, those are the first words out of her mouth. She realizes what she's done and says, "You don't even know me, and this is how I greet you? I am *so* sorry. Let's start again. I'm Dr. Apelbaum." She explains that I have suspicious microcalcifications "all over" that need to be removed and examined. I tell her I just had that done. She shakes her head so vigorously she needs to re-ponytail her hair. She tells me the microcalcifications still show up on my mammogram. She says I need to have them removed and repeats her original mantra: "You can't walk around like this." I tell her I have an appointment next week with a breast surgeon that Dr. Berns wants me to see. She asks which surgeon, and I check my folder. (Yes, I now have an [ever-expanding] folder of doctors' names, numbers and addresses, plus extra copies of pathology and mammogram reports.) I tell her I'm scheduled to see a Dr. Goldberg. She says he's great. (Heard that before.) Then she tells me that she'd like me to have a breast ultrasound done and she'll check to see if they have time to squeeze me in today. Before she leaves, I ask her to check the lymph node that Dr. Berns told me to keep an eye on. It still feels inflamed to me; it feels completely normal to her. She wins.

I'm told that Dr. Markey has time to see me. (Apelbaum's the radiologist who does the mammos; Markey is the radiologist who does the ultrasounds.) Still wearing my charming exam gown, I'm asked to relocate. They move me down the hall, where they tell me to wait — in a dressing room. It's not even a dressing room, really. It's more of a closet, with an accordion door. Another 20+ minutes pass. I've got to pee, *again.* I know they think I'm a nut job, because I've already gone to the bathroom about 7 times since I've been there. Part nerves, and part just me. (Have I told you that I pee a lot?) Anyway, I return from the bathroom, and the doctor's waiting for me. Sorry, Doctor. (I've been waiting how long, and *I* apologize to *him?*) But he seems very nice and asks me to tell him what's been going on, beginning with when I found my lump. Hearing myself repeat the whole story makes it more real, but it also makes me aware of how convoluted this whole process has been.

Markey puts cold goop on both of my breasts and begins the ultrasound. (The second the goop hits my body, I've got to pee again, but no way am I going anywhere.) My right breast appears fine. He does the left breast. He keeps stopping and going over some spots. Again. And again. I silently remind myself that he can't possibly see anything. After all, when I went to the ultrasound place in Westchester (to have my

[non] cyst aspirated), the radiologist there also went over — and over — and over — my breast and never found anything, *including my lump.*

After listening to my saga and ultrasounding both breasts, Dr. Markey starts stroking my arm and tells me that I seem like a nice lady and he feels really terrible about everything I've already been through. Then he says that he needs to spend some more time with me, "to do this right," and would I mind waiting for him a while longer? He's holding my hand when he explains that he needs to see a couple of patients who've been waiting. (Excuse me, but what have I been doing?) He says that once he gets rid of these two patients (his exact words) he'll have the time he needs with me. I'm confused about why he wants/needs more time, but I don't say anything. (Dishrag!) Instead I gather my belongings, make a pit stop in the bathroom and return to my closet.

It takes about 15 minutes before I realize that I'm not going anywhere in the near future, so I use my cell phone to call home and ask the housekeeper if she can stay late. (Fortunately she gives "flexible" new meaning and says that it's no problem.) Once I know that Wendy and Gregory are covered, I call Michael and tell him that I'm still in the city and will probably be on his usual train, the 5:39 P.M. He says to meet him in the fourth car. (In case you think I've gotten off the track here [no pun], I haven't. This is pertinent to what happens later, so bear with me.)

119

After I've done my time in the closet, Dr. Markey is ready for me. He starts stroking my arm again as he explains that there are some areas in my left breast he'd like to biopsy. He injects me with some Novocain, then shows me another needle that he says he'll use to remove some cells. (Thanks to you, I was already familiar with the core-needle biopsy.) Mild discomfort, but not too bad, considering the process involves needles. He does *two* of the core-needle biopsies. I'm concerned that he's found *two* lumps' worth biopsying (is that even a word?), and in the last ultrasound place they were looking for one lump and found *none*. (Do these things pop up overnight?) Markey interrupts my thoughts when he says that he'll have my results sent directly to the surgeon's office (so Dr. Goldberg will already have them when I see him next week). After he completes both needle biopsies, Dr. Markey starts moving the ultrasound paddle around the area of my surgical biopsy. Then he starts touching my scar with his fingers.

DR. M: What's this lump here?

ME: Where?

DR. M: *(He takes my hand and puts it on my lump.)* Here. Do you feel that?

ME: Of course I feel it. That's the lump that sent me to my gynecologist in the first place. But the surgeon, Dr. Walker, he told me that he removed it. Now you're asking *me* what it is? I don't know. Is it scar tissue from the biopsy?

That's what I thought. *(He doesn't respond.)* I don't know what it is.

DR. M: Well, I could be a hero here. . . . It needs to be removed. But I'd rather not disturb it. Dr. Apelbaum told you that you need more surgery anyway, because of the microcalcifications? *(I nod.)* So let's just leave this alone for now, and Dr. Goldberg can remove it when he does your surgery.

Susan, when he started with the *I could be a hero* line and then stopped, I just know that he thinks that lump is cancer. I could tell by his face. I didn't have the guts to ask him directly, though. (See, I really am a dishrag.)

That was it. Dr. Markey told me that I shouldn't have any troubles where he did the core-needle biopsies, but gave me his home number just in case. What a nice man. (I'd wait hours for him any day.) Then I paid an enormous bill (thank goodness for insurance), took the copies of my *new* mammogram report for my ever-growing folder and hustled out of there so I could meet Michael on the train. On the walk to the station I practically inhaled the hard-as-a-rock bagel that I'd had with me since the A.M.

I find Michael who — get this — *doesn't even sit with me.* He's got a regular card game that he always plays with his buddies on the 5:39 train. So, as usual, he sits with the guys! I'm steaming, until I realize that he doesn't know anything about the day I've just had. Then I'm relieved that he's occupied with the boys, since I don't want to recap my day while we're on the train anyway. I decide that I'll tell Michael about things after Wendy and Gregory go to bed. But then I realize, *I don't know what to tell him.* If I tell him that *I think* that the *doctor thinks* that I *might* have cancer, he'll think I'm really being paranoid. But we're making strides. At least I'm fairly confident that Michael won't fall apart on me. He's getting used to the routine. "Honey, I might have cancer. But then again, I might not. Well, on second thought . . ." Still, I decide that once we get home I'll refrain from saying anything to Michael about my day. He's already stressed out enough over events he can't control. (His junior accountant — with the preemie — is still keeping sporadic hours, which is resulting in even more work/headaches for Michael. But the baby's hanging tough, God bless her.) I figure that it's only a week before I'm scheduled to see Dr. Goldberg, and I should have something more concrete to tell Michael then. Until that time my lips will remain zipped. You'll keep me company while I sweat out the week in breast purgatory, won't you?

Susan, this is no fun. But if I'm forced to admit the truth, I'd tell you that while I'm still scared, I am no longer hysterical. Maybe after all this time — and all the back-and-forth about you're fine, oops, no you're not — maybe I'm just getting used to the idea that I might have cancer. Still, it's like I'm outside my body watching this happen to someone else. It's weird, and I'm having trouble explaining it. But look who I'm talking to. Maybe I don't have to explain anything. Maybe you know exactly how I'm feeling.

Anyway, that's it. I think. All the details, as well as I can remember.

Subj: Your news
Date: 01-14
From: Susan_P@aol.com
To: cre8f1@mindspring.com

Dear Lara,

I'm sorry that you're having to go through all of this, but you shouldn't go through it alone. Talk to Michael. You don't have to tell him that you think the doc thinks you've got cancer, because you're right — that's starting to sound like a broken record. But you should tell him what you know to be fact: The doctor says you have microcalcifications that must be removed — and that will require more surgery. Promise me to (at least) tell him that.

Thank you for giving me all the details about your appointment. You're right, I would have bugged you with a million questions if you didn't — and this way I got your great play-by-play. I could just picture you sitting in the closet, in that pathetic dressing gown with your boobies hanging out, on your cell phone trying to arrange child-care coverage. I hope you won't be angry, but you gave me quite a chuckle.

When (exact date, please) do you see Dr. Goldberg?

I've got a job interview next week. I can't believe I forgot to tell you I quit my job. I could have sworn I mentioned that I was going to wait until after my bonus. Well, I did wait, and I did quit. They asked me why, and I told them that my new supervisor was a bitch and a half and if it was the last job on the planet, I wouldn't keep it.

Not true. I told them that I just felt, after ten years, it was time for a change. (Now who's the dishrag?) Anyway, the interview for next week has some possibilities. A small local manufacturer is looking for a programmer. I told him that I was only interested in part-time and he said let's talk. So we're talkin'.

Speaking of talking, Gabby and I aren't. She had a game last night. With only seconds to go, her team (the Freedom) trails by two. One of the players on the other team fouls Gabby. She's at the foul line. She makes the first shot, and the place goes wild. (It's a home game.) She *misses* the second shot. After the game I go to comfort her and say, "It's OK, honey. Everyone knows you tried your best." She absolutely erupts and starts ranting about how I don't know that, I don't know anything, in fact I'm completely stupid and I should never speak to her again. So now, being the mature adult that I am, I have decided to take her up on her offer and not speak to her . . . until she apologizes. It's been two days. The quiet is actually sort of refreshing.

Sue

P.S. Got the results of my bloodwork back. I'm fabulous. (But then again, you already know that.)

Subj: Deal?
Date: 01-15
From: cre8f1@mindspring.com
To: Susan_P@aol.com

Dear Susan,
1. So glad you're healthy.
2. I've got a deal for you.

I'll tell Michael about my most recent mammo/ultrasound appointment if you talk to Gabby. You may not want to hear this, my friend, but I'm voting with Gabby on this one. Your intentions were honorable, and she *did* overreact, but you need to give the poor girl a break. The sting of defeat was still so fresh. She was just blowing off steam, and you just happened to be there. Now her pride won't allow her to give in to you. So be the *grown*-up and *give* up.

Subj: It's over
Date: 01-16
From: Susan_P@aol.com
To: cre8f1@mindspring.com

On 01-15 cre8f1@mindspring.com wrote:
>*So be the* grown-*up and* give *up.*

Too late. By the time I got your e-mail, I'd already apologized to Gabby. That does not let you off the hook about telling Michael, however.

Subj: A Done Deal
Date: 01-17
From: cre8f1@mindspring.com
To: Susan_P@aol.com

I'm LOL. I already told Michael all about my appointment. In fact, I told him *before* I wrote to you proposing the deal in the first place. (I just wanted to make sure that you cleared the air with Gabby.) What's that they say about two peas?

Michael took the news very well. He's definitely getting used to all this "let's just wait and see" stuff, but then again he's always been a more patient person; I'm the better-in-a-crisis spouse. Anyway, I'm sure you'll be thrilled to know that Michael's going with me to Dr. Goldberg's office on the 21st. I made the appointment in the A.M. so we could take the train into the city together. I'll be back before the kids get home from school. (I'd *better* be back; the housekeeper won't be here to bail me out this time. She only comes on Wednesdays.)

I'm glad you and Gabby are speaking. Whatever happened with your interview for the new job?

Subj: Jobless
Date: 01-19
From: Susan_P@aol.com
To: cre8f1@mindspring.com

Well, Lara, it looks like I'll be a Lady of Leisure a while longer. The interview was fine. It was weird, though. I hadn't been on an interview in 10 years. But the man really needs someone full-time. And I really feel strongly about being here with Gabby. (BTW, since I apologized to her, she's been so loving it was getting scary. Then all of a sudden she exploded again. "You don't love me — you never listen to me. You're so unfair!" She storms away. And just as I'm thinking how crazy she's acting, she comes to me and tells me that she thinks she just got her period! Outwardly, I remained calm, but let me tell you, I was going nuts inside. Trust me, having a daughter who's getting her period makes you feel very old very fast. Anyway, for now it appears that the only "outside the home" work I'm doing is simply volunteer (the support group). I'm back to reading the want ads. I'll let you know if I'm wanted.

127

Subj: Congratulations!
Date: 01-18
From: cre8f1@mindspring.com
To: Susan_P@aol.com

Mazel tov on having a menstruating daughter. Give her a good slap across the face for me. (It's an old Jewish custom. I'm not sure why, but when your daughter tells you that she's gotten her period, you're supposed to smack her!) Anyway, congrats on the big event. Was she excited, now that she's officially turned the corner to womanhood?

I'm excited. (No, not about Gabby getting her period!) I just got a big job. A couple of men have recently left a large bank in the city to start their own financial investment company. They need everything: a name, business cards, stationery, logo design, brochures. And they hired me to handle the entire shebang. The bad news: I hate writing financial copy, it's so boring. The good news: It'll pay for Wendy's sleep-away camp. (Gregory's day camp was paid for by my last three jobs *put together,* if that gives you any idea of how huge this new job is.) BTW, what does Gabby do over the summer?

Subj: Summer?
Date: 01-19
From: Susan_P@aol.com
To: cre8f1@mindspring.com

Congrats on your new assignment. That's great. But give me a break, winter's barely begun and you're already thinking about the summer? I know you New Yorkers have a reputation for living life in the fast lane, but you're pushing it just a bit, aren't you?

But since you asked: Gabby stays home all summer. If she went to sleep-away camp, who would pick fights with me? Actually, sleep-away camp isn't something that's really done much by those of us in Canton. None of Gabby's friends go away, so she usually just hangs out with them and spends a lot of time at the community pool. But this summer she might also want to take a basketball clinic. We'll see if she's still really into it. (She certainly is now. She's even redone her bedroom to reflect her new love. She bought a bunch of WNBA jerseys and strung them up so they hang from her ceiling!)

Actually, now that I think of it, maybe I'll encourage Gabby to apply for a summer job as a CIT (counselor-in-training) at the nursery-school camp that's run by our church. But I'll have to wait for the right time to bring it up. God forbid I should tell her what to do! But I figure if she's busy, she'll have less time to fret over her wicked mother. Geez, it seems like I spend a lot of time complaining about our relationship. It's really not that bad either. It's just that it's changing. You know, now that she's becoming a full-fledged teenager, she's flexing her muscles. (Unfortunately, the muscle she flexes most often is the one attached to her jaw, resulting in Giant Mouth Syndrome.) Today the giant mouth was filled with disdain because I forgot to give her a phone message. We won't even attempt to add up the number of times that same giant mouth has made the very same mistake about delivering my messages.

I know the 21st is around the corner. Update me after your appointment with Dr. Goldberg. Oh, and one more thing. Good luck!

Subj: Needles and Knives
Date: 01-21
From: cre8f1@mindspring.com
To: Susan_P@aol.com

My surgery is all set for the 28th. (He was able to squeeze me in, since biopsies don't take very long.) Dr. Goldberg is like a caricature. He practically leapt into the examining room and waved both of his arms in the air and said, "Dr. Goldberg here." I thought he was fooling around, but apparently that's just him. But then the very next thing he did (after flying into the room) was grab my hand, look me right in the eye and say, "You know that you're going to be OK, right?" I nodded. Anyway, from that moment he had my heart, and my trust.

The bottom line is this: He needs more information about the microcalcifications (and the lump that Markey did not biopsy), and the only way to get it is to go in there and remove more breast tissue. (His words.) He says he's not going to make any guesses (re: cancer) because it's pointless. He says that if he knew anything for a fact, he wouldn't have to do the surgery. So I'm going in next Friday. He explained everything in great detail. Unfortunately, I'll need another needle localization before the surgery. He said that he'd like Dr. Markey to do it because, quote: There's no one better. (I agree!) I told him that having the mammogram the previous week nearly killed me, and I didn't think I could stand another needle localization. He wrote me a prescription for a painkiller and told me to take it one hour before my appointment :-) Don't worry. This time I'll remember!

The Plan: Michael and I will get up at the crack of dawn on Friday and drive into the city to Dr. Markey's office. He'll do the needle loc (see, I'm learning all the medical lingo), then Michael will drive me all the way crosstown to the hospital, where Dr. Goldberg will be waiting for me. That's it. All I know. Correction, that's not all I know. The two core-needle biopsies that Dr. Markey did last week were normal. Yeah for that. (He faxed the reports to Dr. Goldberg's office, who had them in my chart when I arrived. Such efficiency.) Two lumps down, one to go.

Well, now that really is it. Before signing off, I want to check out some websites and read up on microcalcifications. Then I have to do a Net search on mutual funds. (Fun, fun.) I'm trying to get a serious jump on my work for the new financial group. After the biopsy on Friday I figure I'll be hurting (again) and too sore to work for a few days. Bye.

L.

Subj: Good thoughts
Date: 01-22
From: Susan_P@aol.com
To: cre8f1@mindspring.com

Hi, Lara.

You seem amazingly calm. That's good. Like the doctor said, it's just a fishing expedition. Let's hope he comes up with nothing but a big rubber boot. Just the same, I'll keep my fingers crossed and say a prayer. Question: If you've got to be in the city so early, who's gonna be with the kids? I wish I lived close enough to help you out.

Since I can't baby-sit, allow me to distract you:

Remember I told you about the interview I had with the manufacturer who really needed a full-time programmer? Well, he called yesterday and told me that after meeting me he's rethought the position. He said that I was right — it really is a full-time job — but he's willing to hire two part-timers and see how things work out. And the best part is, the reason he's restructuring the job is because he was so impressed with yours truly. Not to toot my own horn, but H-O-N-K! I can't help myself. As much as I love being a wife and mom, I still get great pleasure from hearing that my brain is a valuable and sought-after commodity. Sorting whites from darks just doesn't give me the same thrill. Nor does darning socks. Go figure. Needless to say, I said yes. I'll be working four days a week, until 1:00, with Thursdays off for bad behavior. (Hah!)

Anyway, I hope you really are calm and it's just not a front you're putting on. I'm off to basketball. The Freedom is on a roll. Won 5 of their last 6. (You *know* which game they lost.) Gabby and I now joke about the missed foul shot. In fact, now, whenever someone misses her foul shot, Gabby and I laugh about it later and say, "Did you notice when So-and-so missed her shot? Guess she was having a Gabby Moment."

Subj: Tomorrow
Date: 01-27
From: Susan_P@aol.com
To: cre8f1@mindspring.com

I haven't bugged you because you said you had a lot of work to do. But good luck tomorrow, Lara. I'll be thinking of you all day. And I'll be waiting by my computer for the good word. {{{ }}}
   Susan

Subj: Fasting
Date: 01-28
From: cre8f1@mindspring.com
To: Susan_P@aol.com

It's 5:07 A.M. Michael is having some break-fast. I'm not allowed to eat or drink anything until after the surgery. Not entirely true. I just popped two pain pills and took two sips of water to wash them down. Needle localization — ready or not, here I come.

I thought I'd collect my e-mail before we leave. One of our neighbors (and good friends) slept here last night. Her husband is getting their kids off to school, and she's doing the same for me.

Gotta go. Michael's ready. I'll let you know when I know. Thanks for your thoughts and hugs. Much appreciated.

L.

Subj: Results
Date: 01-28
From: cre8f1@mindspring.com
To: Susan_P@aol.com

I was in the recovery room when Dr. Goldberg woke me up. Very calmly he said the words I've sort of been expecting, yet dreading, for months. "Lara, it was malignant. It's cancer." Then he told me:

1. He removed the lump and had it analyzed

(preliminary) while I was still on the table in the operating room, and that's how he knows *for sure* that it's cancer.

2. He already told Michael.

3. The lump was most certainly the one I'd felt from the very beginning.

4. Once I get home I should call his office to schedule an appointment for either Wednesday or Thursday, since the full pathology report should be ready by then and we'll be able to talk about my options.

And then he put one of his hands on my shoulder and said:

5. "I'm so very sorry."

You won't believe this, but I was still so out of it from the anesthesia that once he left, I actually went back to sleep. I don't know how much longer I slept, but when I woke up I had to pee and was able to convince one of the nurses in the recovery room that I wasn't too groggy to walk to the bathroom. (I lied, but give me a break — she was pushing for a bedpan!)

Once I wobbled out of the bathroom (which was all the way on the other side of the recovery room, naturally), another nurse pointed toward 6 to 8 reclining chairs (complete with built-in ottomans) that were arranged in a semicircle. She asked if I felt like I could sit up to eat and drink a little something, since, she said, I wouldn't be discharged until I did so. (Like I needed motivation to get out of the hospital. Puh-*lease*.)

As I moved toward the only available chair, I noticed that everyone else who was sitting was male. Each guy was holding an ice pack against some body part. Mostly knees, and I forget what else. I do know, though, that I was clear-headed enough to envy every one of those guys, nursing what I'm convinced were (only) newly repaired athletic injuries.

I leaned back into the recliner, and the nurse handed me a cup of warm cranberry juice. I asked her if I could see my husband. She told me that visitors weren't allowed in the recovery room. That started my head spinning. I couldn't stop thinking about Goldberg telling Michael. I could just see Michael tightening his jaw, nodding, showing no emotion, seeming to be OK. Then Goldberg would walk away. That's when Michael's mouth would fall open, his tough-guy face would disappear, and his eyes would start to get red (because he always uses the back of his hand to wipe his tears). I couldn't stand the thought of Michael somewhere in the hospital, alone, sobbing. I knew that if he could just see me, he'd feel better, so I asked again. I was surprised to hear my voice crack and my question sound almost like begging. "Please, could I just see my husband? Just for a few minutes. Please." That's when the other nurse (the one who let me use the toilet instead of the bedpan) practically screams across the room to the other nurse. "She just found out she's got breast cancer. Let her husband come in and be with her a few minutes."

I could feel the eyes of all the ice-packed men on me. It was so . . . I don't know — embarrassing isn't the right word. But it made me feel awful. I could feel tears starting to collect in my eyes, but I didn't want Michael to see me crying, and I somehow managed to blink them away right before he walked through the recovery-room door. He looked so scared and pale (except for his eyes, which were red, as I expected). I asked him if he was all right. He nodded. "Are you?" was about all he could spit out. He was trying so hard to be so brave. I told him that I'd be fine. And then, I don't know if it was the anesthesia or seeing the spooked look on Michael's face, or maybe it was the warm juice, but suddenly I felt nauseated and started to vomit. Getting sick like that made my incision hurt, and I started to cry. (Or maybe my tears weren't about pain at all. Maybe I'm just using them as an excuse.)

About an hour later they let me go. The drive back to Armonk was uneventful and unusually quiet. I don't think that either Michael or I knew what to say and didn't want to risk upsetting the other by saying the wrong thing. *(And we've been married how long? Oh, only 18 years.)* By the time we got home, I was pooped out again, so Michael curled up with me and we took a short nap. It felt so good to be close to one another and just (carefully) cuddle.

I've got more I want to tell you (and even more that I want to ask), but all of that will have to keep. It's almost 5:00. Michael and I need to talk about what we're going to tell the kids. They should be home from their play dates in a half hour. That was a last-second change of plans — to have Wendy and Gregory go over to friends' homes after school instead of directly home. (Do you think that deep down in my gut I knew that I'd need some time to regroup?) Bye for now.

Lara

Subj: re: Results
Date: 01-28
From: Susan_P@aol.com
To: cre8f1@mindspring.com

Lara, I can't tell you how upset I was to hear the news. But now you know. So now you can do something about it. Breast cancer, found early, is *very* curable. And you said it yourself, the lump was teeny-tiny and didn't even show on your mammogram . . . so there's every reason to believe that you really did catch it early. Let's hear it for breast self-exams.

So now that you think you've heard the worst possible news in the world ("It's cancer"), let me switch into my "I'm a survivor, but you can call me Pollyanna" mode.

- Breast cancer does *not* mean you're going to die. I can't repeat that often enough.
- Breast cancer is *not* synonymous with mastec-

tomy. (Lumpectomies with radiation have been proven to be as effective as mastectomies for long-term survival. Example: Me!)

- Breast cancer does *not* necessarily mean you'll even need chemotherapy.

Those are the facts, Lara. And the facts will get you through all of this. That, along with Michael, who you know you can count on to be there for you and the kids, in spite of his fears.

As you wait for your appointment with Goldberg (Wednesday or Thursday?), try to stay calm, take lots of breaths and gather as much information as you can. That way you'll be able to make informed decisions every step of the way. But just in case you think that by quoting facts I'm not outraged, you're wrong. And to prove it, I will bite my tongue no longer.

What the hell did Walker do if #1: he didn't remove your lump, and #2: he left you filled with all those microcalcifications?

Subj: Good questions
Date: 01-28
From: cre8f1@mindspring.com
To: Susan_P@aol.com

On 01-28 Susan_P@aol.com wrote:
> *What the hell did Walker do if #1: he didn't remove*

>your lump and #2: He left you filled with all those
>microcalcifications?

You're asking *me?* Ask Artie. I think I want to sue the bastard.

Subj: The kids
Date: 01-29
From: cre8f1@mindspring.com
To: Susan_P@aol.com

Dear Susan,

We told the kids yesterday. Wendy got home from her friends' first. She already knew I had an early-morning doctor's appointment and that was why Lucy (our neighbor) slept at our house the previous night. Anyway, I sat Wendy down at the kitchen table and told her that I had some not-so-good news. Then I simply said, "I have cancer." I tried to keep my voice steady as I stuck to the facts: The doctor removed a small lump from my breast, and it turned out to be cancer. I told Wendy that's all we know for now, but I'm seeing the doctor next week (Wednesday) to decide what the next steps will be. I said that I knew for sure I'd be needing more surgery but didn't know what kind of operation it would be or when I'd be having it. Then I told her the good news: "We are lucky because we found the cancer early, *so I am not going to die.*" (God, please don't make me out to be a liar. Amen.) Wendy had no questions. (Strange, she always has questions.) I told her if she thought of any questions later, she should just ask. That was it. NEXT —

Gregory. He's so young, it wasn't like I had lots of choices about what to say. I told him that I had a boo-boo on my breast and that I just had an operation and needed to have another one, too. I said that means he needs to be careful giving Mommy hugs, but he must still be sure to give me lots and lots of hugs, which, God bless the little angel, he did immediately. I started sobbing, almost uncontrollably. He wanted to know why I was sad. Michael interjected, "Those are happy tears, Gregory, because Mommy is just so glad to have such a wonderful and loving little boy." I nodded and finally composed myself enough to ask Gregory to promise never to stop hugging me, even when he's a grown-up. It was his turn to nod. I started to wonder if I'll even be around when he's a grown-up. Then I had what must have been a panic attack, because all of the sudden I couldn't breathe.

Oh, Susan, it's all so unfair. A 5 ½-year-old child shouldn't have to go through this. What am I saying? *No* child should have to go through this. No adult should either, although Michael is doing surprisingly well. It's amazing when you consider how far he's come since falling apart over my very first suspicious mammogram.

Michael's taking care of the kids tomorrow so I can have some time alone and get some rest. They're going on a temple outing to the basketball game in the city. (Besides being Yankees

141

fans, the Cohens are also big Knicks fans.) Maybe I'll write more when everyone's gone. In the meantime . . .

Thanks for your words of encouragement, but I'm afraid my stiff upper lip is starting to quiver. I'm sorry, but I guess that right now I'm just feeling pretty sorry for myself.

Subj: You're allowed
Date: 01-30
From: Susan_P@aol.com
To: cre8f1@mindspring.com

Dear Lara,

Don't apologize. Right now you have every reason to feel sorry for yourself. But the way I see it, you have every reason to feel grateful, too. I mean, think about it. What if when Dr. Walker told you that you were fine (but had some atypical cells) you simply said OK? What if you didn't call Dr. Berns? What if Berns hadn't sent your slides to the guru? What if he hadn't insisted you get another opinion? What if . . . Well, you see where this is headed.

THANK GOD you have a suspicious mind. And you should be thankful that Dr. Walker talked to you like you were a moron. Just think, if he'd been wonderful about answering your questions, you may have never reached for the phone to call Dr. Berns.

Anyway . . .

I could just picture you telling your kids, and it simply broke my heart. You're right, no one should have to do that. But it's better if they know. It's hard enough having to cope with cancer — having to hide it from the kids is practically impossible. And even if you try to hide it, kids can always sense when something's up. We tried to keep the truth from Gabby. But then I went and shrank her favorite shirt in the wash, which caused her to complain and caused me to completely lose it. No joke. Poor Gabby didn't know what was up, watching her mom decompose over a lousy T-shirt. She kept asking, "Why are you crying, Mom? What's wrong?" When I couldn't stop wailing long enough to answer her, she ran for cover. It must have been a weekend, because Gabby found Artie, who took her out on a "date" to Dairy Queen and explained everything.

After that day Gabby and Artie shared a closeness they never had before. He was really there for her the whole time I was undergoing treatment. They went to some movies together, he took her out to her favorite joints for dinner, and he spent countless hours playing all the different "ball" sports with her. You may find this hard to believe, but I don't think Artie was home later than 7:30 P.M. more than a handful of times that entire year! But then I got well, and things between them sort of drifted a bit. If that all sounds wistful, I don't mean it to be. I'm glad that I'm well and we could return to the same-old, same-old around here. (Translation: me being the primary caretaker and Artie being the primary workaholic — oops, I mean, breadwinner.)

But seriously, deep down I really believe that the bond formed between Artie and Gabby during my cancer days will never be broken. That's the kind of thing that sticks with a kid, don't you think? Anyway, it was a great (and unexpected) upside to see the father/daughter knot being cemented like that. And who knows, maybe things between Artie and Gabby will move back again someday. Maybe they only drifted in the first place because she got older and she's "of that age," and it had nothing whatsoever to do with my recovery. We'll never know. But that's not the point. The point I was trying to make was about keeping secrets from the kids, remember? And the fact is things will be different around the house, no matter how much you and Michael try to keep them the same. (Remember Gabby's poem?) But because you told your kids (even though it was painful), at least they'll understand (somewhat) why their mommy isn't so happy or is so tired and why their daddy seems preoccupied. Hopefully the Knicks game was a good distraction for them. But how about *you?* After a day to think about everything, how are you holding up?

I talked to Artie about your desire to sue the young Dr. Walker before you kill him. (Notice that I took the liberty of adding Walker's death to your wish list.) Artie says that when you see

144

Dr. Goldberg on Wednesday you should ask him if the months that have passed (since Dr. Walker said he removed your lump but didn't) have had any impact on your treatment options or overall prognosis. (I'm gonna butt in here — that's not something Dr. Goldberg will be able to answer until after your next surgery, so you may want to wait until then to ask him.) Artie's point is this: You could certainly prove negligence — the guy obviously blew the biopsy, big time. But in order to prove damages (and collect any monetary compensation), you must be able to show that Walker's screw-up affected the outcome, i.e., your prognosis. If it didn't, you have to ask yourself if you want to sacrifice the time, money and emotional turmoil of a legal case just to hear a judge or jury say that Walker made a mistake. (We already know *that*.) And if you still want to sue him, do you want to do it *now?* Artie suggests making no decisions right now, but instead focus all time, emotion and physical energy on a full and complete recover. I agree with my husband. (And no, this isn't a first.)

Artie wants to make sure you know that he's not licensed to practice in New York State. But if you decide to pursue a lawsuit and need the name of a great NY malpractice attorney, Artie can provide one for you. (If you want a great attorney but cannot afford one, you're screwed. Too bad, but that's our legal system for you.) Anyway, I don't mean to joke about something so serious, except that I will not allow you to lose your sense of humor. You'll just have to trust me on this one, but, as a person who's already been through much of what you have waiting in front of you, I can tell you that a sense of humor will take you a long, long way. Even though you don't feel like it, smile a lot over the next few days. I guarantee it will help alleviate some of the stress that I know you're feeling. Write soon.

Suz

Subj: Knicks
Date: 01-30
From: cre8f1@mindspring.com
To: Susan_P@aol.com

Dear Susan (Now you're *Suz?!* — my, oh, my, how you keep me on my toes),

I just got home from the Knicks game. I decided that I didn't want to be home all alone, so I called the temple and was able to buy one of the extra tickets. I think it was really good for Wendy to see her mom out and about and acting (somewhat) normal. I could almost read her mind: "If my mom was *really* going to die, she wouldn't be at the game right now screaming at the referee." It was the right thing. Also by doing "normal life," I felt normal. Sort of. I still have that out-of-body experience from time to time. You know, like I'm watching this happen to me instead of it really happening to me. I'm rambling. Forgive me.

Michael took the kids to the movies on Friday night. (The night of my A.M. biopsy.) When they returned, I was in bed watching TV. Wendy slips under the covers and says, "You never even had a mole, did you?" She's got this real accusatory tone and repeats the question. I admit that she's right; I never had a mole. She tells me that she's mad I didn't tell her the truth in the first place. I apologize but explain that I really didn't think it was anything, that in fact, the doctor told me it was nothing and I was fine. But I assured her that now, today, as of this minute, I was telling her the truth — the whole truth and nothing but the truth — so help me God — and since it was the Sabbath, I would not think of lying to her or lying to God. She seemed reassured. That's another reason I decided to go to the game today. I wanted to show her I was OK. And God willing, I will remain that way. (Funny, I don't think I've ever thought so much about God or prayed as much as I have recently. Yeah. It's funny, all right. A laugh riot.)

Lara

Subj: You're Wonderful
Date: 01-31
From: Susan_P@aol.com
To: cre8f1@mindspring.com

Lara, you're the best. Any woman who can put a smile on her face, go to the ball game *and* yell at the ref less than 24 hours after learning she has cancer is going to be fine. Do you hear me? You'll get through this and you'll be fine. You're remarkable. And I'm sure that it was great for your children (and Michael) to see you acting like yourself — normal, healthy you — which you will be again, even though it doesn't feel like it right now.

I know what you mean about the God thing. We've become more observant Catholics since my plea bargains with the big guy upstairs: Please, God, let me live and we'll start going to church again. Please, God, let me have a full recovery and I'll be a better example of a good, practicing Catholic for Gabby. Please, God . . . Well, you get it, I'm sure.

I start my new job tomorrow. I'll check my e-mail the second I get home. Maybe I'll even sneak a peek at work — depending on how the day goes. If you don't feel like writing, though, I'll understand.

Sue

P.S. Gabby's jealous that you get to see the Knicks. (She wants to know if you ever see any WNBA games.) Artie used to get tickets to some of the Cleveland Cavalier games. I was never interested, so he took Gabby. Maybe that's what sparked her love of the game. Who knows? But the Cavs are not the same as the New York Knicks. Trust me.

Subj: Stuff
Date: 02-01
From: cre8f1@mindspring.com
To: Susan_P@aol.com

Sorry to disappoint, but tell Gabby that we have not been to a WNBA game. Yet. (But Wendy's been bugging.)

I hope you're not getting sick of me and all my troubles, because I plan to write to you a lot over the next few . . . well, however long this whole thing takes. I really look forward to your letters. Always have. But something tells me that I'll *really* look forward to hearing from you now — both as a mentor and as a survivor. (It's sort of the "she did it; so can I" mentality.) Anyway, I just thought I'd say thanks and thanks. The first thanks is for everything you've already done. And the second thanks is for everything I'm sure you'll continue to do. Please stop me. This is getting entirely too mushy.

I hope you're having a good first day of work. I've had a couple of days to sort things out, and the more I think about this entire saga, the angrier I get. I keep replaying Dr. Walker's words: "This isn't something to keep in the front of your mind. . . ." What an asshole.

I realize that I never updated you about my second biopsy. Since we already know the end of the story, let me just share a highlight.

Dr. Markey was an absolute doll. He did my needle localization using *ultrasound,* not the mammography machine. It hardly hurt at all. He triple-checked to make sure the needle was in the right spot, then apologized for being anal. (His word, not mine.) But he kept saying that after everything I'd been through, he wanted to be certain that everything was being done right. Then Markey walked me into the waiting room so he could meet Michael before we left for the hospital. He told Michael what a lovely woman I am (thank you, thank you) and then wished us the best. He asked if I still had his home number. (I did — my ever-growing folder, remember?) He asked me if I'd call him at home after my surgery to let him know how everything goes. I promised, and you know what *that* means.

I just called him. He already knew the results. He said that Dr. Goldberg phoned him right after leaving the operating room. It blows my mind that there are some doctors who really do care. Anyway, Markey couldn't have been nicer. He told me that it's all out of his hands now, but if I have any questions about anything that's going to come up in the next couple of months, I should feel free to call him. Susan, I've decided:

No woman should ever have to be told she has breast cancer. But if she's going to have to hear those words, she should hear them from doctors as compassionate as mine. I'm going to phone a couple of the cancer organizations listed in some of my breast cancer books and make contributions in honor of Berns, Goldberg and Markey. It'll do more good for more people (hopefully) than if I sent all the doctors thank-you notes or potted plants!

Subj: Hmm?
Date: 02-01
From: Susan_P@aol.com
To: cre8f1@mindspring.com

This Dr. Markey sounds too good to be true. Are you sure he doesn't just have a giant crush on you? Hey, lady, I've seen your family photo and you're no slouch. Just asking. Inquisitive minds want to know. (Does that expression bother you as much as Gabby? She always teases me about it and says, "Whoever said you had a mind?")

The new job is a hoot. I met three people that I'm going to be working with and couldn't imagine spending my time with three funnier or nicer people. (I know this from only one day, but I'm an excellent judge of character. Keep in mind that I knew that my old supervisor was a bitch from a single raised eyebrow!)

I think your idea of making contributions to thank your doctors is great. In fact, I'm going to mention it tonight to all the women at my support-group meeting. (And starting next year, I'm going to give my docs contributions in lieu of Christmas presents.) Listen, if I'm gonna be on time for my meeting, I've gotta run. Good luck with Goldberg tomorrow. I'll be here. Waiting.

151

5

Subj: The Deal
Date: 02-02
From: cre8f1@mindspring.com
To: Susan_P@aol.com

Dear Susan,

We're back. I'm amazingly OK. I think it's because *now I know.*

Dr. Goldberg says that I am not a good candidate for a lumpectomy and that any surgeon who says I could have one is a bad doctor. He removed the lump (which he now calls a "tumor") but explained that I did not have clean margins. After (re)reading all my books about BC over the weekend, I knew what that meant but Michael didn't, so Goldberg gave us a crash course in terminology and treatment options. He even showed us a copy of the X-ray they took during my biopsy to show us what microcalcifications look like — little white dots. (No wonder deodorant is such a no-no before mammograms.)

Anyway, the cells around my tumor were not normal, healthy cells (so I have dirty margins, not clean). Goldberg explained that he could try again to remove more even tissue and hope to get clean margins, but the microcalcifications are also an issue. Apparently they're sprinkled throughout my breast, and they also need to be removed and examined. So the bottom line is this: I need to have my left breast removed. He's also going to remove a few lymph nodes from my armpit area (a sentinel-node biopsy) to see if the cancer has spread (although he doubts it).

Since rereading the books (and surfing the Web), I learned more about lobular carcinoma in situ (LCIS). I reminded Goldberg that LCIS was found in my second-opinion pathology report from Dr. Berns's guru. (Goldberg didn't need to be reminded.) He asked me what I knew about LCIS. I told him that I understood it was a marker and that my chances for developing breast cancer in my other breast sometime in the future were greatly increased because of LCIS. He said that I was correct and told me that the odds were about 30% higher that sometime in the coming years I'd develop "carcinoma of the right breast," as he so medically put it. I asked him if I was being hysterical to suggest removing my right breast *right now.*

Susan, let's face it, the odds that I am currently hitting are much less than 30%. To recap:

- 80% of the time lumps are benign. (Not mine.)
- More than half of all breast cancers happen in women over age 60. (Not mine.)
- Exercise and a low-fat diet are supposed to help reduce a woman's risk. (Not mine.)
- Pregnancy and breast-feeding reduce risk. (Not mine.)
- Beginning menstruation late reduces risk. (Not mine.)

- And doesn't low alcohol consumption also reduce risk? (Not mine.)

Do you see a pattern emerging? And let's not forget, I have no family history of breast cancer although I know that most people (85%) who develop BC don't have a family history either. I am Jewish, though, and I know that increases your risk a bit, but *come on*. Still, you know what really gets me? When I think back to all the doctors who told me that I was fine. And there I was, sitting in Goldberg's office talking about having a *double mastectomy*.

Anyway, Goldberg told me that if I had not brought up removing my other breast, he would have. He said that if I went to good breast surgeons for second and third or even fourth opinions about my case, everyone with any credentials would tell me that a mastectomy, not a lumpectomy, should be done on my left breast. No choices there. But he was honest and said that I would find differing opinions about the right breast. Some doctors, he said, would tell me to leave it alone but continue to watch it very carefully. But Goldberg explained that he personally counsels women to consider prophylactic mastectomies (another new term) when they have a huge family history of breast cancer or when they already have cancer and LCIS. He told me to think about it. I told him that I didn't need time. I knew. I wanted it gone. Maybe if I'd been able to have breast-conservation surgery (still showing off my knowledge of medical terms) performed on my left breast, I wouldn't have been so cavalier about removing my right one, too. But 30% sounds SO high. I don't want to wait for cancer to strike again. Michael had been pretty quiet throughout the meeting, but he turned to me in utter disbelief when I said that I wanted both breasts removed. He said, "We'll talk about it."

Goldberg gave me the names of two plastic surgeons that he likes to work with. Unfortunately, one is out of town right now. He told me to go talk to the first one and if I didn't like him, to wait until the other one returns from vacation. He says they both do excellent work, and even if I'm not interested in reconstruction (I am), he won't operate on me until I at least *talk* to a plastic surgeon.

That's it. Except that when we left Goldberg's office, I asked Michael what he thought. You know, I think I know him so well, and then he surprises me. He says that he can't believe I would just decide "like that" *(fingers snapping)* to remove a perfectly healthy body part. I tell him I can't see holding onto a perfectly *useless* body part that just might kill me. We are definitely not on the same page with this one. He was a honey, though, and said (in front of Dr. Goldberg, who asked Michael what he thought about all of this), "Lara is one of the smartest people I know. I know she's been reading about breast cancer and researching it on the Internet. It's her body, and I trust her to make the right decisions. I guess what I'm saying is that I'll support whatever she decides." (Except that if "whatever she decides" involves removing my right breast; then he's not so sure.) I'm confused and need some time to think. I thought that by trying to explain it all to you it would become clearer in my own mind. I thought wrong. I welcome your opinions.

Subj: Facts, please
Date: 02-02
From: Susan_P@aol.com
To: cre8f1@mindspring.com

Lara, look on your copy of the pathology report. What was the size of your tumor? Also, do you have a copy of your first pathology report, the one from Walker? What does it say about your microcalcifications? You know me, inquisitive minds . . .

Well, I'd say that Michael is holding back on you. He must have read a book or two about being a supportive partner. ("I'll support whatever she decides." Sounds good to me!) I also love that Michael is so proud of your intelligence. It takes a strong, secure man to marry a smarty-pants. Lara, I wouldn't worry about his reservations about your choice to remove your right breast. He'll come around to see things your way. And if he doesn't . . . Well, it *is* your body, and you're the one who will have to live with your choices. If you don't feel like you can deal with the anxiety of waiting for the other boob to turn (my variation of "the other shoe to drop"), then get rid of it. I can't make that decision for you. Just remember, a mastectomy is not a guarantee that you will never again develop breast cancer. They can't ever remove *all* of your breast tissue. In fact, just the other night one of the women in my support group informed us that she's had a recurrence in her mastectomy scar. I know you may not want to hear such news right now, but our entire relationship has always been honest and direct. You deserve to know the facts, even if the facts are frightening, so you can make the best decision *for you.*

However, I will speak from personal experience and tell you that my docs and I watch both of my breasts very carefully. I'm diligent about doing my monthly breast self-exams, I have clinical breast exams done by my breast surgeon every six months, and I have mammograms done every year. The hope is that if something does happen, we'll catch it early. I've learned to live (relatively calmly) with that. Except the week before each doctor's appointment, when, as you know, I tend to freak. But I truly believe I would do that even if I'd had a double mastectomy. That's me. BTW, in medical jargon, which I see you're starting to master, a double mastectomy is called a *bilateral* mastectomy. And as long as we're talking lingo, is the doctor you're going to see a *plastic* surgeon or a *reconstructive* surgeon? There's a difference, you know? Someone who does great nose jobs may be a disaster at rebuilding breasts, so just make sure you're seeing someone who does plenty of boobs. (No pun intended.)

Also, are you getting another opinion before proceeding? I know, you've had a lot of opinions already. I keep forgetting about the very first breast surgeon you saw who told you he could tell by feeling your lump that it was nothing to worry about. Then there was Walker, and now Goldberg. (BTW, I think you should write the other two quacks and let them know that the lump *was* something to worry about — something like cancer!) Listen, I'm not going to bug you about seeing another doctor if you don't want to. I know that you now know what questions to ask, based on your reading, the Net, etc. I also know from what you've told me that Goldberg is right. Not everyone is a good candidate for lumpectomy, and the reasons he gave you for needing to do a mastectomy are correct. Besides, it seems to me you mentioned that you're not very large-breasted — or was that my own personal observation based on your holiday card? :- o Either way, at some point removing more and more breast tissue will leave you looking deformed and better off with the mastectomy/reconstruction scenario anyway.

Whatever you decide, I know you're making an *informed* decision, and that's the important thing, not only for your short-term health but for your long-term peace of mind.

I'm sending good vibes,
Susan

Subj: Ring, ring, ring
Date: 02-05
From: cre8f1@mindspring.com
To: Susan_P@aol.com

Hi Susan,

What a wonderful letter. Thank you. You always seem to say the right thing. I'm sorry it's taken so long to get back to you. The phone has not stopped ringing. That's what happens in a small town — bad news travels fast, even in February, when it's cold, snowy and everyone tends to stay holed up inside. All I can say is it's a good thing that I told the kids, because the answering machine is in the family room, and the kids are always nearby when I play back my messages. (You wouldn't believe the messages some people have left: "I just heard that you've been diagnosed with cancer. . . .") I shouldn't be complaining. The outpouring of support from our friends has been very comforting. This is especially true since my family lives so far away. Our friends really *are* our family. (Michael's parents have been gone for years, and he was an only child, so my family is *it*.) Telling my parents and my sisters was almost as hard as telling Wendy and Gregory. My dad took it particularly hard. He wants to know what's going on but doesn't feel comfortable talking about it. You know, his generation of men doesn't discuss "breast" cancer. I wasn't sure what to say — he seemed so embarrassed by the whole thing — so I was direct and brief: I have cancer and am going to have both of my breasts removed. (I'm not winning any sensitivity awards over that one, I know. But kids aren't supposed to have to tell their parents they're seriously ill — it's supposed to happen the other way around.)

I've decided that I'm not going to see another breast surgeon. I called Dr. Berns. He assures me that Goldberg is one of Manhattan's very best. Besides, Goldberg *was* my second opinion. (And my third. It all depends whether you count Crumb, the first yo-yo who could tell by feel, rather than biopsy, that my lump was fine. I can't believe you forgot about him . . . the doctor who lived up to his name.) Then there was Walker. Oops, I knew there was something I forgot to tell you. Let's just file this one under the category of A Point Worth Noting:

Before discussing anything about my biopsy or pathology report, Dr. Goldberg took me into one of his exam rooms and had me take off my shirt so he could check my biopsy. He picked up a syringe and told me that I'd feel a little stick. Before he poked me, I asked him what he was doing. (Call me peculiar, but I don't like to be stuck for no good reason.) Goldberg explained that whenever a surgeon removes tissue, it leaves a vacancy, and fluid collects to fill the empty cavity. You'll never believe this, but Goldberg also said that *this can be very painful.* "If I leave the fluid, it will be absorbed by your body eventually. But until that happens, you could have a lot of discomfort. It's easy enough to remove some fluid, so I usually do. I've discovered that it makes my patients much more comfortable." That's almost a direct quote. So, Susan, what do you think? That little shit of a doctor (Walker) *could have* done something about all the pain that I complained about after his biopsy. Do you think that he (A) simply chose not to or (B) is stupid and doesn't know that draining away the fluid would help? Or you could pick (C) both A and B. It doesn't matter. A, B or C — he's incompetent.

Moving right along — the info you wanted. (I'm copying it off the pathology report that Goldberg gave me.)

Tumor Type: Infiltrating duct with intraductal carcinoma, solid and comedo type necrosis
Tumor Size: 0.6 CM Infiltrating duct, multi-focal DCIS
Nuclear Grade: Moderate to Poor

Is this what you wanted? If not, there's more. Just let me know. I'm not sure what it all means, so if you want to shed any light, feel free. (Especially the nuclear grade. I don't like seeing the word "poor" on any piece of paper that's about me.)

You also asked what it said about microcalcifications on the old pathology report from Walker . . .

It doesn't use the word "microcalcifications,"

but under Gross Pathological Diagnosis it says "Questionable calcium." Oh, man. *Now* I get it. I feel so stupid. It was right in front of my face this whole time, but I didn't know what it meant. "Questionable" means that the pathologist wasn't sure the tissue he was looking at even had calcium in it. Doesn't it? And that means that Walker knew he may have missed the lump but he never said anything to me about it, doesn't it? And Dr. *Goldberg* knew that — that's why he *showed* Michael and me my X-ray with the microcalcifications. He wanted to prove to us that, unlike Walker, *he* had not missed it.

I need a break. Bye.

Subj: Sorry
Date: 02-06
From: Susan_P@aol.com
To: cre8f1@mindspring.com

Dear Lara,

I'm sorry if I upset you. You're right. I was trying to determine if Walker knew he messed up. I shouldn't have tiptoed around it, though. I should have been straight with you and told you what I was looking for. And after I'd just written about how direct and honest our relationship has been. I feel terrible, and I promise I'll be more direct and more honest in the future.

Your pathology report from Goldberg is consistent with everything he told you. He's obviously a good doctor and a straight shooter. Your tumor was small. (My tumor was considerably larger, over 2 CM.) So you really did find yours early. That's good.

Nuclear grade is a way of measuring how aggressive your cancer is. Don't worry that yours is listed as "moderate to poor." That's not unusual in a woman your age. (That's a compliment, not an insult.) See, you are young for breast cancer. And, unfortunately, most cancers found in younger, premenopausal women tend to be more aggressive (faster-growing) than breast cancers found in older, postmenopausal women. This makes the fact that you discovered your lump early all the better. But try not to jump ahead and worry about any of that right now. After your mastectomy and sentinel-node biopsy your doctor will have much better and more accurate information about the properties of your breast cancer and what additional treatment, if any, you'll need after the surgery. In fact, because your tumor was so small, if your lymph nodes are negative, you may not even need chemotherapy. (See, and you thought that you either have breast cancer or you don't. Little did you know there are different types of cancer with different attributes and behaviors.)

Have you made a definite decision yet on what you're going to do about your right breast? (BTW, my right breast was my bad one.)

I'm glad your phone is ringing. You'll find that many people will ask what they can do for you. At this point there's not much, but there will be soon enough. The best advice I can give you is to let them pitch in. Not only will it be a help to you and your family, it will make your friends feel better. People feel so completely helpless when someone they care about is sick. Giving friends errands to run or tasks to do makes them feel like they're contributing rather than just standing around. Keep a list by the phone of what you need; that way when people ask what they can do, you can promptly answer, "Well, we could use some milk" or "If you wouldn't mind picking up our dry cleaning . . ." I often asked for rides for Gabby, dinners, that sort of thing. (I never had the guts to tell anyone that what I *really* wanted was a foot massage. Somehow I felt that would be pushing it!) Listen, Lara — I know you're not the type to ask for help, but this is the time to change your thinking. By letting others pitch in, you'll be doing *them* a favor. And yourself. Trust me . . . S . . .

Subj: My life
Date: 02-08
From: cre8f1@mindspring.com
To: Susan_P@aol.com

Breast cancer has taken over my life. It's all I think about. All I talk about. I hate this. Please write me a nice, long letter and don't even mention it. OK?
Lara

Subj: Your life
Date: 02-09
From: Susan_P@aol.com
To: cre8f1@mindspring.com

Dear Lara (who isn't thinking about breast cancer),

Pretty silly, huh? You can't hide from it, kiddo, but you're right — it doesn't need to rule your life either. So let me distract you by telling you about life in Canton.

We're pretty boring, thank goodness. (We like it when things *aren't* happening.) Artie is working a bit less this month (so far), and that makes Gabby much happier. (Me, too.)

Gabby is busy and doing well in school. (Can I brag? 3 A's and 2 A–'s on her last report card.) Basketball is still in full swing. I've stopped going to all of the away games. Too much driving. So now if it's a home game or if it's being played relatively nearby, I'm there. If not, I make sure one of her favorite meals awaits her instead. She seems OK with the change of plans. But lest you think she's not mad at me, you're wrong. I picked her up at the orthodontist's earlier today. She greets me with "Thanks for being late." I remind her that I told her I would be late when I reminded her about the ortho appointment in the first place. She has no recollection of that conversation ever taking place; therefore, according to Gabby, the aforementioned conversation never *did* take place. So what else is new? (Any idiot could tell you that *everything* is my fault.) Can you stand it? I can't win. Thank goodness I get to go to work four mornings a week, where I can occasionally be right *and* have people actually listen to me when I speak *and* remember what I've said!

The new job doesn't feel so new anymore. The other part-timer that I share the job with is a bit of a mess. She'll grab something she needs from one of my files and not return it, that kind of thing. I think we just need to establish some rules and better work habits and we'll be OK. She's nice enough and would be amenable to any routine/procedure I propose (I think). We just have different styles. I'm neat and organized — she's not. Still, she gets her work done and does it well, so who am I to dictate how she functions? ANSWER: I'm the one who has to share her pigsty of an office, so I've decided that it's time to speak up! But don't worry. I promise to tread softly.

Subj: Neat Freak?
Date: 02-10
From: cre8f1@mindspring.com
To: Susan_P@aol.com

First you complain about your daughter's room being a mess. I don't give that a second thought, because I know that teenagers often have messy rooms. But now you're complaining that your co-worker isn't tidy enough for you?

Are you sure you're just not a little compulsive when it comes to being neat and tidy? In other words, are all of the items in your lingerie drawer neatly folded, or are they just tossed in there with undies to the left and bras to the right?

Subj: Undies
Date: 2-11
From: Susan_P@aol.com
To: cre8f1@mindspring.com

My dear Lara,

It is none of your business what my lingerie drawer looks like, but you forgot to mention half-slips, which are folded in quarters and in the back right-hand corner of the drawer. Does that tell you everything you need to know? ;- 0

Speaking of clothing . . . Ever since you told me that you're having a mastectomy, I've been meaning to ask you about your selection of shirts, and I keep forgetting. Do you have any soft button-down shirts? Does Michael have some you could borrow? If not, I suggest you pick up a few flannels. Let me explain: After a mastectomy and reconstruction many women have problems lifting their arms. By having a shirt that buttons all the way down the front, you'll find it easier to dress yourself. Also, thanks to modern medicine, managed care and the fact that men run this country, you'll probably be sent home from the hospital with your drains still in. They'll be easier to deal with in a roomy button-down shirt. (You'll be able to pin the drains right inside the shirt.) These are things that doctors would never think to mention, but women who've been there know how important all these little details are when we're trying to recover, function and regain our independence. So, Lara, this is your excuse to do what many women feel is the best therapy of all: Go Shopping!

Subj: Rule breaker
Date: 02-12
From: cre8f1@mindspring.com
To: Susan_P@aol.com

I'm not like most women. I hate to shop. (Lucky Michael.) Since my diagnosis, though, I've increased the time I spend at the *gym*. I take my cancer books with me. I prop them in the book holder on the treadmill and spend hours walking mile after mile. I think I've developed shin splints trying to walk off all of my hostility, anger, fears — whatever I happen to be feeling at the moment. I've dropped out of my tennis league. My mind kept wandering, and I found myself making all of these unforced errors. Then I'd lose and be angry with myself for playing so poorly. It's almost laughable, isn't it? I've got cancer, I'm awaiting surgery to have both my breasts removed, and I'm getting in a pissy mood because I'm double-faulting and dumping volleys into the net! This has got to be what they mean by the term "transference." Gotta go. I'm meeting my friend Karen — *at the gym.* :-)

Subj: A Quickie
Date: 02-13
From: Susan_P@aol.com
To: cre8f1@mindspring.com

I've got 15 minutes before I have to leave for my pelvic ultrasound. Once you're a BC survivor, you have an increased risk for developing ovarian cancer (aren't I just full of good news?), so every six months I see the radiologist to have my ovaries scanned. After the ultrasound I've got an appointment for a haircut. Love these days off from work that are filled with appointments, don't you? Speaking of, when is your appointment with the plastic/reconstructive surgeon?

Subj: Great idea
Date: 02-14
From: cre8f1@mindspring.com
To: Susan_P@aol.com

A haircut, huh? Anything drastic or just a trim? You inspired me. I just made an appointment. Actually, I was overdue for a trim but have had so many doctors' appointments that the thought of one more appointment, even for the sake of beauty, was one too many.

My meeting with the reconstructive surgeon was this morning. (Sorry, I thought you knew.) His name is Donahue. He seemed nice and very capable. Framed newspaper clippings of his many accomplishments adorned his wall. (Years ago a tractor severed a man's arm, and Donahue was the superstar who performed the microsurgery needed to reattach it.) He's a plastic *and* reconstructive surgeon, and he does lots of breasts. He especially likes working with Goldberg because "He leaves me a good amount of skin to work with, so I can give women better results." (Imagine, Susan . . . some doctors don't leave enough skin! Sorry to be so glib, but it helps me cope. Sometimes. Sort of.)

I tell Dr. Donahue that I've decided to have both breasts removed. He says that's good, because reconstructing both breasts at the same time yields better results than doing one breast now and the other breast years from now. Well, isn't *that* good news?

Since you had a lumpectomy, you didn't have to worry about reconstruction. But I know that you get a lot of information about all kinds of breast-cancer-related things from your support group. Still, I don't know what you know about reconstruction and what you don't. So forgive me if all of this is beneath you.

Dr. Donahue described some reconstruction options:

TRAM flap. TRAM stands for something, but I forget what. It's when he takes muscle, tissue and fat from the woman's abdomen and uses it to create her new breasts. I don't have enough body fat for this option. Lucky me. NEXT.

Butt Flap. (My term.) Dr. Donahue told me that instead of my tummy, he can use the tissue from my rear end (again, my term). He assures me that he could build me "beautiful breasts" (his term) from my backside, but *each breast* would require 8+ hours of surgery. I must admit, I sort of like the idea that whenever Michael would kiss my new breasts he'd really be kissing my ass, but 16+ hours of surgery is too much for me. Besides, I don't really need beautiful breasts, do I? I mean, it's not like my job as a nude model is in jeopardy here now, is it?

Option three is implants. Saline or silicone. Donahue assures me that silicone is OK. I don't believe him and told him saline sounded fine. He explained the process.

Donahue will be in the operating room, and once Dr. Goldberg removes my breasts, he (Dr. Donahue) will take over and begin my reconstruction. He can't just pop in implants because there's not enough room. To make room, he says that first he has to stretch my skin. This is accomplished by using tissue expanders, which he'll place under my skin right after the mastectomy. A tissue expander, says Dr. Donahue, looks like a diaphragm. He puts a little saline into each expander before I leave the operating room so I won't be concave; instead, I'll have breasts like a man (again, his words). Every few weeks I'll visit Dr. Donahue's office and he'll inject more saline into each expander. (He explained that the process is similar to a balloon being filled with water.) I'll continue getting the saline injections until I become the size I want to be. (When I told Michael this, his eyes lit up. He's got images of I-don't-know-what floating in his head. Hey . . . the man can dream.) Once I'm satisfied with how I look, I have to have another operation where Donahue will remove the expanders and replace them with the real things — well, not exactly. He'll replace them with the falsies — the saline implants. Nipples are added later, which he says is when we'll talk about them. Anyway, before I left his office, I met with the woman who handles his surgery schedule and his billing. My new breasts will cost about $25,000. (Thank goodness for insurance!) She asked me if I wanted to take some time to think about everything. I told her no, that I liked Dr. Donahue and she should go ahead and book me. She said that she needs to talk to Dr. Goldberg's office first, since both doctors need to be available at the same time. They're going to call me sometime in the next couple of days and let me know when they can "do me." That's it.

Oh, almost forgot. The nurse asked me if I wanted to see any pictures of women who'd had bilaterals done by Dr. Donahue. I did. And you know, they didn't look so bad. Actually, they looked good. She also gave me the card of a woman who is a private-duty nurse and takes care of a lot of Dr. Donahue's patients. She told me that once I know when I'm having the surgery, I can call this nurse to see if she's free to come take care of me. Do you think it's necessary? They're calling my insurance company to see if they'll cover it, in case I decide I want it. But Michael has already told me that if *you* think I should have private-duty care, we'll get it, even if insurance won't pay for it. (I'll bet you didn't know that you had such influence over my hubby, did you, Susan?)

And finally: Happy Valentine's Day. I sent you a card over the Net. I hope you find it funny. I sure did.

Subj: V Day
Date: 02-14
From: Susan_P@aol.com
To: cre8f1@mindspring.com

Happy VD to you, too. Very funny.

Yes, get a private-duty nurse. Line her up for your entire hospital stay, if you can. After all, what's the worst that could happen? You'll feel great and tell her that she can leave when her first shift with you ends? How long do they think you'll be in the hospital anyway? Every place is different, but they all rush you out.

Also, I haven't wanted to push, but have you

given any thought to attending a local breast cancer support group? It could help, and it's not too early. (A lot of women think they shouldn't go until after their surgery. Not true.)

Sue

P.S. As far as my haircut, it's just a trim. (I'm still growing *back* my hair after chemo, remember?)

Subj: Busy, busy, busy
Date: 02-15
From: cre8f1@mindspring.com
To: Susan_P@aol.com

How insensitive of me! You know, I forget you were once bald (and it wasn't that long ago either). It's just that I've got that Christmas photo of you (complete with a cute do) blazoned into my pea-sized brain. Sorry for the faux pas. It won't happen again.

I've been busy with doctors' appointments, so I haven't wanted to try to squeeze anything else into my days — or nights. So no, I haven't pursued anything about support groups. Maybe after my surgery.

I've been busy with work, which makes for some real insanity. But I made a commitment to those financial guys, and they've got big bucks sunk into their new company. I can't bail on them. Besides, I think it's good for me to focus on something besides my cancer, and writing does take my mind off my troubles, at least temporarily.

I've been busy with — I don't remember what else I was going to say that I'm busy with. The phone just rang and interrupted my train of thought. The call was from Dr. Donahue's nurse. I'm scheduled for the 21st — the second surgery of the day. She explained that the doctors like to do the more complicated surgeries (like mine) early in the day so they don't get backed up. (And that's supposed to make me feel better?) Until the phone rang I was doing so much better. Now that it's real, suddenly I'm not so fine. You should see my fingers shaking on the keyboard. I need to call Michael. I'll write later.

Subj: A Date
Date: 02-15
From: Susan_P@aol.com
To: cre8f1@mindspring.com

Oh, Lara, I wish there were something I could do or say to help you relax a little. But I can't think of anything. Right now it's all in your doctors' hands. Or God's. It depends on how you look at it, I suppose. Can I at least try to cheer you up with a funny Gabby story?

She brings home a quiz from school. The quiz is designed to evaluate how well you know your parent and how well your parent knows you.

Since Artie was working (what else is new?), I was the parent of choice. Anyway, the quiz has two columns. Column A is a series of questions about me, column B is a series of questions about Gabby. Each of us has to complete both columns of questions (without showing the other one our answers). It sounds confusing because I've done such a lousy job explaining it. (I'm the computer programmer — *you're* the writer, remember?) But basically it was simple. It asked things like, What's your favorite food? Your favorite TV show? Your least favorite movie? Keep in mind I had to answer each question as it pertained to me *and* to Gabby. She had to do the same. Then we got to compare our answers.

Her least favorite food? She's written down vegetables. I've said that her least favorite food is fish.

GABBY: Well, we're both right. I don't like either one.

ME: Yeah, but Gabby, you eat *some* vegetables, like corn. You don't ever eat any fish.

G: You're right. I forgot.

Then we move on to her favorite movie. She's written down that she doesn't have one. I start humming "The Sound of Music." Again she says she forgot.

Then we have to name her favorite pastime. She's written down basketball. I've written down "arguing with her mother." (She cracks up.)

176

The 15th question was the best: What's your least favorite type of music? She's written down country. I've said that she hates Spanish music. This, too, makes Gabby laugh. (It's an old joke. Artie's parents live in Akron, so Gabby gets to see them fairly often. Years ago, when Gabby couldn't have been more than five, she was going somewhere with her grandpa and he had his car radio turned to a Spanish station. She asked her grandpa if he could understand what they were saying. He confessed that he couldn't speak or understand any language other than English. So naturally, the Giant-Mouth-in-Training asked him *why* he was listening to a station that he didn't understand. He told her that it wasn't usually talking . . . mostly they played music, and he likes Spanish music because it has a good beat! Gabby claims to suffer every time she gets a ride from her grandpa, which these days she accepts only when she's absolutely desperate.)

The last quiz question had to be completed after Gabby and I finished comparing answers. It read: "So, how well does your parent know you?" You'll never believe this, but laughing the entire time, Gabby writes, "Better than I know myself!"

I got a kick out of it. I hope you do, too. I don't know, now that I've typed it, it doesn't seem so funny. Maybe you had to be there. Or know Gabby. (But after typing up the whole darn story, I'm sure as hell not gonna delete it now!)

Subj: Ramblings
Date: 02-16
From: cre8f1@mindspring.com
To: Susan_P@aol.com

Thanks for the cute story about Gabby's quiz. It *did* make me laugh. See, she really does love and appreciate you!

I've been doting over Wendy and Gregory for weeks. I am constantly thinking, What if something happens during the surgery? What if it's worse than everyone expects? What if I don't have that much longer to live? I know that "what if" is not a particularly constructive game to be playing right now, but I can't help it. I know that if something happens to me, Michael will be OK. I mean, he loves me and he'll miss me, but eventually he'll get on with his life and find someone else. But it's my kids I'm upset about. No one will ever love my kids the way that I do. Not ever.

I find myself thinking about all the times I've been so critical of my mothering skills. You know, all the times I should have been more patient with them or all the times I didn't spend time playing with them or reading to them or whatever. Now, when I consider the fact that I might not be the one to be here for them, all of a sudden my "infractions" don't seem to be such a big deal. I've realized that I've been a really great mom and that is why (or partly why) I have two really terrific kids. I just can't imagine that anyone could take my place and do the kind of job with them that I can. I've been begging God to give me the opportunity to finish raising my kids. Gregory is so young. I keep thinking that if I don't make it, he won't even remember me. I'll just be that woman in the silver frame that Michael will put on Gregory's nightstand.

This is all too awful. Please, do me a favor and don't embarrass me by addressing anything that I've typed in this entire letter. I mean it. I needed to get it off of my chest, and it was easiest to tell you. Probably because I could do it without looking you in the eye or worrying that you'd hear the tears in my voice. But it's over now. I've had my breakdown and expressed my deepest, darkest fears. Don't make me regret such painful honesty. Thanks.

Lara

Subj: Re: Ramblings
Date: 02-17
From: Susan_P@aol.com
To: cre8f1@mindspring.com

{{{{{{ }}}}}}
Love,
Susan

Subj: I'm better
Date: 02-18
From: cre8f1@mindspring.com
To: Susan_P@aol.com

Well, I'm calmer now. I've got my button-down shirts and have typed out everyone's schedule for the days I expect to be in the hospital (3 to 5, they say). Our housekeeper is going to sleep over Sunday night and work for us on Monday instead of Wednesday this week. We have to leave for the hospital very early Monday morning, and she'll get the kids up and off to school, but it's up to Michael starting Tuesday and until I come home. I've given him a list of his duties while I'm away. He's wearing his I'm-annoyed-with-you face (nostrils flaring, lips pursed, eyebrows scrunched together), because he says that I'm treating him like he's a moron. Not true. Well, slightly true. Here's a cut-and-paste of part of the list I'm leaving for him:

TUESDAY

6:30 Wake Wendy for school.

6:35 Now go back into her room and wake her up again.

7:05 Wendy leaves for the bus. *Remind her* that after school Karen will be picking her up and driving her to Hebrew school. *Remind her* to thank Karen for driving.

8:00 Make Gregory's lunch, which includes a container of vanilla yogurt, a plastic spoon and napkin, chocolate-chip cookies and grapes. Be sure to toss in a freezer pack to keep everything cold. Put the lunch box in the *large* zippered compartment of his backpack.

180

Also put Gregory's sneakers in the same compartment. He'll need them — Tuesday's gym day.

Put a bag of chips, which Gregory likes for morning snack, in the *front* pocket of the backpack. Also, put the note I've written (it's in the top drawer of my desk and dated 2/22) in the *front* pocket. It's his bus pass that will allow him to go home with Justin after school.

8:15 Wake Gregory. Dress him and give him breakfast. (He'll say he isn't hungry. Make him eat anyway.) If there's *any* snow on the ground, he should wear his *snow boots* to school, otherwise they won't allow him to leave the blacktop during recess.

Remind Gregory that his sneakers are in his backpack. Also *remind him* that he's going home with Justin after school and that his note is in the front pocket of his backpack.

8:45 Help him brush his teeth. Give him a vitamin.

8:50 Leave for bus stop. (We always drive down the hill to the bus, but that's because I'm lazy. :-) Just get him there.)

5:30ish Pick up Gregory from Justin's house. (34 Laurel Way)

6:15 Pick up Wendy from Hebrew school.

Dinner for everyone. (I usually grab a pizza on the way home from Hebrew school.)

REMEMBER: Unpack Gregory's lunch box and put the freezer pack back into the freezer so you can use it again tomorrow. Be sure to look for any notices that he brought home. (Do whatever the notices say. Parents who don't respond to notices are despised by teachers.)

7:30 Bath for Gregory. (Remind Wendy to bathe, too. She sometimes "forgets.")

8:00 Bed for Gregory.

9:00 Bed for Wendy.

Nighty-night, Michael. In case you're wondering, the "dead" time during the day is when supermarket shopping, laundry and all of my writing gets done. And let's not forget that Karen doesn't usually drive our daughter to Hebrew and Gregory doesn't always have a play date after school. But fortunately we've got good friends willing to help you out. Regardless — welcome to the life of a mommy. Get some sleep. I can't wait to see you tomorrow morning. Love, L.

So, Susan, what do you think? Will he get it right?

Subj: Your Instructions
Date: 02-19
From: Susan_P@aol.com
To: cre8f1@mindspring.com

There is absolutely no doubt in my mind that Michael will get every single instruction 100%

correct. He'll be fine. After all, you left him instructions that "a moron" could comprehend. Shame on you!

You made me wish that I'd saved the instructions I left for Artie when I went into the hospital. Resembled yours. Too closely. I hope you don't mind, but I printed out your list and showed it to Artie. He howled. Also, we both got a kick out of your note to remind Wendy to bathe. And all this time we thought only Gabby "forgot."

Well, kiddo, not much longer. I know you'll be relieved to get Monday behind you. You'll be in my thoughts. And my prayers.

With love — from me.

Subj: Prayers
Date: 02-20
From: cre8f1@mindspring.com
To: Susan_P@aol.com

Everyone's praying for me. I just got a call from our rabbi. He's been so wonderful. He's called several times since he heard about my diagnosis but called again today to wish me luck tomorrow. He also said that he will continue to pray that I have a full and complete recovery.

Amen.

I called both kids' schools. I spoke to Gregory's teacher and the guidance counselor at Wendy's school (who promised to get word to all of Wendy's teachers). Anyway, I told them what was going on and asked them to let me and/or Michael know if there are any changes in Gregory's or Wendy's behavior.

Who knows what's going on in little Gregory's head? He knows I'm going to the hospital for a few days, but he doesn't know what an operation is or what cancer means. He's the lucky one. Poor Wendy. Unfortunately, my little bookworm is a big fan of this author who writes books about terminally ill teenagers. (Why Wendy finds this desirable reading I've never understood, but she owns every book this author has written.) This makes Wendy too knowledgeable about cancer, chemo and who knows what else. I thought that someone at her school should know what's going on at home.

I guess that's it. I'm to have nothing to eat or drink after 9 P.M. It's 8:45, so I think I'll go feed my face. Something nice and fattening, too. I'll be in touch as soon as I'm home. Thanks for everything. You've been nothing but wonderful to me — and *for* me. I mean it.
Love,
   Lara

6

Subj: Today
Date: 02-21
From: Susan_P@aol.com
To: cre8f1@mindspring.com

Dear Lara,

Well, today's the day. I know that you won't be getting this letter until you come home from the hospital, but I wanted it to be there waiting for you when you returned. I hope that all went well and you're not in too much pain. They say that a mastectomy alone isn't so painful — it's the reconstruction that's a killer. I'm keeping my fingers crossed that your surgery yielded no surprises and you're feeling like your old self in no time. Write when you can.

Susan.

Subj: Day 2
Date: 02-22
From: Susan_P@aol.com
To: cre8f1@mindspring.com

I just thought I'd tell you that I miss you. We were so stupid. Why didn't we discuss giving Michael my e-mail address so he could let me know how you did? Clearly we were not thinking, and we pride ourselves on being so completely organized. (At least I do.) Well, I just wanted you to know that I'm thinking of you. Again.

Subj: Hello?
Date: 02-24
From: Susan_P@aol.com
To: cre8f1@mindspring.com

According to my calculations you might be coming home today. I hope so.
Me

Subj: I'm waiting
Date: 02-26
From: Susan_P@aol.com
To: cre8f1@mindspring.com

Lara, I'm starting to get concerned. Are you OK?

Subj: Lara?
Date: 02-27
From: Susan_P@aol.com
To: cre8f1@mindspring.com

I can't stand it. I'm giving you one more day, then I'm calling directory assistance.
Sue

Subj: I'm home
Date: 02-28
From: cre8f1@mindspring.com
To: Susan_P@aol.com

I can't lift my arms.I can't even reeach the keybrd. Michel had to put it in my lap.it hurts. Bad. my sister's here. she flew in yesterday to help. we diddn't know it would be this bad

Subj: Thanks
Date: 02-29
From: Susan_P@aol.com
To: cre8f1@mindspring.com

Thank you for writing. I was really worried about you. I'm sorry that you're having such a difficult time. Ask your doctor to write you a prescription for physical therapy. It will help you regain your range of motion. I'm glad your sister is there to help. I wish there were something that I could do. I've missed you. Feel better and write more when you can.

My thoughts and prayers remain with you.
Susan

Subj: Lara's sister
Date: 03-01
From: cre8f1@mindspring.com
To: Susan_P@aol.com

Dear Susan,

I'm Erin, Lara's (middle) sister. She asked me to write to you and thank you for the deli platter. They delivered it yesterday. We all enjoyed it. (And it was doubly exciting when the doorbell rang and for once it wasn't flowers.) Lara's house looks like a funeral parlor.

She's in pretty bad shape and has a lot of pain trying to get into and out of bed, since she still can't use her arms. Michael ordered a hospital bed from a surgical-supply pharmacy that's somewhere near here. They delivered it yesterday. Michael and I thought that because you can use a hand control to move the head portion of the bed up and down, it might make it easier for Lara. It's definitely better, but not good. She asked me to tell you to stop worrying about her and to assure you that she's in good hands. But maybe you know: Is it *normal* to be in so much pain? She can't even drink coffee from her ceramic mug. She says it's too heavy and hurts her incisions. (She drinks everything from paper or Styrofoam cups.) Besides the hospital bed, is there anything else we can do for her?

I almost forgot. She asked me to tell you that her lymph nodes were all negative. She said to tell you that the "sentinel node biopsy" didn't work. (She spelled that for me so I'd be sure to get it right. A sign that she is feeling at least a tiny bit better?) But they removed her lymph nodes the old-fashioned way. She said you'd know what that means. I guess that's it. If you want to write back, I told her that I'd check her e-mail again tomorrow.

Erin

Subj: Thanks
Date: 03-01
From: Susan_P@aol.com
To: cre8f1@mindspring.com

Dear Erin,

Thank you so much for your letter. Now that you've proven that you're qualified to deliver telegrams for Western Union :-) would you do me a huge favor and please print out this letter and give it to Lara? Thanks.

Susan

Dear Lara,

Well, doll, you made it. You may feel lousy, but negative nodes! That's great news. (I had six positive nodes.) Did anyone explain about lymph nodes to you? If so, just skip this next part. But I've got time, and you aren't going anywhere very fast . . . so allow me to give you a broad overview about such magnificent news!

No one ever dies from breast cancer. They die from breast cancer that has spread outside of the breast and invaded some other body part or organ. *Today* the best way the doctors have to determine if microscopic cancer cells have spread beyond the breast is to check the lymph

189

nodes in the underarm area. And *today* the sentinel node biopsy is the best and least invasive way to get to those lymph nodes. (I'm curious as to why it didn't work for you.) Thanks to my love for the italics icon on my computer screen, you probably noticed that I kept saying *today*. That's because things in the breast cancer arena sometimes change rapidly. For instance, I also had my nodes removed the old-fashioned way. (It's really called an axillary lymph node dissection.) But that's because the sentinel node biopsy wasn't "invented" when I had my surgery. (Ah, what a difference two years can make!) But the good news is that since you wound up having the same procedure that I did, I'm better able to give you the whole scoop. (No pun intended, which you'll understand as you read on.)

Unfortunately, nodes are tiny and embedded in fat. So the surgeon doesn't ever know how many nodes he's removing. He just grabs/scoops out tissue from where the nodes are located, and the pathologist wades through all the fat to find, count and examine the nodes. A good sample is at least 10, but I know some women who've had more than 20 nodes removed and one woman whose doctor removed more than 30! Anyway, the pathologist analyzes them, and if they're all negative, then you can feel pretty confident that cancer wasn't transported out of the breast area. That's you, Lara. Thank God. That's YOU!

Dr. Goldberg probably only removed nodes from your left breast, since your right breast was removed prophylactically. (In other words, since there was no cancer in your right breast, he didn't need to check to see whether the "no cancer" had spread. Get it?)

Once you've had lymph nodes removed, you're more susceptible to infection, since the nodes are active participants in your body's immune system. (That's why doctors wouldn't want to remove all your lymph nodes, even if they could find them all.) Anyhow, because you've had some of your nodes removed, from now on (and for the rest of your very long life) you'll need to take certain precautions with your left arm and left hand to prevent infection. Getting your cuticles trimmed during a manicure, for instance, may be something you want to rethink, because any cut is an invitation to infection. Whenever you do get a cut on your left arm or hand, you should apply some sort of antibiotic ointment, just to be safe. (Careful shaving your underarms.) You also shouldn't have your blood pressure taken or blood drawn from that arm anymore. Instead use your right arm. All very doable, wouldn't you say?

You don't have to answer that. In fact, you don't have to write until you're feeling better. But now that I know Erin is there and you can receive e-mail, I'll continue to babble on until you write back to me and tell me to shut up. I'm just so relieved that you're OK.
Love,
   Susan

Subj: I'm back
Date: 03-02
From: cre8f1@mindspring.com
To: Susan_P@aol.com

Hi, Susan, it's me. Congratulations are in order. If I go slowly, I can now lift my arms to just above my waist (so no more typing with the keyboard wobbling in my lap). Dr. Donahue says no physical therapy for another week or so. (I saw him a couple of days after being discharged from the hospital. He needed to remove my drains. OUCH!) Anyway, he said that he doesn't want me doing too much with my arms yet. He's afraid that I'll mess up his reconstruction. He showed me one exercise he'll let me do, though. I stand facing the wall and, using walking motions (with my index and middle fingers), I try to walk up the wall. I don't get too far, and it hurts like hell, but I'm climbing the wall (pun intended) at least 5 times every day. Donahue says that the sentinel node biopsy would have been easier to recover from (arm-wise) since they don't have to go in as deep. But Dr. Goldberg tried it, and it didn't work (something about too much scar tissue from my previous biopsies), so — it is what it is.

I can't believe that I'll ever lift my arms high enough to slip into a turtleneck again, let alone play tennis. But Dr. Donahue assures me that it simply takes time. (And pain. And tears. He didn't mention those.) I'm seeing him again today to remove some stitches. It hurts just thinking about it, so I won't.

Erin went back to Illinois. She's got three kids of her own to take care of, and they're little — all three are between Wendy's and Gregory's ages. I started calling Erin "Flo," short for Florence, as in Nightingale. She really was a lifesaver, not only for me but for the kids. She drove them to their activities, cooked, ran the house and basically just took over. This was good for Michael, too. It helped ease his guilt over having to work. It's already tax season, and this is Michael's busiest time of year. He has no choice: He can't stay home and take care of me. The good news is that at least Elliot's resumed normal hours, so he can help out. (The baby's home and "doing better than expected." I'm not sure exactly what that means, but that's what Elliot told me when I asked him how she was doing. I didn't press him.)

My youngest sister (Nora) also volunteered to fly in and help me out for a few days. But she'd have to bring her two-year-old terrorist — uh, daughter — with her. Thanks, I think I'll pass. My parents won't drive here because they're afraid they'll get lost on all the winding country roads. I told them if they can't drive, they won't be a help, and if they can't help, they can't come. I said all this nicely, of course.

So now it's up to me, myself and I. And Michael . . . in the evenings . . . after work. But I'm getting by. Sort of. I can now dress myself. Sort of. It only takes 10 minutes for me to maneuver into a button-down shirt. Before he leaves for the train, Michael puts an empty bowl on the kitchen counter. That way I can pour Gregory his cereal without having to reach up to cupboards to retrieve dishes that may as well be perched on top of Mount Everest, they're so unattainable. Michael also puts milk in a cup in the refrigerator so I don't have to lift the heavy bottle. Necessity may be the mother of invention, but Michael is the dad with all the good ideas. My friend Karen, on the other hand, is the *friend* with all the good ideas. She's already divvied up dinner-duty between my girlfriends. Every day at 4 o'clock someone appears at my house to deliver the evening meal. Karen says that she's already "assigned" this week and that we'll see how I'm feeling before she lines up next week's dinners. (I knew that would please you, Mrs. Crocker.)

My brain is still anesthetized. I swear, I can't think. (I'm also taking pain pills when the kids are at school. I'm sure those aren't helping when it comes to my brain drain.) But thinking is just one of many things (more like *most things*) that I can't do. Needless to say, I can't drive — so every other day one of my girlfriends who's not assigned to meal-duty (gotta spread the wealth) takes me to get my hair washed. I still can't lift my arms high enough to wash it myself, even if I bow my head down. The beauty shop (what a misnomer!) is no picnic either. It's too painful to sit in the chair and lean my head back into the shampoo bowl, so I stand facing the bowl and bend over at the waist to have my curls cleaned. Who knew that virtually every activity pulls the upper torso/breast area? Even picking up a coffee cup strains those muscles. But I've graduated. Today I drank my morning coffee from my favorite mug — something I couldn't do last week. I'm trying to stay positive by measuring my progress from week to week. Day-to-day changes are too subtle to notice.

The hospital was a nightmare. I plan on writing a scathing letter to the president of the hospital later in the week. I'll send you a copy.

Thanks for the crash course about lymph nodes. No one had given me the full scoop (!) yet. I'm sure Dr. Goldberg will cover the precautions, though; he's so . . . cautious. I'm going to see him for a post-op checkup sometime next week. Today I'm only seeing Dr. Donahue. Somehow I've managed to go full circle and end up back at having those stitches removed. (OUCH again.)

I can't believe I almost forgot to tell you: When Goldberg told me that my lymph nodes were all negative, he also told me about my right breast. He explained that the cells had already started to change. "I call them precancerous," he said. Those were his exact words. He had a big smile on his face when he said it was a good move to remove it. Hooray for my gut instinct.

Michael's been unbelievable. I didn't see what I looked like before leaving the hospital. It's not like it is in the movies, where they unwrap the bandages and the woman, gazing into a mirror, bursts into a smile followed by tears of joy. No, they had bandages on me, all right, but they didn't remove them until an hour before I left. Then once they did remove them, the mirrors in the room were all too high for me to see my reflection. No one offered me a hand mirror, which I would have declined anyway. When we got home, I told Michael I needed a shower and shampoo. (I really did, too. Sponge baths don't cut it, especially when you consider that just one day after my surgery, I got my period. I'm catching no breaks, Susan. Absolutely none.) Anyway, Michael undressed both of us, got into the shower with me and washed my body and my hair. After the shower he pulled back the curtain, and all of a sudden there I was. The wall opposite our shower has a huge mirror on it, and I was forced to face my reflection. It was awful. Black stitches run *all the way across my entire upper torso.* They begin under each armpit and run horizontally across to the center of my body. The two lines of stitches don't meet, though. They come within an inch of one another and stop. It looks like there are millions of stitches, too. Without breasts I look all bony and emaciated. In fact, I look just like the pictures I've seen of the men in the concentration camps.

I tried to look away. But Donahue had given me an antibiotic ointment to put on the sutures after bathing. I had to look. I put the ointment on my finger and tried to rub it on my stitches. Susan, it was so revolting. Each stitch is individually tied. The knotted ends that stick out feel just like pieces of barbed wire. And I could feel the stitches poking the pads of my finger, *but I couldn't feel my finger touching my skin.* I started hyperventilating, crying, shaking. I was standing there naked, having as big a meltdown as I think I'm capable of having without crossing over into a legitimate nervous breakdown. I was so scared. But Michael was wonderful. He very calmly (and carefully) wrapped his arms around me and just hugged me. When he let go, he took the tube of antibiotic from me, squeezed some of it on his finger and rubbed it gently, a little bit at a time, across my deformed body. Susan, if he was disgusted, even a little bit, he didn't show it. And I kept watching his face for a sign. Nothing. I wonder if I could have done the same for him. I don't think so. If any good can come from any of this, that moment was it. In the course of daily life (and being married so many years) I guess I'm guilty of having lost sight of what a truly extraordinary and good man Michael is. That moment was a reminder. And just like the births of Wendy and Gregory, those brief minutes in the bathroom with Michael will stay with me forever.

I've been sitting a long time. I need to rest. Please write me one of your terrific, long letters. A good Gabby story, too. (But not *too* funny. It hurts more when I laugh.)

Lara

Subj: Welcome Back
Date: 03-03
From: Susan_P@aol.com
To: cre8f1@mindspring.com

Lara, it was great to hear from you. I know that you don't feel anything close to yourself just yet, but your letter sounded *so* much like the old you. It made me feel much better.

This weekend we're going on our annual ski trip to upper Michigan. Well, Artie and Gabby are the skiers. I just sit in the lodge and read trashy books. I don't ski because I never learned how, I hate the cold, and I'm afraid of heights and the chairlift. (You can pick any excuse you like — over the years I've used them all.)

It's my job to pack for everyone. This caused me to have to enter Gabby's room. A horrifying experience. I still have not recovered. Lara, you can't even imagine. Every week she has to put away her laundry and pick up her room. This would lead anyone to believe that her room is neat and tidy. Stupid. And to make matters worse, a month ago she forbade me to enter her room. "It's my room, and I can keep it the way I want. Besides, I'm not a baby. I can take care of my own room." Lara, that's a direct quote. Humor her, Artie says. She's getting older. I give in. Stupid again.

What I discovered when I opened her bedroom door is not to be believed. I will tell you, but you'll think I'm making it up or exaggerating. I'm not. I promise. Let's start with her closet and drawers. Forget her drawers — they were stuffed so full of balled-up clothes that I'd need a crowbar to pry them open. When I think of the time I spend each week folding her laundry, I could do her serious bodily harm. But the drawers are just sloppiness. The real disgusting part came when I discovered items that should have been thrown out but were instead stashed in drawers, corners of the closet, or just deposited on the floor. The assortment contained: Q-tips and tissues (both *used*), snipped-off price tags from newly purchased items (along with the plastic thread that attaches them to the garment), empty gum and candy wrappers (I don't allow food in her room). Well, I would have hit the ceiling, except that I'm afraid of that ceiling. All those basketball jerseys are still hanging from that ceiling. I'm sneezing just thinking about the dust that must have accumulated on them during the last month. Lara, I can't remember ever being so furious with Gabby.

She came home from school two hours ago. As you can probably tell, I'm still steaming from our argument. If I believed in hitting her, I would have. But I've never hit her and vowed I never would. So I yelled. A lot. And really loud. Then she looked me right in the eye and told me she hated me. And you know what? I know that she really means it. At least at this moment she does. And I don't care. She's supposed to hate me.

Sometimes. I also hated my mom when I was a teenager. Plenty. But I did not give my mom the kind of aggravation that Gabby gives me.

It's so unfair. (God, that's Gabby's favorite line.) But it really is. Now she'll spend this entire weekend chumming around with her dad, having a grand old time. Because they ski and I don't, I'm the one who's going to be left out. She'll be on her best behavior, so she and Artie will have no problems getting along. This will make him an easy target when she begins to manipulate him (a role she mastered during my BC treatments when the two of them bonded). She'll cry her heart out to him and complain that I overreact and am impatient with her. He'll tell her that he'll talk to me. Then it will be *my* problem. Then I'll be angry with Artie because he doesn't get it. (He was never a teenage girl; how could he possibly understand?) I'm ranting, and you probably don't even know what I'm talking about. See, it's this: She's going to win. And I just hate that. Especially when she's wrong. There should be some consequence here. Artie would kill me if I canceled the weekend, so that can't be the punishment. Geez, Lara, what's a mom to do? No one ever told me that being a mom would be so difficult. And so thankless. I feel like crying.

Well, when you asked for a Gabby story, I'm sure this isn't what you had in mind. Sorry. I'd better go if I'm going to get us packed up before Artie gets home. I'm not taking my laptop, so I'll

200

write to you when we return. Hopefully I will have calmed down by then.

Subj: Crystal Ball
Date: 03-04
From: cre8f1@mindspring.com
To: Susan_P@aol.com

Hi Susan,

I hope you're enjoying your weekend. Thanks for the glimpse into my future. Wendy's already a slob, and I can easily imagine finding her room in such a state sometime in the next couple of years. I don't blame you for being mad, but it sounds like the confrontation with Gabby ended up hurting you much more than it did her. As far as what you can do about that, I'm afraid I don't have the answer. But you're right. You can't just ignore it. Perhaps you can do the old "link the punishment to the crime" routine, though. You know, if she can't take care of her clothes, don't buy her any more new ones. If she can't throw away her used tissues . . . Man, I don't know what kind of punishment fits *that* crime. That *is* gross, but it could be worse. . . . Never mind, I don't want to go there.

Wendy and I are getting on famously. Too well, in fact. She's treading lightly. I think she's still afraid that I'm going to die. I got a call from her Language Arts teacher yesterday. I told Wendy to stay after school for the movie. (Every other Friday the school shows a movie. It's their way of giving the kids something somewhat social to do after school. Plus, it keeps the kids out of the town, which the local merchants really appreciate.) Anyway, you're supposed to send a note if your kid is staying. I gave Wendy the note before she left for school. Around lunchtime the teacher calls and tells me he's noticed that Wendy has been pretty "fragile" all day. He says the math teacher has also noticed and even thought at one point Wendy was going to cry. The teacher says he thinks Wendy just needs to be home with me and would it be OK if she came home on the bus instead of staying for the movie? I told him it was fine.

Foiled by my good intentions. Since I'm still not doing too well, I figured that it was better if the kids were busy or away and didn't have to see me so incapacitated. After the movie ends, it's only a few more hours till Michael gets home, and then he can handle everything. At least that was the plan. It's obviously backfired. Now it seems Wendy is feeling like I'm pushing her away, and that's making her even more worried and upset. Apparently she needs to see for herself that I'm OK. Or that I'm going to be OK. Or just to be with me. I don't know. You're right. Being a mom is confusing, and no one told me that either. But still, it's worth every struggle, isn't it?

Susan, I hope I'm not prying, but I couldn't help noticing — you've mentioned Artie's family in some of your letters but never your own. And then in your last letter you wrote that you also hated your mom from time to time but never gave her the kind of trouble that Gabby gives you. Are your parents still living? Any siblings? If you'd rather not answer, no problem. I just thought that since you finally brought it up, you might feel like sharing . . .

Subj: We're Back
Date: 03-06
From: Susan_P@aol.com
To: cre8f1@mindspring.com

We're home. And believe it or not, a good time was had by all. As we were packing up the van to leave for Michigan, Gabby asked if she could speak to me, *privately*. Artie raised an eyebrow but for once in his life didn't ask any questions. Anyway, she apologized. Just like that. She told me that she was really sorry and that she knew she was wrong and that when the weekend was over she was going to spend a few hours cleaning up her room. And then she said, "I love you, Mommy." Not Mom, but Mommy. Just like a little girl. And she looked like one, too. I was caught so off guard. Where have the years gone? When did my little girl turn into a young lady? To have that reminder, just a glimpse of when Gabby was little and always called me Mommy . . . well, I melted. I gave her a long hug and told her that I loved her, more than she could even understand. And because I was feeling generous, I told her that I probably overreacted a *tad,* and if she was especially wonderful the rest of the weekend, I just might consider helping her clean up that junkyard she calls a bedroom. She laughed, and that was it. We locked up the house and had a great couple of days away. Clearly, the time together was much needed.

Let's see, my family. You're right. I've avoided it. But we've known one another long enough, and I think you should know. And I (subconsciously) must need to tell you, and that's why I mentioned arguing with my mom when I was a teenager.

My mom died when she was 52. (I was 30.) She had breast cancer. We were very close, and it's taken me a very long time to get over it. Actually, I'm still not over it — I just deal with the loss a little better. My mom was a really great lady. She had the most wonderful sense of humor. She used to turn every argument, every tense moment, every frustration into laughter. And there was nothing she couldn't handle. Once when I was young, we were shopping, and when it was time to go home, she discovered that she'd locked her keys in the car. No problem. Mom said that clearly we were meant to spend more money. Without missing a beat, she grabbed me by the hand, turned me around, and we headed right back into the mall, where we shopped until my Aunt Betsy arrived — with a wire hanger. You should have seen the two of them trying to break into our car. It could have been a Lucy/Ethel bit, and to this day it remains one of my happiest memories, as well as one of the funniest things I've ever seen. Just writing about it, I'm grinning ear to ear.

Aunt Betsy was my mom's sister. She died two years after my mom. Breast cancer also. Do you think that a day slips by when I don't look at Gabby and wonder what sort of legacy I'm leaving her? I keep hoping (and legitimately praying) that by the time she's old enough to become a potential victim of this horrible disease, breast cancer will be a thing of the past. Unfortunately, Gabby keeps getting older, and that vaccine (or cure) remains undiscovered.

Anyway — my mom always took everything in stride. Until the cancer. That was something she couldn't control, and she hated it. She always had solutions to every problem, but by the time they discovered her cancer, there was no solution. Today they probably would have done some designer chemo or a stem-cell transplant, and who knows? But that wasn't even an option back then. So she had the standard chemo, even though we all knew it was too late. The treatments were awful, and she turned into someone else. I sometimes wish she'd skipped the heroics (i.e., chemo) and just died. At least I wouldn't have any memories of how the chemo ravaged her body — and her spirit. I could go round and round with this one. But what *I* think or what *I* wish doesn't matter. It was her choice to try everything possible until the bitter end. And it was bitter. To this day I can't help but wonder what really killed her: the chemo, the cancer or the fact that she'd lost all control over her life and hated living that way.

You'd think I'd feel grateful to have had my mom all the way into my adult life. But I don't. It wasn't long enough. (Is it ever?) Besides, I still miss her too much to feel grateful about *anything* that ends with her dying at age 52.

My mom was so happy when Gabby was born. She said that only by being a parent to a little girl would I be able to unravel the complexities of the mother/daughter relationship. Then and only then, she promised, would I truly understand how much she loved me. Boys are terrific, she said (I have an older brother), but there's something magical that happens between a mother and her daughter. She was so right. But she died before I was able to form the kind of relationship with Gabby that she was talking about. It's the kind of relationship that would have made me appreciate my mom's love and devotion even more. As Gabby passes through each stage of development, I discover so much more about myself, my mom and our relationship. And that only makes living without her all the more difficult. And you know what's really weird? Even though she's been gone for years, I *still* find myself making mental notes of things I want to remember to tell her, and occasionally I still even reach for the phone to call her. I really miss hearing her voice. Sometimes I pop in videotapes of my wedding, just so I can hear her and see her smiling and dancing. She was so healthy and carefree. So *Mom.* I'm especially sad that Gabby doesn't have any memories of her. She would have just adored her grandma, and my mom would have really loved Gabby's spunk. Mom always believed that women should speak up for themselves, and she would have praised Gabby's mouth as one of her greatest assets. (Then she would have winked at me and said something funny, like "It's such a joy to be the grandma instead of the mom.")

Anyway, three years after my mom died, my dad remarried a woman named Polly. I was OK with him remarrying — it was Polly I wasn't OK with. I'm still not. (It's complicated, and probably just me having trouble with someone stepping into my mom's place, but it's the way it is.) Still, my dad and I talk on the phone a couple times a week, even though we don't get together as often as we should/could. (He and Polly live in Cincinnati, which is where I'm from. Artie and his family are the ones originally from Canton, which is how I got here.) Gabby spends at least one of her school vacations every year with my dad and Polly, so that's nice. Gabby is clueless that I have any problems with Polly. (Do you think that would make Gabby like Polly more or like her less? Inquisitive minds . . .)

My older brother, Peter, lives in California, which makes getting together problematic. But we're very close, and even with the time difference, we manage to talk to one another no less than three times a week. We e-mail a lot, too. Gabby's always begging to go visit Uncle Peter — and if *we* can't go, can *she?* I've resisted sending her out there alone, since Peter is unmarried and has no children. (He's gay.) I thought she'd be too much of a handful. But now that she's getting older and can take care of herself (for the most part), I might give in.

Well, there you have it: the entire Washburn family tree. I've got to run. Thanks to the ski weekend, I've got a mountain of laundry. I hope you're feeling better. Let me know what's going on.

Susan

Subj: The Washburns
Date: 03-07
From: cre8f1@mindspring.com
To: Susan_P@aol.com

Dear Susan,

Thanks for the family bio. Your mom sounds like quite a lady. Funny, capable, liked being in control — I know you may find this hard to believe, but you sound a lot like her. It's apparent that the two of you had a special relationship. My mom and I get along but aren't very close, mostly because we're just very different people. I love to read; she doesn't. I love to play sports and be active; she knits. I enjoy my work; she never had a career. I'm ruled by my mind; she's ruled by her emotions. I'm pragmatic; she's artistic. Are you noticing a trend? Still, I know just what you mean about really understanding your own mother only *after* having a daughter of your own. As Wendy grows and our relationship changes, I do have a much clearer and better understanding of my mom. And I do appreciate her more. But I'm the lucky one. My mom is still living. That doesn't mean I take the time to share my innermost thoughts — or my feelings of deep appreciation — with her. But after reading your letter, I decided to call her and do just that. Unfortunately, life got in the way. I got her answering machine. Isn't that always the way it goes? I just hope that when Gabby and Wendy are adults, they grow to understand us — and when they reach for the phone to tell us, we'll be home. :-)

Enough mush. Susan, I was more than a little upset when I read about your family history with breast cancer. You never mentioned it before, and I was really caught off guard. I don't know what to say — especially when it comes to understanding Gabby's risk.

It's ironic that you should write about the genetics of BC, because I had a rather convoluted conversation on this very topic with Wendy a couple days after I got home from the hospital.

WENDY: You know, Mom, I'm really lucky.

ME: How so, sweetie?

W: Well, I know that you didn't have breast cancer when you were pregnant with me, did you?

M: No, honey. I didn't.

W: Well, we just finished a unit on genetics in Miss Fischer's class. So now I know.

M: Now you know what, Wendy?

W: *(Like I'm an idiot for not immediately understanding, she says)* Well, since you didn't have breast cancer when you were pregnant with me, you couldn't have passed it on to me. *(She continues to look me in the eye, pausing the longest time, and then in the littlest, thinnest voice, she asks)* Right?

Susan, I was so tempted just to smile and tell her that she was right and that she doesn't have to worry about breast cancer ever hurting her. But I couldn't. She's too smart, and I'm too afraid that if I don't correct her notion of genetics and how things are passed along, she'll accuse me of not being truthful. (And after the whole mole story, you know, I *promised*.)

I gave her a brief lesson in genetics, complete with a Punnett square (remember those?). Then I told her that since there was no one else in our family with breast cancer, the odds were that my cancer wasn't something that's inherited anyway. But then I got your letter. What do you tell Gabby? Has she asked? How does a young girl grow up and look at her breasts as anything other than ticking time bombs when so many women in her family have developed breast cancer? I understand your fears. And guilt. What kind of legacy are we leaving our daughters and granddaughters if we don't do everything we can to stop this disease from claiming more lives? I feel the activist in me stirring. That's good. The "old" Lara is starting to surface. When I'm well, maybe the two of us could put our heads together and think about ways we can focus more attention on this disease. But not yet. I still feel too lousy. But I've graduated. I am no longer taking pain pills. I've moved on to Tylenol by day and a sleeping pill at night, which is the only way I can sleep. I've always been a side or tummy sleeper, but Donahue wants me flat on my back. He says absolutely no sleeping on my "breasts" (Lara repeated, as if she had a wishbone lodged deep in her throat).

I can now put on a button-down shirt without histrionics and am also getting *smoother* (but not yet higher) arm motions. Tomorrow morning I'm going back to the city to see Dr. Goldberg, Dr. Donahue and last, but never least, Dr. Berns. Then I'll come home and take a nap!

Lara

P.S. AN IDEA: Consider using a solo trip to visit Uncle Peter as an incentive for Gabby to keep her room clean. You know, "When you prove to me you really can pick up after yourself and wouldn't be a problem for Uncle Peter, then and only then will I even *think* about allowing you to go out west for a visit." Just a thought.

Subj: Basketball
Date: 03-07
From: Susan_P@aol.com
To: cre8f1@mindspring.com

The Freedom made the playoffs. Gabby's thrilled. So am I. I love your idea about her bedroom. You're obviously a very capable mom. Let me know how it goes tomorrow. I'll write more then. I'm too rushed.

    S.

Subj: Appointments
Date: 03-08
From: cre8f1@mindspring.com
To: Susan_P@aol.com

As expected, I'm pooped. Three doctors in one day is too many.

Dr. Goldberg says that he's done with me for a while. He wants to see me again after the tissue expanders come out and the implants are in. He says he could make a case for or against chemo, but it's something I should discuss with an oncologist. He recommends Dr. Berns. (No kidding.)

And now the news we've all been waiting for:

Goldberg says that the time I lost because of Walker's botched biopsy had no affect on my treatment. I would still have needed a mastectomy. Walker's mistake also does not affect my prognosis, which Goldberg assures me is excellent. He did add, however, "If you had waited a year before coming to see me after your first biopsy, then your prognosis would have been greatly affected and we would be having a very different conversation from the one we're having now." That's scary stuff. But the bottom line remains as Artie explained: I can sue Walker and prove negligence, but I can't receive damages ($$) because Walker's mistake didn't affect my life span. (Thank God!) Needless to say, Michael and I do not want the emotional and financial burden of a lawsuit that will give us nothing more than the satisfaction that we hauled Walker's sorry ass into court. So while I've warned my gynecologist not to refer any more of his patients to Dr. Walker, there's nothing else I intend to do. NEXT —

Dr. Donahue (who has this annoying habit of calling me Laura, instead of Lara) opens my gown, stands back and admires his handiwork. He says that I look great. (Do I get a vote?) He gives me the OK to start physical therapy but warns me not to overdo. (Yeah, like how? I can barely brush my teeth!) He says that he'll see me in two weeks for my first injections of saline. NEXT —

Dr. Berns. Well, this appointment isn't so matter-of-fact. After taking a few minutes to look through my pathology report (3 pages long!), Berns starts explaining all of the terminology to Michael and me. (Yes, Susan. Michael is with me. He's more than with me. He's sitting next to me on the love seat in Berns's office *holding my hand.*) Berns dances around the issue for a while and then asks what *I* think about chemotherapy. I tell him I'm not sure but want to err on the side of being overly cautious. I explain I've got little kids I want to raise, and whatever will give me the best odds of being around to do that is what I want. He explains that my survival stats without chemo are already greater than 90%. (Say it again. And again.) But he also says there are a couple of things in my pathology report (like the S phrase??) that indicate that my cancer is a very aggressive type. He points out that I've gone the extra step from the very beginning (starting with my questioning of the diagnosis of atypical cells and ending with my decision to remove my so-called healthy breast, that turned out to be not so healthy after all). He says in light of a few suspicious items in the pathology report, maybe I shouldn't get conservative now. I think about everything he's said. I decide if I'd been conservative, I might have ended up dead. That does it. I ask him to tell us about the chemo.

Berns makes it clear: There's no such thing as "preventive chemo." Chemo, he explains, is given to kill any cancer cells that may have escaped from my breast and found a home in some other part of my body. He says because all my lymph nodes are negative (and he reiterates how that's the most important of all prognosticators for survival), we can hope that no cells escaped — and skip the chemo. Or we can look at those suspicious areas of my pathology report and take the necessary steps to kill any cancer cells that may be lurking in my body. He says there's something called light chemo (CMF) that's often given to node-negative women who opt for chemo. (You must have had the CAF chemo, which he says is usually given when the lymph nodes are positive.)

THE ROUTINE: Dr. Berns says I'd have a total of eight treatments of intravenous CMF. I'd get the chemo every three weeks for six months. He gives the treatments in his office, so I wouldn't have to go to a hospital or somewhere else, where I might be treated anonymously. He tells me that since I'm young and healthy (yes, I've got cancer, but I'm considered *healthy!*) he expects I'd have very little trouble with CMF, and *if,* after four rounds, I thought it was god-awful, I could always stop. He says the biggest side effect for me would probably be tiredness; the treatments would leave me exhausted for around two days.

Then we move on to hair. Berns explains that with CMF I should not go bald (but with CAF you always lose your hair). He says I should expect hair thinning, but just how much varies. And just as I'm silently thanking God for my long, thick hair (which could actually use a little thinning), Berns says the hair loss wouldn't be as severe (or as noticeable) if I reduced the weight and pulling of my hair. He *strongly suggests* I get a short haircut. (Gulp.)

During the entire lowdown about chemo-therapy, Michael's been holding my hand, which is by now sweaty. (Not mine. His.) He's been amazingly silent. But now it's clear that we've reached the point in the conversation where it's time for us to say something. I look at Michael, and he lifts his eyebrows (which is his "I don't know, what do you think?" look). I take a minute to think about everything Berns has just told us. Then I tell him that I think I want to go ahead with the chemo. Michael gives my hand a gentle squeeze. Berns asks if I want to have my first treatment. I'm caught completely off guard. "You mean, like *now?* Today?" He tells me that this way I can get one treatment out of the way. He says he has time. What do I think?

I think that I'm a dishrag. I chicken out. I tell him that it's been a long day and I'm not mentally ready for chemo yet. But before leaving his office, I make an appointment to get my first treatment. I make it for next Wednesday, knowing that the housekeeper will be around for the kids.

I've got nothing else to tell you. I'm tired, and I've got to read *Corduroy* to Gregory before he goes to sleep. I promised. Bye.

Subj: Choices
Date: 03-09
From: Susan_P@aol.com
To: cre8f1@mindspring.com

Dear Lara,

I agree. Go for the chemo. You've done everything you possibly can to assure your full and complete recovery from this disease; you may as well not stop now. Besides, I know you. If, God forbid, you should have a recurrence sometime down the road, you'd be second-guessing yourself and wondering if it would have made a difference if you'd had the chemo. I have a great deal of respect for Dr. Berns, too. Many oncologists are insensitive clods who wouldn't allow you to be a partner in the decision-making process. They just lecture you and then say do it or don't. Dr. Berns sounds like a honey.

You're right. I had CAF. (That's 'cause I had six positive lymph nodes, remember?) And it's the A (adriamycin) in CAF that causes the baldness. Most of the women in my support group who have/had CMF did pretty well with it. They complain that it makes them really, really tired, but besides that, they're basically OK. Hopefully, you'll be like them.

BTW, have you done anything as far as joining a support group? I know you may not think you're the support group type. Neither did I. But it can really help. I wish my group had been around when I was going through my treatments. The next six months will not be easy. Even if you sail though chemo, which I expect you will, it's a constant reminder of what you've had to face — what you're still facing. And then there's the reconstruction. It may be helpful to talk with other women about how you're feeling, your new body, and whatever else comes up. I'm trying not to push. It's hard. So I'll simply say, "Think about it." OK?

7

Subj: PT
Date: 03-13
From: cre8f1@mindspring.com
To: Susan_P@aol.com

Today my friend Donna picks me up to take me to physical therapy (PT), which is two towns away (20 minutes from my house). She walks me in (which is a mighty good thing, because the door into the building was too heavy for me to push open all by myself). Donna says she'll be back for me in an hour. (Gee, thanks, Mom.)

My physical therapist, Randi, asks me to give her my medical history before she evaluates me. Once that's complete, she very gently reaches for one of my arms. I warn her that I can't move them very well. She says that it doesn't matter, that is after all why I'm there. (She's got a point.)

Anyway, she barely moves my arm, and it hurts so bad that I start to cry, which I'm sure isn't so unusual either. But then the unusual *does* happen. I can't stop crying. It's like a flood. (I'm talking biblical proportions here, too.) And it seems that the harder I try to compose myself, the worse it gets. And so for the rest of the appointment I learn arm exercises and bawl my head off. Randi is a doll and acts like this happens all the time. (Oh, sure.)

I guess I've just been holding back so many tears for so many weeks that once I started, there was just no stopping me. It was *so* embarrassing. After the appointment, Donna took one look at me and said, "Oh, no. It must have hurt a lot." It did hurt — don't misunderstand. But from my red face and puffy eyes Donna must have thought that Randi abused me. I'm going back to PT on Thursday. (I promised Randi I'd get a grip before then.) But first I've got a chemo treatment to get through on Wednesday.

I'd better get going. Another friend (Jane) is picking me up in 20 minutes, and I really should fix my tearstained face before she gets here. Jane's taking me to the hairdresser's for my new chemo cut. When I told Randi about the new do I'm getting, she said that if I continue to do the arm exercises she showed me, by the end of next week I should be able to wash my shorter tresses all by myself. From her mouth to God's ears.

Subj: Tears
Date: 03-14
From: Susan_P@aol.com
To: cre8f1@mindspring.com

Crying's good. And remember, Lara, there are no extra points for bravery *or* bottled-up emotions. My advice? Invest in some waterproof mascara and let the tears flow. Good luck with the chemo tomorrow.

Sue

Subj: Treatment
Date: 03-15
From: cre8f1@mindspring.com
To: Susan_P@aol.com

Hi, Susan.

I just got home from my first treatment. Michael volunteered to go with me, but I didn't want him to come. I'm not sure why. Yes I am. Michael's already had to take off too much time because of me, and April 15th is exactly a month away. Need I say more?

My friend Barbara drove me into the city and back. I wouldn't let her walk me back into the house afterward though, since I'm feeling perfectly fine. Berns's nurse gave me some pills to take in case I get nauseous. She said not to take them unless I feel bad, though. Actually, I feel good. I just *look* bad. I was never meant for short hair. Michael: "It will grow back." Wendy: "Now I know why you've always had long hair." Even my little Gregory: "Mommy, I liked you better the old way." Me, too, sweetie. In fact, I liked *everything* better the old way.

My mind is racing. It feels like I'm on speed (except I never took speed, so I don't really know what that feels like). I'll keep you posted.

Subj: Great!
Date: 03-16
From: Susan_P@aol.com
To: cre8f1@mindspring.com

Glad it went well. Congrats. One down. Seven more to go.
Me

Subj: Foster Parenting
Date: 03-17
From: Susan_P@aol.com
To: cre8f1@mindspring.com

Hi, Lara.

You're not going to believe this. Yesterday our priest called. He wants to know if Artie and I would be interested in being foster parents to a 7-year-old girl. The girl's mom died a few years ago. She had breast cancer, which is why Father John says he thought of us. (And that's supposed to be a *good* thing?) Apparently the girl's dad has been raising her, but he was just sentenced to two years in jail for committing some white-collar crime. Can you imagine? They're looking for a temporary home for this poor little girl. I have such mixed feelings. I keep making lists in my head of the pros and the cons. (No pun intended.)

Last night we had a Peterson powwow to discuss everyone's feelings about the matter. Gabby wants to do it. She thinks it would be fun to have another girl in the house. Images of the younger sister she never had, I suppose. In a way, I think she could really benefit from having another child in the house. In Gabby's life everything is always about Gabby. This little girl would change that. (Whether Gabby would quickly grow to resent that, who knows?)

Gabby also has images of a cute little 7-year-old running around. I asked her how she would feel if the girl weren't cute. What if she were ugly or fat or foul-mouthed or not very smart? Would Gabby want anything to do with her then? *I* don't even know the answer to that, and I know Gabby well. Better than she knows herself. Remember?

Artie is in the middle of the road. He says he likes the family the way it is but wonders if this isn't some sort of omen or something. You know, all those years we tried to have another child and couldn't, and now another child is offered to us — by a man of God, no less. I think he's almost afraid to say no, so Artie does what he does very well — he keeps trying to pass the decision-making onto me. Well, onto Gabby and me. "It's really up to you two. You're the ones who will spend the most time with her." He's right about that. He works such long hours, this would have a much greater impact on my life and Gabby's than on his. But I keep stressing that even though he wouldn't be here physically, this child would still need and deserve his emotional support. And could we count on him for that? Could we?

I have no doubt that Artie and I could love this little girl. Gabby could *probably* love her. But I keep coming back to two things:

1. The baggage. This is a child who watched her mom die and is now losing her dad. To jail! There are tons of issues that this child would be bringing with her. (And those are only the ones I can imagine.)

2. Saying good-bye. I don't know if I'm capable of opening my home and my heart (mostly my heart) to a child for two years and then saying good-bye. The truth is, I can't even watch those made-for-TV movies where a couple adopts a child and years later the court rules that the child must return to her biological parents. I used to cry my eyes out over such stories — now I refuse to even watch them. To *willingly* put myself in such a similar position, to even be considering it — I must be crazy.

After talking about it last night, we all decided to sleep on it. This morning it's not much clearer. The only thing I know for sure is if I don't leave now, I'll be late for work. Hope you're feeling well.

Susan

Subj: I'm Vertical
Date: 03-18
From: cre8f1@mindspring.com
To: Susan_P@aol.com

Dear Susan,

It was awful. About two hours after sending you my e-mail telling you how great I was doing, the chemo hit me. Hard. I spent the next couple of days in bed. Every time I stood up (like to go to the bathroom), I was overcome by nausea and started vomiting again. I thought I had bad morning sickness with my pregnancies — that was nothing. The pills the nurse gave me for nausea did no good. Michael (who didn't go in to work on Thursday because I was too sick to be left alone) called Dr. Berns, who phoned in a different prescription to the pharmacy. Michael wouldn't even leave me to go pick up the pills; he had one of my friends do it. It didn't matter, though; those pills were also useless. I was really scared. I felt like someone had poisoned me and my body was trying to get rid of all the toxins — and if it didn't get them out soon, they were going to kill me. In fact, for a few hours that day I truly thought I was going to die.

Gregory came running into my bedroom as soon as he got home from school. All he wanted was to give me a kiss so I would feel better. Michael had gotten him up and out that morning, and told him that Mommy would be awake, feeling better and waiting for a kiss by the time he got home. (Two outa three ain't bad. What am I saying? It was worse than bad. It was horrendous.) Gregory came to a halt halfway into the bedroom, and in his best whisper-voice (that I'm always begging him to use whenever we're at temple, but he never does) he asked if he could give me a kiss. Susan, just the sound of his voice and seeing that little face peering at me from behind his brainiac glasses made me feel better, I swear. From my lying-down position I opened my arms and told him that I would love a kiss from him. But as he leaned in toward my cheek, I got a whiff of him and immediately started to vomit. (I usually *love* the way he smells.) I tried to get to what we now call the "puke pot" on my nightstand, but Gregory was standing there, and I couldn't shove him out of the way fast enough. He ran out of our bedroom, splattered in my vomit, scared and screaming for his daddy. Michael came in and asked if he could bring me some tea. Just hearing the word made me sick again. I hate to be so graphic, but are you getting the picture? I want to make sure you *really* understand, because I'm not being a baby.

The next day (Friday) I was still too sick to get Gregory ready for school. Michael had a client meeting that he'd already rescheduled once and couldn't postpone again, so he woke Gregory a little bit earlier, dressed him and dropped him off at our neighbor's house. (That way Michael could still catch the 8:27 train, making him late to work, but not for his 10:00 meeting.) Lucy (our neighbor) gave Gregory breakfast and walked him down to the bus stop, along with her own kids. All I can say is, Thank God that at least Wendy is old enough to dress and feed herself *and* make it to the bus alone. Amen.

I've discussed my chemo nightmare with Dr. Berns. He says that the anti-nausea medication works by blocking the nausea signal from reaching the brain. The pills somehow prevent the brain from getting the "I feel like puking" message. The pills didn't work for me (he says) because it was already too late when I took the first one. My brain had already gotten the message that I was sick as a dog and wasn't about to forget it, no matter how many pills I took. So for my *next* treatment Berns doesn't want me to wait until I get sick. I'm to take the anti-nausea medication every four hours even if I have no symptoms. So, one might ask (as I surely did), "Why did your nurse tell me to wait to take the pills in the first place? Why didn't you have me take them, just in case?" Berns says that many people don't need them, and 1) they're very expensive (more than 50 bucks *a pill*), and 2) the pills have side effects, so there's no reason to take them unless they're needed. Needless to say, they're needed.

I'm still not feeling myself yet, but I'm upright and able to eat clear chicken soup.

It's not that I'm not interested in your foster-parenting opportunity. I just needed to get my chemo story off of my chest. (Pun? No pun? Who knows?) So now let's talk about you . . .

Have you made a decision yet? You seem to have thought through a lot of the issues. I couldn't believe that you were so clearheaded about the pros/cons after only 24 hours. (See, you *are* your mother's daughter.)

I have so much admiration for you for even *considering* becoming foster parents. We could never. I love my children dearly. But I'm not a child lover in general. You know those women who want to hold every newborn they see? That was never me. To me, babies all look like bald little men. Except mine. Wendy was gorgeous right from birth. And after too many hours of pushing, Gregory's chin was mashed in, leaving him looking like a baby bird. (But he quickly improved until he became the cute little guy he is today.) That's not to say that I couldn't adopt and love a *newborn*. I could. And I'm sure I would love that baby as much as I love Wendy and Gregory. But I don't think I could learn to love an *older child*. Not unconditionally. Not like I love my own children. It's not something I'm real proud of, trust me. It's just the way I am. I wouldn't admit it to just anyone. (But you stopped qualifying as "anyone" months ago.) At least I know that about myself. And about Michael. He would be even less willing than I to consider temporarily raising someone else's kid. I hope you don't think less of me for being so . . . I don't know, so closed-hearted. I'm hoping I've got other redeeming qualities that will cause you to forgive such character flaws.

Thanks to my severe reaction to chemo, I had to cancel my last PT appointment. I'm still doing my exercises at home, though. Three days in bed did nothing for my mobility, so I'd better go spend some quality time with the wall and my latest gadget: an over-the-door arm pulley that Randi made me buy.

Lara

Subj: Guilty
Date: 03-20
From: Susan_P@aol.com
To: cre8f1@mindspring.com

I feel so guilty. We decided not to proceed with the all the forms, house visits and every-thing else needed to become a foster family. Gabby's furious with me. She thinks it would be so wonderful, and "You never listen to my opinion anyway, so why did you even ask me what I wanted?"

Why, indeed? What it finally came down to was my belief that in two years I'd grow too at-tached to this child. I have trouble with partings. That's partly why I still have such trouble coping with my mom's death. But even when my brother, Peter, comes out for a visit, I always get teary when I drop him off at the airport. I just don't do good-byes well. Besides, I've had enough heartache over the last few years.

I can't believe what a hard time you had with your treatment. I'm so sorry. Have you tried eating potatoes or bread? I did well with both. It's like the bulky nature of those kinds of foods helped absorb some of the toxins from my body. You know, sort of spongelike. This is entirely unscientific and completely untrue . . . but it's how it made me feel when I ate those kinds of foods. (And how you *feel* is what it's all about.)

I'm sure that you'll have an easier time of things next time if you take the anti-nausea medicine (they're called antiemetics) before you feel sick. Did any of your friends offer you pot? I was shocked at the number of people I knew who offered it to me when they heard I was sick from chemo drugs. I didn't know I even knew so many people with such "access." You may want to consider it, though. It helped me. (There's also a pill form of marijuana that may help. It's apparently not as effective, but you may want to ask Berns about it.)

Subj: Hospital Stay
Date: 03-22
From: cre8f1@mindspring.com
To: Susan_P@aol.com

Dear Pot-smoker (who knew?),

Well, I finally had the time and energy to write my hospital complaint letter. It wound up being 8 pages (single-spaced, too!). That's ridiculously long, I know, but I didn't want to leave anything out. The president of the hospital should know that as bad as breast cancer may be, his hospital only made matters worse. I don't want to bore you with the entire letter, so I've cut-and-pasted some of the highlights. (It's *still* long.) Read it and weep. I did. But it also made me feel better to vent. And maybe after reading my tirade, they'll change their hospital policies so some other woman won't have to go through everything I did. Hey, I can hope. (NO! I am not smoking any of that pot that YES! two of my friends have already offered me. I couldn't believe it.)

Dear Mr. Rosenfeld, [FYI, Susan, he's the prez of the hospital],

Two weeks ago I had the misfortune of having a bilateral mastectomy at Mount Cedars Hospital. I could be flip and say that I don't know which was a more horrific experience, undergoing disfiguring surgery to rid my body of cancer or the way in which I was treated (or ignored) in your hospital. But instead I am going to share with you the many, many ways that Mount Cedars fell short in helping to ease my pain and suffering.

- My husband waited in the designated area during my surgery. At one point he asked a nurse to get some information about how I was doing: Was the surgery complete? Was I in recovery yet? How much longer did they expect things to take? Before he knew it, my husband tells me that a gate went up. It was "closing time." My husband was left waiting behind a locked gate with no information about me — and no one from the hospital to ask for help. As

231

time passed, however, three different men and women in scrubs came by. My husband asked each of them, "Could you please get me some information about my wife?" Each time he was told that it wasn't that person's job. "But there's no one here," my husband pointed out. *"Whose job is it?"*

- Thankfully, I had been forewarned by my reconstructive surgeon's office to hire private-duty nurses during my hospital stay. But the best nurses in the world (which I believe I had) can't provide care without the necessary supplies and equipment. It seems that every time my nurses tried to get something for me — to ease my pain or increase my comfort — they were blocked. Examples:

1. My private-duty nurse explained that following a mastectomy a woman should have her arms slightly elevated and supported by pillows at all times. She then left my bedside to get them. She came back empty-handed. The nurses on the floor (and the housekeeping personnel) claimed that there were no pillows available. My nurse told me that she couldn't understand what was going on. She'd worked in your hospital before and never had this problem. However, my nurse was creative. If we couldn't support my arms with pillows, she explained, rolled blankets would do. But blankets were also not available. This became an even bigger issue that

evening when the room became quite cold.

2. Knowing that my reconstructive surgeon likes his patients doing breathing exercises immediately after surgery, the private-duty nurse woke me every hour to do them. Every hour she promised a barometer-type machine to make it easier to measure my breathing and to see if I was making progress. Every hour she explained that she still had no success getting the machine delivered to the room. She finally was able to secure one — but only because she went down to respiration therapy and got it herself.

3. By lunchtime I was being encouraged to eat; however, the anesthesia had left me nauseated. Fish, which I don't eat under normal circumstances, let alone when I'm queasy, was delivered for lunch. My private-duty nurse called food service and told them that she also noticed cheese blintzes on the delivery cart. *(SUSAN: Blintzes are a Jewish food; they're mild and similar to a crêpe.)* She asked if they could serve me blintzes instead. But your food-service personnel told my nurse that since I had not requested kosher meals when I was admitted to the hospital, I wasn't entitled to one. I agreed instead to eat a fresh-fruit plate with cottage cheese. It took more than an hour before it was delivered — *without utensils*. (I ate the fruit with my fingers and was forced to pass on the cottage cheese.)

• Toward the end of my first 24 hours in Mount Cedars (YES, all this happened during my first day!), a supervising nurse appeared and wanted to know if I'd been walking in the hall yet. I told her that I'd been up many times to use the bathroom and had walked *into* the hall but not up and down it. I explained that the pain medication and the remaining effects of the general anesthesia had left me too dizzy and unsteady to walk the hall. The supervisor then proceeded to warn me that I'd better find a happy medium between the amount of medication it took to control my pain and what made me dizzy, since I needed to be up and walking in the hall. *I was less than 24 hours post-op and she was giving me grief about taking pain medication?* I may have been on pain medication, but I knew enough to feel outraged. Sadly, however, feeling extremely vulnerable and wanting to get out of Mount Cedars (the hospital with no supplies and food rations), I started to take Tylenol. Needless to say, that did nothing to ease my pain and made me more miserable than I needed to be.

- I had private-duty nurses around the clock. Yet at 1:30 A.M. a large man came charging into my room. (My nurse had just left to get some pain medication for me. The Tylenol was ineffective, and I figured I could "sleep off" the dizzying effects of the medicine by morning — leaving me capable of walking the ever-so-important hallway.) Anyway, without warning this man grabbed my right arm. (Remember, my mastectomy was *bilateral*. Moving either arm, even gently, caused me great pain.) But your nurse was far from gentle. He yanked my arm and at the same time knocked the IV needle, which my private-duty nurse had recently reinserted. (It had to be reinserted because my original vein had become so irritated that another one needed to be used. The new vein had not worked out well either, so my nurse capped off the IV, hoping for permission to pull the needle first thing in the morning.) I tell you all of this because that little needle in my arm was responsible for a lot of discomfort . . . but not as much discomfort as that male nurse caused when he grabbed my arm from under the blanket, knocking the needle.

Is there no way to mark a room — or a patient — who has private-duty care so your staff doesn't need to intrude and repeat procedures the private-duty nurse has already done? My private-duty nurses took my temperature and blood pressure numerous times (never causing me the slightest bit of discomfort). But twice Mount Cedars nurses managed to get to me and both times hurt me by grabbing and pulling at my arms as if I were incapable of feeling pain.

I'm getting angry just thinking about everything that happened to me at your hospital, so let's just jump ahead to my last day:

My original roommate was discharged that morning. By afternoon I watched as a patient from another room (not a *new* admission) was wheeled into my room. Sadly, this woman was missing a leg. Sadly for me, the bed she was being wheeled into was the window bed. As the nurse wheeled her past the chair I was sitting in, she banged the wheelchair into my chair. This of course jostled my arms and sent pain shooting though my upper torso. "Oh, no," I said to my nurse. "Every time she needs to use the bathroom, she's going to bang into my bed or my chair." My nurse eased my mind by telling me that the bathroom in our room wasn't wheelchair accessible, so the patient would be using a bedpan.

Wrong. My new roommate was in the room for less than an hour before she buzzed for a nurse to bring her the wheelchair. I lay in my bed as her wheelchair first hit the side guardrail and then the foot of my bed *three times* before she was able to get to the wheelchair-accessible bathroom *in the hallway*. With each bump of the bed I was in pain (especially since I was taking only Tylenol). I was crying (again), and my husband left my bedside to visit the nurses' station and demand an explanation along with a relocation or reshuffling of beds.

Why, I wondered, didn't they move *my* bed next to the window and allow the wheelchair patient to have the bed closest to the door? That way, whenever my roommate needed to get up, she could do so without disturbing me.

The reason, I learned, was that the woman with the wheelchair wanted a bed with a window view! *That's what this was about. She* wanted a window. But what about *me?* Who was worrying about what was good for me? My husband, that's who. He insisted that I be moved to another room. A hospital administrator appeared to explain that the only available bed in the hospital was on the medicine floor. She said that the medicine floor was not an appropriate place for me. As I sit at my keyboard writing this, I'm struck by the irony that *anything* could have been less appropriate for me than the situation I was in.

(SUSAN: There's more, but if you'll forgive the sloppy transition, I'll just cut to the conclusion.)

It is my hope that my complaints will dramatically affect hospital policy and that other patients, or at least other women faced with the struggles that breast cancer presents, can be helped not just by your doctors but by your hospital. (And if you can't provide better help and care, you should at least take the steps necessary to prevent causing these patients *additional* pain and hurt.) There is no reason anyone should have to endure anything close to what I suffered through while at Mount Cedars.

Frankly, I'm appalled that I never received a written apology addressing the verbal complaints I made while I was a patient at your hospital. But I can't say that I'm surprised. It's so terribly consistent with everything else I experienced at Mount Cedars.

Before I left the hospital, my private-duty

nurse found a cabinet containing all kinds of booklets about breast cancer, reconstruction and chemotherapy. She took it upon herself to grab an assortment of the literature for me. Those booklets can provide all kinds of useful information and resources to help a woman with breast cancer on her long road to recovery. I can't help but wonder, If the hospital has such material, why isn't it being given to the patients? Why does it sit on a shelf in a closet, where it does nobody any good? And then it occurred to me — the simple act of taking the time to assemble the booklets, visit the patient and offer the patient the material requires effort. And someone who cares.

Well, Susan, that's it. The *abridged* version. So I got a little carried away. But without all the gory details, how can they make the necessary changes?

Subj: Your letter
Date: 03-24
From: Susan_P@aol.com
To: cre8f1@mindspring.com

Where did you stay? In the hospital from hell? Thank goodness it's over. But let me tell you — the next time I need a letter of complaint written, I know who to ask. Wow.

Subj: Progress Report
Date: 03-27
From: cre8f1@mindspring.com
To: Susan_P@aol.com

Dear Susan,

Well, I just got back from PT. Randi is such a doll. I'm amazed at how much I hate everything she does to my body but how much I love *her*. A typical session: I come in and use the overhead pulley to loosen my shoulders. Then I go into one of the private rooms, where I undress, put on an examining gown (which I can do *all by my lonesome*, because it has a slit all the way up the front, just like my button-downs). I lie down on the table (on my back). One of the assistants puts heat packs on both shoulders. After 20 minutes Randi comes in to abuse me. She does a series of exercises with me. My personal favorite (hardly) is when she grabs my hand and lifts it toward the ceiling, which moves my arm upward. I tell her when it hurts, and she keeps going anyway. We pretty much get to the point where I scream out in pain. Only then does she put my arm down and let me rest for a few seconds. Then she does it again. Whoever referred to physical therapists as physical terrorists must have been a bilateral-mastectomy patient. Anyway, it hurts, but I'm seeing results. And I have to admit it's happening faster than I expected.

After doing my arm exercises, Randi massages the incisions. Now, one might think that having another woman massaging your "breasts" would give a heterosexual woman the heebie-jeebies. Not true. Probably because I don't think of the tissue expanders as breasts. They don't look like breasts, they don't feel like breasts. In fact, they look and feel like scars. Period. But Randi says that by keeping the skin moving, the scar won't adhere to my body and everything will heal better. She's the expert, so I do what she says. After spending a few minutes using her fingers to move my scar around, Randi leaves me to get dressed. Anyway, that's the drill. Today, once I was dressed I grabbed my latest something-to-make-life-a-little-easier piece of equipment: a belly-pack. (I still can't carry a purse; it's too heavy, and I can't easily get it up and around my shoulder yet.) I click the belly-pack together and just like I've been doing it my whole life, I reach into it and search for my keys *so I can drive myself home.* Save your applause. On second thought, don't. Driving again was a huge accomplishment. The hardest part is turning the wheel, so I made sure I found *two* parking spaces, where I could just pull forward and not have to worry about backing out when I left. This took me back to when I was 16 years old and I used to park that way all the time. And forget parallel parking. I wouldn't even consider going anywhere that required that skill. I still avoid it whenever given an option. Anyway, I'm filled with optimism and a great sense of accomplishment. In fact, tomorrow morning after I shower *and wash my own*

240

hair, I'm going to try to put on one of Michael's large sweatshirts. See, Miss Marijuana Smoker, I, too, am filled with surprises!

Subj: Congrats
Date: 03-29
From: Susan_P@aol.com
To: cre8f1@mindspring.com

Lara, what a great letter. It's so good to hear you sounding so much like your old self. I've missed your sarcasm.

It sounds like Randi's got you moving in all the right directions. Literally. Shampooing your own hair, driving to your own appointments and maybe even wearing a sweatshirt — did you ever think you could find such joy in such simple acts? Yes, breast cancer changes how we see *everything.*

My lymph node removal left me with a little stiffness in my right shoulder, but I never had to go through anything like you've described. (A week or two of the climbing-the-wall exercises and I was A-OK.) Your reconstruction is probably making your recovery harder, especially since Donahue told you *not* to do much moving right after surgery. (A sure way to get stiff, no?) Regardless of why you're having so much trouble, it sounds horrible. Especially since you're used to such independence.

You haven't mentioned work in a while. Are you still writing, or have you taken time off?

(Actually, that was a selfish little transition that I interjected so I could share my good news.) I got a raise! No joke. I haven't even been there two months, but Walter (he's the owner) said that he wanted me to know how pleased he is with how I'm doing and how I've managed to save the company so much time and money that he thought I deserved to be recognized. Hence, the raise. I was shocked. This is so far from how I was treated at the tire factory. Just goes to show, you never know. What do you think? Should I write the supervisor from the tire factory a thank-you note for being such a bitch and forcing me to quit my job? Joking, of course. But I just love it when life throws you a problem that seems so unfair at the time, and somewhere down the road you can look back and see that what you thought was so terrible was actually a blessing. I try to frame my cancer in the same way. I truly do enjoy many things today that I used to take for granted. I'm going about this the long way, I know. Thanks for bearing with me. What I'm trying to tell you, Lara, is that the little accomplishments you're achieving are not so little. They are huge, because they are reminders of how much of our life — and how much of our living — we all take for granted. And we can joke about it, but simply being able to wake up in the morning, shower and dress ourselves is a pretty great thing to be able to do, *and* it's nothing you would have thought about if it hadn't been taken away. Something worth pondering.

Subj: I'm back
Date: 03-29
From: Susan_P@aol.com
To: cre8f1@mindspring.com

Excuse the mini-lecture of my last letter. I didn't mean to sound so preachy. I just wanted to point out how far you've come, and I think I got a little carried away. Sorry.

Also, I forgot to mention (please forgive me) that the Freedom has advanced to the regional finals. Gabby's thrilled but a PITA because she's so tense about the upcoming game. It's this weekend. April Fools' Day, no less. Wish us luck.

Suz

Subj: Score Please
Date: 04-01
From: cre8f1@mindspring.com
To: Susan_P@aol.com

So how'd the Freedom do? And what's PITA?

Well, I got my first injection of saline. (Actually my second. He did the first one when I was asleep on the table in the operating room, though, so that one doesn't count.)

Donahue again greeted me as Laura. I corrected him. He laughed. (I'm not sure if he laughed because he doesn't think it's a big deal that he can't remember how to pronounce my

243

name or because he's laughing at himself for being such a dullard. Time will tell.)

I told him that I've started chemo. He told me he doesn't like to do the surgery to replace the tissue expanders with the implants until after the chemo treatments are over, since chemo slows down the healing process. So, lucky me, I'm going to have the expanders in for the next six months. He said that he'll fill them with saline every three or four weeks in order to keep the skin stretching. As I get close to the size I want to be (he thinks that I should be a B cup), he'll slow down and inject less saline. The goal is to time it so my injections and my last chemo treatment coincide. Then I can have the surgery to have the expanders taken out and the implants put in. Oh joy!

The Saline Injection Process:

I change from Michael's sweatshirt (thank you, thank you) into the gown we all know and love. Donahue's nurse (her name's Sandy) does the injections. She opens my gown and starts rolling a plastic disk that's about the size of a silver dollar across my scar. I ask her what she's doing. She tells me that before she can inject the saline, she needs to find the valve of the tissue expander. The valve is magnetized, and the plastic disk is also a magnet. She says that once she feels the two magnets "connect" she knows she's in the right place. Using a pen (not very high-tech, is it?) she marks the spot with an X. I immediately think about one of those divining rods they use to find water or mine for gold. It's probably just nerves, but I can't get the image out of my mind, and I get the giggles. I stop laughing immediately, however, when I see Sandy loading up a huge syringe with the largest needle I've ever seen. I panic and ask her to please stop and explain what's going to happen before she does anything else. She seems to take my request (i.e., panic attack) in stride and tells me what to expect; I give her permission to continue. She begins.

Sandy shows me a small needle and tells me she's going to insert it through the X on my skin. She reassures me that I won't feel it, though, because the doctor cut all of my nerve endings during my mastectomy. (She's right. I don't have any feeling in my skin, and that's why I couldn't feel myself touching my stitches when I tried to put on the antibiotic ointment. All the pain I feel is *internal*, not external.) Anyway, next Sandy attaches a plastic tube to the end of the small needle. The large needle (the one that caused me to make her stop and explain everything) never goes into me. It's part of a "feeding system." The large needle goes into the plastic tube that delivers the saline through the small needle that's inserted through my skin into the tissue expanders. ("The ankle bone's connected to the knee bone. . . ." Feel free to join in and start singing at any time.)

Once I was convinced that Sandy wasn't going to hurt me, I felt better, but I didn't like *thinking* about what was going to happen, so I asked her to distract me by talking to me. She didn't shut up, and by the time she was done, I'd learned that she's single, has never been married (even though she looks like she's pushing 50), has no children, but does have a niece whom she absolutely adores. Both women/girls love to go shopping. Sandy's saga will be continued in roughly three weeks, when I go for more saline.

The whole time Sandy was filling me up, she kept mushing the area where my breasts once rested with her fingers. I guess she was trying to feel when my skin started to pull. Whatever. Sandy says that she didn't put in that much saline (it looked like a lot to me), so it shouldn't hurt. But then she asks if I have any leftover pain medication from my surgery? (Not a question that inspires a whole lot of confidence in her previous statement, is it?)

My girlfriend who drove me into the city insisted that we stop for a quick sandwich before driving home. (I may be driving, but I'm not up to driving solo in the *city*.) Fortunately, I've got wonderful friends willing to do the schlepping for me. Anyway, it felt so good to be out, having lunch and talking girl talk. Normal life feels like it's just around the corner.

Lara!

Subj: Season's over
Date: 04-02
From: Susan_P@aol.com
To: cre8f1@mindspring.com

The Freedom lost. But they had a good season, and the coach was wonderful. She kept stressing everything that the team had accomplished rather than what they'd lost. The game wasn't even close, so unfortunately the girls had a lot of time to sit on the bench and come to grips with the fact that they were (most likely) not going to win. I'm bummed. But it's just a game — it's not like it's cancer or anything. :-)

I told you Gabby was a PITA. You asked for a translation: *Pain In The Ass.*

Thanks for the details about your expansion process. I didn't know what was involved. Most of the women in my support group have had lumpectomies, so they haven't needed reconstruction. Two have had mastectomies, but one chose no reconstruction. (Her name is also Sue, and she wears a breast form tucked into her bra.) The other woman did have reconstruction, but she had a TRAM flap. So tell me, O inflated one, how do they look?

Forever inquisitive,

Me

Subj: Next season
Date: 04-04
From: cre8f1@mindspring.com
To: Susan_P@aol.com

Sorry about the Freedom's loss, Susan. I hope Gabby's not taking it too hard. (And if she is, I hope she's going easy on you. And you on her!)

My tissue expanders are hard as rocks. They don't hurt, but my torso feels tight. I guess that's why they put the saline in a little bit at a time. When I inhale, I feel like I'm wearing a corset that's entirely too tight. (Never having worn a corset, I can't be sure about this, mind you, but it seems to be the perfect way to describe it.) Hopefully, my skin will start to stretch, because while it's not painful, it's not exactly comfortable either.

Congrats on your raise. *Very* impressive, Susan. I've continued working but haven't taken on any new assignments. You already know about the big job I had for the new financial company. Well, I'm already done with the bulk of the writing (!), so now it's mostly revisions, proofreading and overseeing the art direction, printing, whatever. Nothing that requires a lot of brainpower, so it's entirely manageable. Thank goodness. Yesterday I wrote a press release for the temple's Passover food drive. Mailed it out of here today, so now, as of this very moment, I am completely caught up. Except for my journal writing. I haven't touched the thing in ages. I was never an everyday writer anyway. But once every week to ten days I'd jot down a few thoughts. Now that I think about it . . . I stopped writing in my journal around the same time I started writing to you. (It's not that I'm calling you a bad influence or anything.) I guess in many ways, *all the important ways,* you've become my sounding board. So, Diary, how does that make you feel?

I've got my next treatment tomorrow. I'd be lying if I said I wasn't nervous, but Dr. Berns has promised me it won't be like last time. I just have to trust him, I guess. However, if I don't answer your letters, you'll know why. Keep writing, though. It'll give me something to look forward to when I'm feeling better.

Subj: Crossed Fingers
Date: 04-05
From: Susan_P@aol.com
To: cre8f1@mindspring.com

Good luck. I hope it's a breeze. And if it's not, I hope it's better than the last time. I'll check in tomorrow.
Fondly,
Your diary :-)

8

Subj: Chemo
Date: 04-05
From: cre8f1@mindspring.com
To: Susan_P@aol.com

Hi there, Susan, Sue, Suz.

I just got home from my second treatment. Two down. Just like last time, I feel wired. (Didn't Dr. Berns tell me that chemo is supposed to make me feel tired?) Go figure.

I've got a funny story. Even though Dr. Berns has a nurse, he's the one who gives me my chemo cocktail. First he puts a needle into my arm. (That's not the funny part. Exactly the opposite, in fact. I've got crappy veins — as you may recall from my hospital complaint letter — so getting the needle in without my vein rolling or collapsing is *never* a laughing matter.) Anyway, once the IV's in, Berns starts by giving me some saline. (Between my breasts and my arm, I'm getting a lot of saline, don't you think?) Next Berns injects an anti-nausea medication into the saline bag and leaves me for about 5 minutes. He returns and tells me that he's going to give me a steroid of some sort. It's supposed to act as a boost to the anti-nausea medication. He warns me that I will most likely feel intense burning from this steroid in my *vagina.* He says that it will last for about a minute and then go away. Berns has a wacky sense of humor, and I think he's bullshitting me. He injects the steroid and nothing happens — for about 20 seconds. Susan, when I tell you that it felt like someone had lit a match between my legs, I kid you not. I start crossing and uncrossing my legs. I lift my tush off the chair. I'm squirming around, and just when I think I can't take it anymore, it stops. Berns is cracking up and says, "I told you."

Anyway, next he injects the 5-fluorouracil (the F part of the CMF). After that he adds the methotrexate (M), and last but not least comes the cytoxin (C). The cytoxin takes the longest to inject, and before the syringe is empty, he asks me if I can taste it yet. I noticed a metallic taste in my mouth that began just as he started his question. Then I become very foggy and light-headed. Berns has asked me something else, but my brain isn't working quickly enough to process what he's said. I suddenly realize he's just asked me if my brain is feeling fuzzy yet. It amazes me that he can know exactly how the drugs will affect me and time each side effect almost to the second. (But then I have to ask myself, Why, if he's so smart, couldn't he anticipate how sick the chemo was going to make me?)

Anyway, here's the funny part. I called Michael when I got home and told him about the burning in my crotch.

MICHAEL: Where was the IV hooked up anyway?

ME: In my arm, where do you think it was?
MICHAEL: Well, I was just wondering!

Can you imagine? Michael believed the IV was inserted into — Well, never mind. You're a bright lady. You get it.

Subj: Poor Michael
Date: 04-07
From: Susan_P@aol.com
To: cre8f1@mindspring.com

I'm LOL. Well, let's just hope that the "boost" does more than burn. Let's hope that it works. Keep me posted.
  Sue

Subj: I'm Boring
Date: 04-08
From: Susan_P@aol.com
To: cre8f1@mindspring.com

Hi, Lara.

I'm sorry that you haven't written. Unfortunately, I have a pretty good idea about why. I just hope that it's not as bad as the last time. Just keep your eye on the end — only six more to go.

Nothing new to report. Artie's working. I just got home from work, followed by errands, and am procrastinating about starting dinner. Gabby's doing homework. I just love not having to run off to basketball games, but my time off for good behavior expires next week, when softball season starts.

I keep forgetting to ask you how your hair is doing? Mine seems to be growing faster than ever, but it's also grayer than ever. I never had to dye my hair before chemo; now it's an absolute necessity. Oh well, I should be grateful that at least I've got hair to dye, right? Of course right. I'll wait to hear from you.

Susan

Subj: Better
Date: 04-10
From: cre8f1@mindspring.com
To: Susan_P@aol.com

I'm back. It wasn't good, but it was better. Though it took me longer to feel like getting out of bed. Does that make any sense? Let me try again: The sickness wasn't as intense this time. (I could actually kiss Gregory without vomiting in his face.) But I felt crummy for more days after the treatment. I took the anti-nausea medication. I didn't throw up but had a lot of dry heaves and was pretty nauseated most of the time. Plus, I had a massive headache. Dr. Berns says the headache was from the anti-nausea medication. So he wrote me a prescription for the headache. My nightstand looks like a pharmacy.

Because my first treatment made me so sick, I decided to be better prepared this time around. I lined up a woman, Michelle, to help out. (She's a lab assistant in White Plains — 12 minutes from my house — who gets off work at 5:00 and was interested in making some extra money.) Michelle arrived here every day at 5:15. She prepared dinner, straightened up and gave Gregory a bath. Technically I suppose Wendy is capable of doing a lot of the stuff around here, but I'm trying very hard not to burden her with (my) adult responsibilities. Besides, it's plenty hard just being a kid and concentrating on school-work (let alone housework) when your mom has cancer. Fortunately, we can afford the outside help, so rather than dumping it all on Michael, I've lined up Michelle for the week following each of my remaining treatments. (Six, but who's counting?) It works out especially well, because the kids really like her. Before she got her job at the hospital, Michelle used to baby-sit for Wendy and Gregory, so it's not like the kids have to deal with a stranger who doesn't even know her way around our house.

Having Michelle here was just another reminder of how much worse this could be. What if we lived hand to mouth and couldn't afford the help? I also think about how many people live without medical insurance. Cancer costs a fortune. I think my treatments are close to a thousand dollars each. My anti-nausea pills are more than fifty bucks apiece, and I use four of them *every day*. And let's not forget my million-dollar boob job. The numbers are staggering. I need all my strength just to battle this disease; I couldn't imagine worrying about the finances, too. That's Michael's job. His most recent problem was with the insurance company. Apparently they didn't want to pay the full price of reconstructing my right breast. They only wanted to cover 50%. *Why?* Because (they said) the surgeon shouldn't charge the same amount for the second breast as he charges for the first breast. He should charge less. *Why?* Because (they said) the surgeon doesn't have to make a separate trip to the hospital, wait while I'm being prepped or wait around for the anesthesia to take effect. Therefore (they said), the second breast goes faster and, therefore, should cost less. According to them, half as much.

Michael said that he couldn't believe he'd understood them correctly. "You mean that if my wife only had a mastectomy on her left breast and had it reconstructed you'd pay 100% of the reconstruction?" They said yes. "And," Michael continued, "if one month later, my wife reentered the hospital, had a mastectomy on her *other* breast and had it reconstructed, you'd pay 100% of that reconstruction?" They said yes again. "But because she had them both done at the same time, you'll only pay full price for one?" They told him that he was correct.

"But that's outrageous," Michael countered. "If my wife did it that way, there'd be *two* separate anesthesiologist bills and bills for two separate hospital stays. That would cost even more — much more than the 50% you're withholding now. And that doesn't even take into account that by doing the surgery as two separate operations my wife would have to undergo the pain and recovery twice, instead of just getting it all over with at once."

Michael says that their response was "I'm sorry, Mr. Cohen. But that's our policy."

Michael tells them that they may want to rethink their policy, since an election is coming up in November and our senator (who happens to very vocal about BC, believing more needs to be done to support/protect women) would be very interested in their "policy." He tells them he will wait for two days before documenting my case and sending the information on to Washington. "I almost hope that you stick with your asinine policy," Michael added. "I'd love to see this made public."

I know you won't be surprised to learn that the following afternoon Michael got a phone call from the insurance company telling him that the check for the previously uncovered 50% of the surgery would be mailed out immediately. Michael knows how to be very persuasive. (Did I mention that he was the one who finally got me the blankets and pillows during my stay in the hospital from hell?) But all joking aside: What about all the unfortunate women with breast cancer who don't have a Michael in their lives?

Subj: A Sad Day
Date: 04-11
From: Susan_P@aol.com
To: cre8f1@mindspring.com

Hi, Lara.

Thanks for the update. I'm glad your chemo was easier this time and hope that it'll continue that way with every remaining treatment. (Feel free to say "Amen.")

You're smart to be grateful for having Michael and Michelle in your life. Friends, family or baby-sitters that you hire — it doesn't matter. Support is support, and you're lucky to have all three. A lot of women don't. (Something else you learn in a support group.) Artie's dad (who's been retired for the last four years) used to chip in by picking up Gabby from her after-school sports on the days that I couldn't, either because of a doctor's appointment or because I was just feeling too crummy. (Hence the ongoing Spanish-music experience.) But as I explained to Gabby every time she opened a mouth to complain about the flamenco music (which was often, remember, it's Gabby I'm talking about), beggars can't be choosers.

I know that I probably shouldn't burden you with this right now, right after chemo, but you're the person I *want* to discuss it with. So I hope you don't mind . . .

I just got home from a funeral. One of the women in my support group died. It wasn't totally without warning. She'd had a recurrence, and her prognosis wasn't good, but she was undergoing treatment, and I guess I just thought that she had more time. Needless to say, it's been a very upsetting couple of days. It's particularly upsetting for me, because, as you know, I don't handle death (or good-byes) very well. Anyway, I had just returned from the funeral and was still all red-eyed and weepy when Gabby came home from school. She asked what was wrong. I told her.

She blew her top.

Gabby started accusing me of caring more about the women of the group than I care about her. She proceeded to tell me that she was sick and tired of hearing me on the phone discussing the details of my personal life with total strangers. Every week I get a phone call from at least one woman who's just been diagnosed with breast cancer. They call me with questions about doctors, treatment options or sometimes just to talk. I try to refer them to the group, but as you know (ahem, ahem), some women are reluctant to go to a group. Many say they prefer the anonymity of the phone; others (who eventually end up at the group) say that they initially resisted coming to the meetings because it made their cancer too real. Similarly, others don't want to come to meetings because then they're admitting that they belong to this group that they really don't want to be a part of. Whatever the reason, the phone rings here, Gabby hears my conversations and apparently doesn't like it. She'd never even mentioned it before, and I had no idea that she had feelings about it one way or another until her explosion. I certainly know now. I just don't know what I'm going to do about it. I want to take her feelings into account, but I don't want her to dictate my life. I've spent a lot of time and energy getting the support group up and running and feel that we provide a service that makes a huge difference in women's lives. But I also don't need to give Gabby (even more) ammunition for some psychiatrist's couch. And I keep thinking about that poem she wrote. I almost said something to her about it but decided that I never get anywhere with her when she's ranting. Besides, I was still rattled from the funeral. I decided to postpone our conversation until we're both in better spirits. I'll try to talk to Gabby about everything tomorrow. (Depending on what kind of mood she's in.) If you have any thoughts on the matter . . .

Subj: My opinion
Date: 04-12
From: cre8f1@mindspring.com
To: Susan_P@aol.com

Dear Susan,
We've known each other how long (?) and you've never directly asked for my opinion about anything. Now you do, and *this* is what you come

up with? You couldn't have started me off with something simple, like a book recommendation (*The Color of Water*) or a gift for a teenage boy (*a gift certificate from a CD store*). OK. No more jokes. It's just that I'm so relieved to be feeling better that everything seems like a joke to me. But this is serious stuff, and I'm flattered that you're even interested in my opinion.

Obviously Gabby doesn't like the situation the way it is now. So change it. No, not by allowing her to dictate your life but simply by making some adjustments, so what you want to do doesn't interfere with what she wants.

From your letters I've come to the conclusion that you have a comfortable life and the ability to solve some of your problems by investing a few bucks, just as I was able to do by hiring Michelle. So toss some dollars at the problem. Install a second phone line. Give out this phone number at your support group. If the support group has a listing in the phone book, again, use this new phone number. There must be people who regularly refer women to you. Give them this new number and ask them to use it in the future. The objective here is for you to be able to know (based on which phone rings) if the call is a personal call or a cancer call. If you hook up an answering machine to the cancer phone (for lack of a better word), then you'll be able to call people back when (A) it's a good time for you and (B) you have privacy, which in this case means out of Gabby's earshot.

But that doesn't solve your immediate problem. I'd begin by explaining to Gabby how much the support group means to you. Let her know how much you could have benefited if such a group had existed when you were diagnosed. And tell her how it makes you feel to be able to help so many women in their time of crisis. Make it perfectly clear to her that you cannot *(and will not)* make changes in your life simply to suit her desires but that what she thinks and how she feels *does matter* to you. (Repeat that sentiment often. Whenever I've pulled rank and "won," it seems to make Wendy feel better when I repeat that it matters to me that she thinks I'm being too strict/mean/inflexible or whatever. But just because it *matters* doesn't mean I'm changing my mind. Ah, the joys of being the mom and the one in charge!)

Tell Gabby about the second-phone-line idea. Explain that it's a compromise you're willing to make so she won't have to hear your conversations. See if you can find out *why* she resents the calls so much. Is it because these strangers matter to you? Is it because you give them more time than (she thinks) you give to her? Is it because she has a Victorian view of breast cancer as something sexual that should remain private? If you can get at the root of what her problem really is, you'll have an easier time appeasing her.

Ask Gabby if she has other "compromise ideas" that would allow you to continue to help other women without infringing on her — Well,

I don't know what she thinks you're infringing on. Her space/life/time? But if you can get her to talk, she may just spill the beans about what's bothering her. My guess is that it has nothing whatsoever to do with the support group, the time you spend there or the conversations you have. My guess is that every time she hears you talking about cancer, she's reminded that she could have lost you, and that makes her afraid. It's also a painful reminder of how little control we have over our lives, and if Gabby's anything like you (and your mother), she hates that out-of-control feeling, too.

Well, there you have it. See, when it comes to solving other people's problems, I have no trouble speaking my mind. (It's only my own problems that sometimes reduce me to dishrag status.) I hope I wasn't too much. But you asked. :-)

Subj: Good Ideas
Date: 04-14
From: Susan_P@aol.com
To: cre8f1@mindspring.com

Dear Lara,
You're *good*. In fact, I suggest you quit your day job. The child psychologists of this world could really use you. And cancel everything I've ever said about how your relationship with Wendy will be when she's a teenager. I didn't know then that you possessed such a talent for

peeking into the mind, body and soul of a teenager. :-)

I love your idea about another phone line. But it wouldn't be our second — it would be our *fourth!* (The primary line is for me and Artie. We have a second line for Gabby, the Giant Mouth, and another for the computer and fax machine. And now a cancer phone?) Still, when you've got three lines, what's one more? Actually, it's a great idea, and Gabby loved it, too.

I also promised Gabby that I would get another woman to co-lead the support group with me. That way all the calls (and the responsibility for running the group) can be shared. I say that I made the promise for Gabby, but actually, it will be good for me, too. As the group continues to grow, it really is too much for me to handle alone (along with my paying job and my wife/mom role).

But you were absolutely right. It's not the calls she resents, it's what they *rep*resent. Unfortunately this is something we'll just have to work through. But at least we're talking about it. Only took 2+ years. But maybe we needed that much time to pass before we felt like the topic was "safe." You know, that I wasn't going to die.

I told Gabby that I read her poem. In fact, when I approached her to begin our conversation, I didn't even say anything. I just handed her the poem, and she started crying. I guess we've got some work to do. But at least now we know.

On to happier things. Tomorrow is April 15th. You must feel relieved. A few of my friends are married to accountants, and they always complain about the months preceding tax day. And Michael had to get through them under less-than-stellar circumstances, wouldn't you say? Plus, let's not forget that in between preparing his clients' tax returns he also had to find time to get on the horn and have a few fights with the insurance company so they'd pay for your boobs. (*They're* the boobs. I've never heard of anything so ridiculous!) Poor Michael. He's been through so much (as have you). But he made it (just as you will). BTW, when's your next treatment?

Sue

Subj: You'll Never Guess
Date: 04-17
From: cre8f1@mindspring.com
To: Susan_P@aol.com

We had a busy weekend. Or at least I did. (Michael did a lot of sleeping, which is typically how he spends April 16.) With treatments every three weeks (my next one's the 26th), and being sick for 3 to 5 days after each one, I've realized that I have to make good use of my two "off" weeks if I want to get everything (or *anything*) done. With that in mind, I spent yesterday doing one of my least favorite things: shopping. For Gregory, mostly. All of a sudden it's spring here, and his old windbreaker has sleeves that only reach his forearms. His lightweight pants extend just below midcalf (but that's only if he wears them around his hips, instead of his waist). The poor kid looked like he was wearing doll clothes. Now he's got a wardrobe that should make the girls swoon, except he suddenly thinks that all girls are yucky, except for his sister, and his best gal-pal Louise — whom he plans to marry one day at the kiddie pool, under a rainbow beach umbrella. (Don't ask.)

Allow me to make your day: The other evening I went to a meeting of our local support group. (It's not *local* local; it actually meets in the library of one of our neighboring towns.) The group meets in the same room where they have programs and story hour for the kids. There are cardboard cut-outs of Chicken Little and nursery-rhyme characters stuck to the wall, so it's cute and cheery-looking. (Unlike the women, who couldn't look "cute" if they tried, thanks to the library's fluorescent lighting that makes even healthy, rested women look washed out, wrinkled and tired. Fluorescent lighting should be outlawed!)

I'm not sure exactly what possessed me to go to the meeting. I think that writing to you about why you shouldn't allow Gabby's feelings to deter you from continuing your involvement in your group may have had something to do with it. Whatever. I went.

I can't say that it provided any real answers or

relief for me, but it was interesting. The leader asked the women who'd been there before to begin by introducing themselves. They went around the circle as each "veteran" gave her name, and her age when she'd been diagnosed and explained her treatment. That's when it got a little creepy. "Lumpectomy with radiation, 1.2 centimeters, 3 positive nodes, four months of CAF." "Lumpectomy with radiation, no positive nodes, no chemo, 5 ½ year survivor." "Mastectomy with TRAM reconstruction, 1 positive node, CMF for six months . . ."

Susan, listening to everyone using the same breast cancer "shorthand" made me aware of our unique sisterhood. We *are* different, aren't we? And we speak our own special language that normal, healthy women couldn't even begin to understand. (Hey, I never wanted to be part of this sorority. Why didn't someone first *ask* me whether or not I wanted to pledge?)

When it came time for the newcomers to give their stats and stories, I shared my chemo troubles with everyone. One woman suggested I ask my doctor for very strong sleeping pills. She said that way, when I felt really rotten, I could knock myself out and try to sleep through the nausea. Not a bad thought. Especially when you're desperate.

Another newbie had a mastectomy a few months ago. She was still having trouble lifting her arm. I suggested physical therapy and even gave her Randi's name. She seemed genuinely grateful and kept saying she couldn't believe that she hadn't thought of it. (I can't believe her doctor hadn't *suggested* it!)

I was surprised that a few of the vets were also young, like me. We were able to commiserate a bit about how we were all struggling to run our households and the effects that our cancer was having on our kids. But most of the women in the group were older. Their kids are no longer at home or if they are home, they aren't as needy. Still, I took the phone numbers of two women who are around my age. They were *very* sweet and said I should feel free to call them if I need anything. The group meets every other week, and I think their next meeting coincides with my treatment, so I probably won't be well enough to attend. But maybe the one after that. We'll see. Nights are hard; I'm so tired.

OK, now you want to know the *real* reason I think the group didn't work any wonders for me? Because I've got you. You are always there for me. You've been with me since the beginning and will no doubt be there for me in the end. You have a lot of answers, and you're always willing to listen. Isn't that the best thing about e-mail? You can go on and on and on (as I often do). But I never have to feel bad about it, because I know that you're free to skim ahead or even quit reading at any time, and who would know?

Lara

Subj: Good Ideas
Date: 04-19
From: Susan_P@aol.com
To: cre8f1@mindspring.com

On 04-17 cre8f1@mindspring.com wrote:
>*But I never have to feel bad about it because I know*
>*that you're free to skim ahead or even quit reading*
>*at any time, and who would know?*

I would know. And I'd never do that. I love your letters. All of them. And I read every single word. Almost. :-)

BTW, I keep forgetting to ask, O curly one: How's your hair doing?

Sue

Subj: Hair & Saline
Date: 04-20
From: cre8f1@mindspring.com
To: Susan_P@aol.com

Hi Susan,

My hair is hanging in. Literally. Every morning I notice more of it than usual (i.e., pre-chemo) around the hair trap in my shower. And after combing through my knotty curls, I notice there's more on my comb than I've grown to expect. But all in all it's only a wee bit thinner (or maybe it's not at all, and I'm just imagining it). Anyway, no one would notice that I've lost *any*.

This is when I can tell that it really pays to have lots of hair, which — thank you grandma — I've got.

I went for a fill-up today. There's now enough saline in the expanders to give me a little shape. Not much, but a little. Actually, now I look sort of barrel-chested. Unfortunately, the expanders aren't exactly symmetrical. The right one looks fuller. Again, though, no one other than me would notice. When I mentioned being uneven to Dr. Donahue, he reminded me that the expanders are not supposed to be breasts, they're only supposed to be stretching the skin to accommodate the implants, which, he assures me, will look like breasts.

Donahue is on my nerves. He greeted me as *Laura* again. I corrected him. He laughed. Again. (He mispronounced my name while holding my chart in his hands. Why doesn't he just write it down? Lara. Rhymes with Sarah. Then at least he could *pretend* to know me.)

It gets better. After calling me Laura, Donahue says, "Let's see, you're not having chemo, right?" I correct him again. And again I wonder why he didn't write *that* in my chart after the last appointment. Better question: Why doesn't he write it down when I correct him this time? (How much do you want to bet that at my next appointment I'll still be *Laura* who is *not* having chemo?)

As she inflated me, Sandy continued her chit-chat about her life as a single woman in

Manhattan. (See, *she* remembered me. She knew that I require distraction when she places needles — that I can't feel — into my skin.) Susan, will I ever get the feeling back? If so, when? And what about under my left arm, where Goldberg took out my lymph nodes? Will I have feeling there? It's so bizarre when I put on my deodorant in the morning. I feel pressure inside my armpit, but I really don't feel the deodorant hitting my skin. What's the deal?

Lara

Subj: The Deal
Date: 04-22
From: Susan_P@aol.com
To: cre8f1@mindspring.com

Lara, I thought you knew. When they cut the nerves during a mastectomy, that's it. You won't ever have sensation in your breasts again. That's one of the things that Sue (the woman in my group who had the mastectomy without the reconstruction) complains most about. She says that after all these years she still has not gotten used to the loss of sensation. She's even shared that when she's "intimate with her husband" (her words) and he kisses her scar or traces it with his finger, she only knows he's doing it if she can *see* him. In other words, if the lights are out, she has no clue. Sad, huh?

As far as your underarm goes, that feeling

should come back. At least some of it. Those nerves are disturbed during the lymph node removal, but they're not all severed. They can take up to a year to regenerate. So whatever feeling you've regained a year after your surgery is it — and hopefully, you'll have complete sensation. If not . . . well, look on the bright side. You'll have an advantage over your kids during tickle fights. I'm super-ticklish under my arms. (See, it's amazing what you can learn about someone over the Internet, if you simply write enough letters.)
Susan

Subj: Cantaloupe
Date: 04-25
From: cre8f1@mindspring.com
To: Susan_P@aol.com

Thanks for your answers about all my numbness. It wasn't what I was hoping to hear, but now at least I know. Don't laugh, but before all this I used to think that having a mastectomy was like scooping out a cantaloupe. Really. I assumed that the surgeon cut a woman's skin in some discreet place, like the crease under her breast. He then peeled back the skin while he scooped out the cancer and all the breast tissue. If the woman wanted reconstruction, the surgeon inserted an implant and resewed the crease so everything, including the nipple, looked just like it did before the surgery. Voilà. The surgeon's done, the woman looks great, and everyone lives happily ever after.

I guess I stopped believing in those kinds of fairy tales on February 21. Little did I know that the surgeon basically hacks off a woman's breast and then has to reconnect the woman by sewing the skin from her collarbone to her rib cage. OK, so maybe it's not that extreme, but it's a hell of a lot closer to the truth than my cantaloupe theory.

I've got a treatment tomorrow. Write to me. Thanks.

Subj: Done!
Date: 05-01
From: cre8f1@mindspring.com
To: Susan_P@aol.com

It took me 5 days to get upright this time. Not good. And I was further bummed to finally drag myself out of bed, back to my computer and find that I had no mail from you. Everything OK?

Well, I've got 3 down. It seems like it should be more. It certainly *feels* like it should be more. I had a tough time. (So what else is new?) But this time I started feeling sick somewhere between the crotch-burning medicine and the methotrexate. Before he injected the cytoxin, Dr. Berns asked me if I wanted a piece of candy. I told you that he's got an unusual sense of humor — but I didn't get the joke. He must have seen the confusion on my face, because he nodded toward a dish of hard candy that was on the counter near my chair. (I'd never noticed it before.) "Some people are bothered by the metallic taste; the candy helps to mask it." That was all he needed to say. He waited while I unwrapped a butterscotch drop and popped it into my mouth before he shot me full of cytoxin. I couldn't taste a thing (!) other than butterscotch, which will be my favorite candy from now on. But just because I couldn't taste the drugs didn't mean I couldn't feel them. In fact, I was pretty green before he even removed the IV from my arm. It started with pressure in my sinuses. Dr. Berns gave me an antihistamine and told me that the next time I should take one an hour before my treatment. He also gave me a different anti-nausea medicine to try — if I wanted. (I want. I want.) I started feeling nauseous in Robin's car. (She was my designated driver this treatment.) Fortunately, I now keep Baggies in my purse.

In addition to all my other symptoms, I've developed mouth sores from the chemo. Berns suggests yet another medicine to add to my collection. (Doesn't he know that my nightstand is already jam-packed?) This treatment also brought with it another new sensation. I started feeling *burning* on the top of my head. No joke. It felt like my brain or hair follicles were being fried (resulting in dead brain cells, more noticeable hair loss or, God forbid, both). All I know is the burning drove me nuts.

I've also noticed that on the third day after my treatment, my chin breaks out. Susan, it's truly like my body is trying to rid itself of these toxic drugs from every possible pore — from the top of my head to the tips of my toes. (Yes, even my *toenails* are affected. They're all dried out and cracking, as are my fingernails. I've cut both very short.) The bottom line is, I'm a mess. In fact, I think it's safe to say that I look almost as bad as I feel. I'm kvetching. Sorry. This treatment is over, and I'm moving on.

Here's some good news: Did I tell you that in December we're going on our temple's biannual trip to Israel? (Well, we are.) Wendy will have her Bat Mitzvah there (along with about 10 other 12- to 14-year-olds from our temple). Last night everyone going on the trip got together for their first meeting. Needless to say, I didn't make it, but Michael brought me back the itinerary. It looks great, and best of all, it's giving me something *big* to look forward to. By December I'll be done with all my treatments. I'll also have my expanders out and my implants in, and hopefully all this will be a bad, bad memory. Anyway, I taped a little sign over my nightstand that says "Next year in Jerusalem." (I'm sure that's meaningless to you, O Catholic one, but it's a phrase Jewish people everywhere say each year at the conclusion of our Passover seders.) And for us Cohens it will be a reality. I've never been to Israel, and neither has Michael. We're so excited. I'm just hoping that Gregory can behave himself on the flight. I think the plane ride is something like 14 hours. Well, whatever it is, it is. But I must admit, I get great joy when I catch myself worrying about something as inconsequential as my little guy's ability to sit still on an airplane.

Subj: Feeling Groovy
Date: 05-03
From: cre8f1@mindspring.com
To: Susan_P@aol.com

Susan, is everything OK? I haven't heard from you in a while, and that's not like you. I'm hoping that you're just having a hard time adjusting to the softball schedule. Wendy plays, too. I don't know how they do things in Canton, but here softball is three times a week, and it's a major nuisance. Fortunately, a girl who lives two minutes from here is on Wendy's team this year. The girl's mom (I don't even remember her name) has graciously volunteered to get Wendy to and from all practices/games whenever I need the help. So many women (who are little more than acquaintances) are being so incredibly thoughtful. This is when it really comes in handy to live in a small town where (almost) everyone knows everyone else's business.

The cutest thing happened this morning. We live on a very steep and hilly road, so every day I drive Gregory down the street to his bus stop. (On the mornings when I'm still too sick from chemo, Michael catches a later train so he can perform my motherly duties.) Anyway, it's a pretty basic routine. We drive down to the bottom of the hill. I turn off the car and walk Gregory across the street, where I wait with him until he gets on the bus. Once the bus pulls away, so do I. However, during breakfast this morning Gregory asked me if he could go down to the bus stop all by his-self. (That's Gregory's variation of "himself.") I, of course, say no.

GREGORY: But, *Mo-om*. Scott Samuels walks down the hill all by his-self. *And* he crosses the street all by his-self. *And* he waits at the bus stop all by his-self.

ME: But, sweetie, Scott is two years older than you are.

GREGORY: Well, if you want to drive me, you can. But can I just cross the street and wait at the bus stop alone?

I think about this for a while. There usually isn't a car in sight, and I *would* be there with him.

ME: OK, big shot. We can give it a try.

He gleefully grabs his jacket, and we drive down the hill. I'm still sitting in the driver's seat, and Gregory is still sitting in the backseat of the car. He's not moving. I finally speak up:

ME: Well . . . go!

GREGORY: Mom, I need help opening the door. Remember?

Silly me. I forgot that our car doors have child

locks. I get out of the car and go around to open Gregory's door.

ME: OK, Gregory. Show me how you cross the street.

The little punk looks both ways no fewer than *seven times* before finally crossing. The self-satisfied grin on his face is too cute.

ME: Remember, Gregory. You don't walk toward the bus until it stops completely. *(This I shout from my designated waiting spot, next to my car, across the street.)*

GREGORY: I know.

He's still wearing that grin. As he waits for the bus, my big shot starts mouthing something to me, over and over. Unable to lip-read, I finally yell, "What?"

GREGORY: Can I do this *every day*? *(His voice is full of hope.)*

ME: We'll see. *(This is what I usually say when I don't want to be accused of breaking a promise that I never wanted to make in the first place.)*

But my "We'll see" is good enough for Gregory. He keeps grinning. And then he starts mouthing to me again. These words I have no trouble lip-reading at all. Over and over again his lips form the words "Mom, I love you. I love you." Then he puts his little hand to his mouth and sends me kisses that have to travel all the way across the street that my little boy has just crossed, *all by his-self.*

Subj: Grieving
Date: 05-04
From: Susan_P@aol.com
To: cre8f1@mindspring.com

That was such a lovely story about Gregory. Thanks for sharing it with me. I wish I didn't, but unfortunately, I also have a story to share.

I haven't written in so long because I've had my hands full. But not in a good way. Artie's youngest brother and his wife, Lisa, were in a very serious accident. Paul (Artie's brother) and Lisa were on their way home from a 40th-birthday party for one of their friends. This 17-year-old boy ran a red light and crashed into Paul and Lisa's car. The boy was driving one of those heavy-duty utility vehicles. Paul and Lisa were in a little sedan. The boy walked away with scratches. Paul died before the ambulance could get him to the hospital. Lisa survived the crash but is not in very good shape. The doctors think she'll recover, but she'll have to be in the hospital, followed by a rehab center, for a couple of months. (She has a spinal-cord injury. It wasn't severed, but she needed surgery to stabilize her spine. They say she'll need massive amounts of physical therapy to be able to walk again.) It gets worse. Paul and Lisa have two children. Jenny is four, and John is almost two. Both kids are living with us (until Lisa's able to take care of them), since we're their legal guardians as well as their godparents.

Oh, Lara, it's been just awful. I didn't think Artie's parents would make it through the funeral. It's just too cruel when parents outlive their children. When I watched the Petersons put their youngest child — *their baby* — into the ground, I was devastated. I still haven't recovered. It's not supposed to work this way. Parents are supposed to go first.

The boy who was driving the car was drunk. The newspapers are filled with stories about what a great kid he is, too. An honor-roll student, class president. If he's such a great kid, what was he doing driving drunk at midnight on a school night? If I sound bitter and full of blame, I am. I have no forgiveness in my heart, and when I look into Jenny's and John's eyes, I don't think that I ever will.

John is too young to understand what's happened but clearly misses being with his parents. The change of environment and routine has definitely upset him. Artie took apart John's crib from Paul and Lisa's house and reassembled it here, but John still has trouble sleeping. We've also been busy trying to childproof everything. Our home is not even close to safe for a toddler, so Artie's been screwing childproof locks into cabinets and drawers, while I try to remove all breakables and choking hazards — i.e., everything! Gabby's room is an accident waiting to happen, so we just put a hook lock on the outside of her door and keep reminding her to lock up whenever she leaves her bedroom. Actually, if there's any silver lining to any of this (and trust me, there's not), it's been the way Gabby has handled herself. She's spending a lot of time with Jenny, reading to her, working puzzles and singing finger-songs. (Jenny's favorites are "Where Is Thumbkin?" and "The Wheels on the Bus." Do those bring back memories or what?) Anyway, for the first time in years I see Gabby thinking about other people before herself. She spends her time after school (when she's not playing softball) with Jenny and John, and Gabby has actually asked me (more than once!) if I need help when she's spotted me sorting through laundry, preparing dinner and doing dishes.

Jenny is having a really bad time of it. She understands that her daddy is not coming back. I think. It's so hard to know what's going on inside the mind of a four-year-old. When Gabby was four, I remember thinking she was such a big girl. Now, all of a sudden, four isn't big at all. Four is helpless and scary and filled with uncertainty. Four is the age when you'd better remember how much you loved it when your daddy "bucked you" during piggyback rides, because you'll never get to ride on his back again. God, my heart is breaking. I've got to go. I could lie and tell you that I have to make dinner, but the truth is, I'm crying. Again. I've never experienced such grief.

Susan

Subj: My condolences
Date: 05-05
From: cre8f1@mindspring.com
To: Susan_P@aol.com

Dear Susan,

I'm still in shock. Your letter caught me completely off guard, which, I know, is exactly how the accident caught you. Please know how very, very sorry I am. You probably feel that because I'm so far away there's nothing I can do to help you during this time. You might be right, but just some thoughts:

A year ago I wrote a brochure for a grief-counseling center. They serve families in Westchester County but also direct people to support groups in other states. Would you like me to see if they know of a grief-counseling center in Canton? I could also search the Internet. Didn't you say you're near Akron and Cleveland? One of those cities must have a group that can help the children through this. (Maybe not John; he's awfully young. But a grief-support group might help Jenny.)

Also, what are you doing to help *yourself?* Have you considered asking your doctor for a (mild) antidepressant? It may help you get through the coming weeks, as you struggle to get the kids settled *and* cope with how the loss is affecting you. I know that you had a difficult time when your mom died. I'm sure this entire tragedy is only re-awakening some of the pain of that loss, too.

281

How's Artie doing? I hope he was able to take off at least a few days of work after the accident. Were he and Paul close? Not that it really matters, does it? It's still a loss. It's a loss to Artie, to his siblings, his parents, to Lisa and to the kids. That's the worst part, isn't it? I can't even imagine having to look into small children's eyes and tell them that they're never going to see their daddy again. You have incredible strength, and you will make it though these months. You just have to believe it. A very wise woman once told me that even when I didn't feel like smiling, I should smile anyway. Eventually, she said, by doing normal things, I could recapture normal life. You were right. It's tough, I know, but try to follow your own advice and please, please let me know how I can help.

Love,

Lara

Subj: re: Condolences
Date: 05-06
From: Susan_P@aol.com
To: cre8f1@mindspring.com

Thanks for your letter, Lara. I know that your sympathy is heartfelt, and it really does help. Perhaps the best thing that you can do for me now, however, is just listen. (Or read.) I mean, don't feel like you need to comment on my ramblings. I'd rather if you tell me about what *you're* doing and just be an ear for me. I think I have a lot of feelings I need to get out — but would rather not *discuss*. Does that make any sense? I hope so.

You should know, that I, queen of support groups, already have Jenny involved with a grief-counseling center. The kids are grouped by age and have their meetings at the same time that the surviving parents meet in another room. I go to the meetings with the parents so I can help Jenny (and John) as best I can. The best point I think the counselors have made is that as of right now, the kids have really lost *both* of their parents. The loss of Paul is forever, the loss of Lisa is tempo-rary, but the kids don't necessarily differentiate. (The kids have seen Lisa, so they know that she's alive, but she's not really there for them, emo-tionally or physically.) So for now, Artie and I are the next best thing to parents for John and Jenny. It's a huge responsibility. Fortunately, just as he did when I was going through my treat-ments, Artie has really stepped up to the plate. He's home every night between 6:45 and 7:00, which is early enough to spend time with all the kids (Gabby included, who, since the kids moved in, is hanging out with us again, instead of barricading herself in her bedroom).

And Lara, get this: Every night while I clean up after dinner, *Gabby* gives Jenny a bath and *Artie* bathes John. And both of the bath-givers, on sepa-rate occasions, have been heard singing through the bathroom door. It's always the same song:

"I'm Gonna Wash That Man Right Outa My Hair." (Of course, Artie couldn't leave well enough alone and took the liberty of poetic license by changing the word "man" to "girl.") I used to sing that song to Gabby every time I shampooed her when she was a little girl. I didn't know Artie was even paying attention. And I find it even more difficult to believe that Gabby actually remembers.

I'm almost afraid to say it (don't want to jinx anything), but with love and patience I'm starting to think that the kids will be OK. And for proof of that belief, allow me to end this letter on a lighter note:

This morning when I helped Jenny get dressed, she wanted to know if I liked her Barbie underpants. I told her that I loved them and that Gabby also used to wear Barbie panties. Gabby chimes in by swearing that she never, *ever* wore Barbie on her butt! This leads to a discussion of poor, defenseless baby John. The girls end up doing a pinkie swear that when John's toilet-trained and wearing big-boy underwear, we must never reveal that he *ever* wore Disney diapers. Suddenly we're all laughing. I know it's dumb, and maybe you had to be there to appreciate it. But it's the first time we've all sat around and laughed since the accident.

Subj: Your request
Date: 05-08
From: cre8f1@mindspring.com
To: Susan_P@aol.com

Dear Susan,

I will (try to) honor your request and not comment on any aspects of your letters where you're simply thinking out loud, as long as you know that you're free to change your mind at any time. Deal?

I don't think that the story about Barbie underwear is the kind of thing you intended that I leave alone, however. Too cute. Gregory sports a full line of superhero briefs. But be forewarned — before wearing the likes of Superman, Spiderman and Batman on his tush, Gregory was first drawn to a bunch of cuddly cartoon characters. Wendy called them wimpy, but Gregory liked having his favorite Nickelodeon characters guarding his jewels. :-) Now, however, when it comes to who graces Gregory's butt, the rule is simple: If he doesn't fight the bad guys, he doesn't get worn.

I get inflated again in two days. I'm hoping the additional saline evens me out a little. I'm pretty lopsided now; the right one's bigger and higher. Only a tad embarrassing, considering the whole world greets me by not-so-secretly checking out my chest, or lack thereof. What's that you're always saying about inquisitive minds?

Subj: The Boy
Date: 05-09
From: Susan_P@aol.com
To: cre8f1@mindspring.com

We were all doing so much better. And then yesterday happened. The boy who was driving the car that killed Paul committed suicide. It was in yesterday's paper. It didn't give the boy's name, but I'm sure it was the same one. The article quoted the parents as saying that their son "was so overwrought and racked with guilt over the death he caused while driving under the influence of alcohol . . ." Well, you can imagine the rest. And how many days ago did I question the same newspapers' reports that this was really a good kid who had simply made a mistake? And wasn't I the one who swore never to forgive him? Now I wonder how I can forgive myself for my vengeful thoughts. I feel incredibly guilty.

I'm grieving all over again. The senselessness of everything has left me feeling very hopeless. Why is life so hard Lara? When did our troubles take on such monstrous proportions? Don't answer. Don't even say anything about the suicide. Just do me a favor and tell me something funny. The next time I turn on this computer, I want to forget. If only for the three minutes or so it takes me to read your letter.

Subj: This is funny
Date: 05-11
From: cre8f1@mindspring.com
To: Susan_P@aol.com

I'm honoring your wishes and will tell you

something funny. In fact, I'll do better than that. I will make you laugh out loud. (I did.)

I saw Donahue yesterday.

He, of course, greets me as Laura. I, of course, respond as I always do, "It's Lara. Rhymes with Sarah." He laughs. I decide to be bold. "Why is it whenever you mispronounce my name and I correct you, you laugh?"

He tells me that he used to date a girl named Lara, so it must just be a mental block. OK. That's acceptable. But then the shithead says, "Let's see, since you're not having chemo . . ." I interrupt him and tell him that I *am* having chemo, that I will be having my fourth treatment on the 17th. He shakes his head and tells me that it's not in my chart! Can you believe the nerve? But get this, he *still* doesn't add it to my chart. Now, you don't need to be a rocket scientist to know what will happen at my next appointment, *again*. Write it down: Lara — Rhymes with Sarah. Chemo — Yes. *I don't understand. Is that so difficult?*

I'm angry. The guy is a reconstructive and *cosmetic* surgeon. His waiting room is packed with beautiful people in search of nose jobs, fuller lips and liposuction. I look around and very rarely recognize the signs of a breast-reconstruction patient. (The stiff arms, button-down shirt, no breasts — you know, the dead giveaways.) How many 39-year-old bilateral-mastectomy patients can he possibly have right now? And he can't remember me? Worse, he doesn't seem to be at all fazed to know that *I know* he doesn't remember me. He seems quite content, in fact, to treat me like nothing but a number. A number, BTW, with huge dollar signs in front of her!

(In case you were wondering, this is not the funny story I promised, although you may, in fact, have found it funny. I assure you, I didn't.) OK. Ranting over. Here's the funny part:

I'm suddenly voluptuous. For real. While Sandy continued her monologue about her life (the niece who loves to shop just charged $200 on Aunt Sandy's credit card, *without permission*), she also filled me up. When she'd finished, I looked down and — whoa, baby. I couldn't believe my eyes. But the best part happened last night.

Michael and I head upstairs at 9:00, my new bedtime, thanks to chemo exhaustion. Well, my bedtime is really 9:15, but we head upstairs at 9:00, and Michael rubs my back for 15 minutes until I go to sleep. Sorry, I digress.

We're in the bedroom and I take off my makeup. Then my jeans and last but not least my sweatshirt. (I stopped wearing a bra the day before I had my bilateral. There's been no reason to wear one, since there's nothing there that needs any support. So when my sweatshirt comes off — that's it. I'm buck naked.) Michael shrieks. "LARA! Look at you. Oh, my goodness, let me see." I'm twirling around, prancing actually, as I model my overinflated tissue expanders (that are pulling my skin like crazy). The smile on Michael's face is boyish. He tries to seem nonchalant as he asks, "Um, Lara, how much bigger are you going to get them?"

I try to sound sincere when I answer, "I'm not really sure yet. What do you think?"

Susan, he buys it, hook, line and sinker. He looks hopeful when he asks, "Would you consider double-D's?"

I told you that I'd make you laugh. I gently broke it to him that he'd have to be happy with basic B's. He looked disappointed but asked me if he could touch them. I couldn't feel his hands on me (but you'd already prepared me for that). Still, one thing led to another, and for the first time in months we were making love. Normal life. I'm starting to regain it, and wouldn't you know, I've got to get chemo'd again in 6 days.

Subj: LOL
Date: 05-13
From: Susan_P@aol.com
To: cre8f1@mindspring.com

Lara, you're a tease. But you're a very funny tease.

We're getting by. Or at least we think we are, and then something happens. Last night Jenny asked Artie if she should call him Daddy. Don't ask me what he said, because I ran out of the room in tears and didn't hear his response. What's more, I didn't have the strength or the guts to ask Artie how he answered. (Does that qualify *me* for dishrag status?)

Jenny and John are doing surprisingly well. Probably because Lisa's doing better. She calls each night from the hospital to say good night to them. Last night she was able to read Jenny a story over the phone. Tiny steps, but steps nonetheless.

I've started seeing a shrink. As you predicted, Paul's death has awakened a lot of feelings about my own mom's death. And having the little kids here has made me mournful of the other children Artie and I tried to have but couldn't. And then there's my bout with cancer. I've got lots of issues to discuss, which is fine, because the shrink has young kids. See, I figure that by the time she helps me put myself back together again, she'll be able to pay for at least one of her kids' college tuitions. *And graduate school.* :-) Truthfully, I don't plan to make a habit of having my head shrunk, but I decided with all the upheaval a little perspective couldn't hurt. What do you think?

Subj: My Thoughts
Date: 05-16
From: cre8f1@mindspring.com
To: Susan_P@aol.com

On 05-13 Susan_P@aol.com wrote:
>*Truthfully, I don't plan to make a habit of having*
>*my head shrunk, but I decided with all the upheaval*
>*a little perspective couldn't hurt. What do you think?*

What I think is that your shrink better be incredibly skilled at what she does, because you're a pretty together lady, and if your shrink doesn't watch herself, you'll be analyzing her and *she'll* be paying for Gabby's post-secondary education, that's what I think!

I'm getting chemo'd tomorrow. I'll be back :-)

9

Subj: Postponement
Date: 05-17
From: cre8f1@mindspring.com
To: Susan_P@aol.com

OH, SHIT, Susan. I was supposed to get a treatment today but can't. Before each treatment the nurse does a finger-stick to check my white count. It was too low for a treatment, which explains why I've been so tired and draggin' ass the last few days. Anyway, the nurse gave me an injection that's supposed to boost my count. (What's that all about?) I've been instructed to return to the scene of the crime in a week to see if my counts are high enough to qualify for treatment number four. Could we please just get on with it?

Now for the good news: Since my chemo was canceled, I was able to make a surprise appearance at Wendy's softball game. Wait a minute. I just said that was good news? I'm in worse shape than I thought. :-)

Subj: Low counts
Date: 05-18
From: Susan_P@aol.com
To: cre8f1@mindspring.com

There's a bad chemo joke that goes:

Q. What's worse than getting chemo?

A. Needing chemo and having your counts so low that you can't get it.

I told you it was a bad joke. But basically, as you've so often remarked, chemo is like poison. They give you the poison to kill cancer cells. Unfortunately, the chemo's not smart and kills good cells, too. When your white count is too low, it's too dangerous to have those toxic drugs in your system. So what they do is similar to injecting you with the antidote to those poisons. Your body then begins to get better. Soon it's well enough to — you guessed it — be poisoned again.

The same thing happened to me during my chemo. Don't be too discouraged. Try to enjoy the extra days and the beautiful spring weather. At least it's beautiful here. As promised, the April showers have resulted in glorious May flowers. Every day Jenny asks if she can pick some yet, and every day I tell her "Soon." Unfortunately, when you're a kid, "soon" takes forever. When you're an adult, it's always *too* soon. Speaking of — my birthday is on the 22nd.

Subj: Birthday
Date: 05-19
From: cre8f1@mindspring.com
To: Susan_P@aol.com

A happy, happy. How old again? 44? 45? Do you and Artie have any special plans? If so, please share. (If not, lie to me and make up something *spectacular*.) Michael and I usually go out to dinner with another couple on Saturday nights or to celebrate b'days. Because he works in the city, it's about the only chance he has to stay connected with our friends in Armonk. But we're not going out much these days. I'm too tired to even *think* about doing anything or going anywhere. But don't worry — I've decided to live vicariously through you.

Lara

Subj: Correction
Date: 05-21
From: Susan_P@aol.com
To: cre8f1@mindspring.com

Excuse me, but I'm only going to be 43 years old, thank you very much. The truth is, I'm not at all upset about getting older. I guess once you've had a brush with the alternative, getting older is great.

My birthday falls on a weeknight, so I'll be where I usually am on Monday nights: the softball field. Actually, it's not so bad. Jenny and John love to go to the games, since Gabby's teammates fawn all over them. (Teenagers love little ones. Especially when they're cute, which J&J definitely are.) Gabby loves having them

there, too. She sneaks over to the bleachers between innings and makes both kids give her
kisses for luck. Jenny thinks she's responsible for
Gabby's triple last Monday night. How can I
complain?

We, too, tend to do the out-with-friends-for-
dinner routine on Saturday nights. We also so-
cialize with one of Artie's sisters and her hubby
fairly often. (She's the one who sent me the
mammogram joke. We obviously get along really
well, but they're the only sibling/spouse combo
that we see regularly. It's not because we don't
get along with the others, though. We all just
travel in different circles.) Occasionally we live
dangerously and catch a movie after dinner. But
only when everyone's feeling energetic, which
isn't all that often, now that we're getting older.
(Ahem.) So you see, dear Lara, life in the suburbs is life in the suburbs, whether you're living
in Ohio or living in New York. As for my
birthday celebration on Saturday night — we
have reservations at my favorite Thai restaurant.
We're going with my best friend and her husband. So in the event you haven't already figured
it out, here's some free advice: If you're interested in living vicariously through another
person, find someone else — and make sure
she's considerably younger than I, very single
and *very* available. ;-)

Subj: Birthday Wishes
Date: 05-22
From: cre8f1@mindspring.com
To: Susan_P@aol.com

Dear Susan,

Happy Birthday to You. And many, many more healthy years ahead.

Amen.

I'm going back tomorrow to try to get my treatment. I'll write when I can. In the meantime, enjoy the day (and the softball game tonight). Give Gabby a kiss for me — and tell her that if she gets a hit, I'll expect a thank-you note.

Lara

Subj: Checkin' In
Date: 05-29
From: Susan_P@aol.com
To: cre8f1@mindspring.com

Uh-oh. It's been a long time, and you're still not writing. But don't worry, I'm not going anywhere. I'll be here when you're feeling better.

Susan

Subj: Awful
Date: 05-31
From: cre8f1@mindspring.com
To: Susan_P@aol.com

It took a full week this time. The doctor assures me that the side effects of the chemo are not cumulative. He's a liar. Aside from the first treatment (which, you'll recall, I endured without the anti-nausea pills), each treatment is worse than the one before. And this one is no exception. But I *am* halfway to being finished. Yeah.

I had all of my usual chemo side effects, but this time my right arm also blew up. My vein must have collapsed or something, because within hours after my treatment I'm lying in bed when my arm starts to hurt. I look to see what's wrong and notice that my arm is the size of my thigh. I call Berns, only slightly hysterical. He tells me to put cold compresses on it and to let him know if it gets worse. It doesn't get larger, but it continues to hurt, so I don't move it. (And I was doing so well with my range of motion, too.) Fortunately, the setback was only temporary. In fact, I just returned from PT, and Randi says that from now on we'll work on rebuilding my upper-body strength, since my movement is so good. Yeah again.

I won't bore you by listing all the troubles brought on by this last treatment, because I don't want to think about them. But know this: I am Super-Woman. At least that's what Berns says when I bitch to him that I'm still getting my periods even though he told me chemo would put a stop to them. That was supposed to be the upside to chemo.

My hair is a mess. It's definitely thinner, even though Michael claims it's only noticeable if you're looking closely. Wendy, who hasn't yet learned the art of diplomacy, chimed in that she could tell. But lately I've been losing more than ever, so I asked Berns if there was anything I could do. He told me to get it cut *shorter*. Strange concept, isn't it? If you want to *keep* your hair, *cut* your hair. But I'm following instructions and have an appointment tomorrow. I should be in a rip-roaring lousy mood by then, because I've got my period, my skin is still broken out, my mouth sores are stinging, and as I think I may have mentioned once or twice, I HATE THE WAY I LOOK IN SHORT HAIR. And just how are things on your end?

Subj: Half Over
Date: 06-01
From: Susan_P@aol.com
To: cre8f1@mindspring.com

Gosh, it's good to hear you bitchin' again. I'd missed all that whining and complaining that you so enjoy when you resurface after your week in chemo hell. Don't allow me to deter you from such ranting either. You're entitled. Besides, I was worse. How, you may wonder, could that possibly be? Allow me to enlighten you:

1. I was completely bald. I didn't just avoid

mirrors. I made Artie remove all that weren't permanently attached to the walls. (I made that request at some ungodly hour when I was too sick to sleep. Bless the man. He got out of bed and went from room to room, confiscating the offending objects of my reflection.)

2. I had a severe headache during one treatment. Migrainelike, I suppose. The light made me worse, so I went in search of the darkest place I could find. It turned out to be Gabby's closet. I hid under her Little Mermaid sleeping bag and refused to come out for *eight hours.*

3. I complained. Incessantly.

4. My wig itched and I didn't like to wear it, but I did so out of respect for others. (Go figure, but some people are actually uncomfortable looking at a 40-year-old woman with no hair.) Anyway, I used to threaten people (salespeople, checkout girls, bank tellers, etc.) that if they didn't do FILL IN THE BLANK I would remove my wig and make a stink. (It's amazing, but most retailers don't want some nut job in the middle of their store flipping her wig. Literally.)

Those are a mere handful of reasons that I not only give you permission to bitch, but encourage it.

Sue :-)

Subj: Shopping
Date: 06-02
From: cre8f1@mindspring.com
To: Susan_P@aol.com

Well, someone is obviously feeling better. Either that or you've just missed me so terribly much that you're overflowing with joy that I'm back.

I hope it's the latter. And the former.

I went shopping with Wendy yesterday. She needed some new short-sleeved shirts. (It's suddenly June and 80 friggin' degrees. I can hardly wait for the *real* summer to arrive. How's the weather in Canton?) Anyway — shopping. Wendy and I are close to the same size and usually shop in the same departments. We always share a dressing room. Yesterday when she finished trying on her tops, I told her to wait outside with Gregory and her dad while I "tried on." She said that it was OK, she didn't mind waiting for me. I told her that I really thought she'd be better off waiting *outside*. She repeated that it was OK, *she'd wait for me in the dressing room.* Susan, it was so obvious that she wanted *to see.* I kept thinking about all the parenting books I'd read years ago. They always said that if a child walks in and catches you naked, not to freak out. If you don't make a big deal out of it, they won't. Or at least that's the theory. (You may want to check that with your shrink next time you go.) No one wrote about what you're supposed to do if your preadolescent daughter wants to check out your (missing) breasts.

It was obvious that Wendy did not want to leave the fitting room. So I figure I had two choices: 1) force her to leave, thereby making a big deal out of it or 2) allow her to stay and act like it was no big deal. I decided to go for option number two.

She couldn't take her eyes off of me. Finally she said, "Oh, Mommy, it looks like it really hurts a lot." (Unlike Gabby, Wendy still calls me Mommy.)

I told her that it *used* to hurt a lot but not so much anymore. And that was it. *Nothing more was said,* although I'm afraid the poor kid will have nightmares. The scars are still pretty red and angry looking. And as I said, they don't look like breasts. And even if they did, there are no nipples or anything, so it's pretty disgusting. But I think it would have been worse if I had forced her out of the fitting room. Still, I guess we won't really have the definitive answer to that one until years from now when she's sitting on some shrink's couch. Speaking of, how's it going?

Lara

Subj: An update
Date: 06-04
From: Susan_P@aol.com
To: cre8f1@mindspring.com

Slowly, Lisa is making progress. She's in the rehab hospital now, and I take the kids over for at least a half hour every afternoon. She's a very brave woman. I'm not sure I'd be holding up as well. Still, I'm not sure that she's given herself permission to grieve yet. She says that it's all she can do to concentrate on getting herself well so she can take care of her kids. Funny, but it's always about the kids, isn't it? Somehow they always get us through.

You were right about the shrink. One day I decided that she wasn't doing any more for me than you do. (No insult intended.) But you're free — she's not. You're always there for me — she requires that I make an appointment. Actually, she helped me sort through a lot of issues that I needed to talk about. I don't have any neat and tidy answers, but I've got a better understanding of the questions. Omigod! I'm talking in shrinkspeak. Please forgive me.

Susan

Subj: Wendy's breasts
Date: 06-05
From: cre8f1@mindspring.com
To: Susan_P@aol.com

On 06-04 Susan_P@aol.com wrote:
>*Omigod! I'm talking in shrinkspeak. Please forgive*
>*me.*

All right. You're forgiven. Just don't let it happen again.

I'm glad the kids are able to see their mom. I'm sure that helps with their recovery, as well as Lisa's. Is she able to walk yet? Do they know how much longer before she can go home?

Shopping again with Wendy. This time for bras. The kid not only looks like Michael, she has his body type. Well, not *exactly*. It's just that she doesn't have mine. I was always little. Skinny and shapeless. In fact, my soon-to-be replacement-part breasts will be a full cup larger than where I began. (Yes, she finally admits to being only an A cup. Almost.) This is not the case with dear Wendy. She is bursting out of her bras. While we were shopping for those shirts, she may have been checking out my breasts (or lack thereof), but I was also checking out hers. They were *spilling* out the sides of her bra. Today we left the boys behind and hit the mall.

We were on our way home (after getting Wendy's breasts properly supported in 34B's), and she asks me when her breasts are going to stop growing. I tell her that I don't know. "If Daddy had a sister, maybe I could answer that question," I say. "But since Daddy didn't have a sister and you've got a Cohen body, not a Feldman body, I haven't a clue."

She waits a few seconds and asks, "Well, Mommy, what if they don't stop?"

I assure her that her breasts will stop growing — eventually. Then I'm struck by the irony. My little girl is growing up and her body is developing at the same time that my body is being destroyed — by cancer and by chemo. There's something profound here, but it's not something I want to dwell on. I just can't help but wonder how my losing my breasts while she's developing hers will affect her image of herself and her feelings about her body. It can't possibly be good.

Lara

Subj: Six weeks
Date: 06-06
From: Susan_P@aol.com
To: cre8f1@mindspring.com

It's hard to believe that it's been 6 weeks since the accident. Yes, Lisa is walking, but she's not terribly steady or very fast. But she's upright, and the doctors all assure us that she's going to be fine.

Today was John's birthday. We had a little party for him at the rehab hospital. That was really hard for Lisa. She kept crying and talking about how guilty she feels because she's not able to be with her kids. I think having John hit a milestone without her really hit her hard. She's also going through a lot of guilt feelings about why she lived and Paul died. I gave her the name of my ex-shrink. The shrink's already familiar with the story (at least from my perspective). I failed (but maybe Lisa can help) to put the good doctor's kids through college. That's mean, and I didn't intend it to be. Lisa's great. She just needs to go through the grieving process, something she's been fighting because all her focus has been on the physical healing she has to do. She just needs time.

At least Lisa hasn't lost her sense of humor. She asked me to toilet-train John while she's in the hospital, adding, "I'm no dummy. I should get something out of this. So go ahead, teach him to pee in a potty." When I told Gabby about Lisa's remarks, she was all excited and said that toilet-training John will be her first project of the summer. That's what *she* thinks. Cleaning her room will actually be her first project. She just doesn't know it yet. :-)

I didn't mean to ignore your bra-shopping saga. It's just that I've got nothing to add. You summed it all up when you said that losing your breasts while she's developing hers was ironic. I don't know about you, but I prefer my irony in books, not in life.

Subj: More saline
Date: 06-08
From: cre8f1@mindspring.com
To: Susan_P@aol.com

I got more saline today. Dr. Donahue greeted me as Laura. I gave up and simply said hello. Naturally he also told me I wasn't having chemo. That I couldn't let slip by. I told him that he was mistaken, that I am, in fact, having chemo. I then whipped out a pen (that I'd strategically placed in the pocket of my jeans before entering his exam room and removing my shirt). I asked him if he would mind making the notation that

I'm having chemo in my chart. He grunted, but he did it.

After groping me, Dr. Donahue announced that since I'm close to having enough skin to accommodate a size-B implant, I'll be coming in less often and Sandy will add less saline. "Just enough to keep the skin supple." The plan is to continue like that until my chemo treatments are over. Then we'll do the exchange. Seeing less of Dr. Donahue isn't exactly a hardship, so I'm thrilled. So was Michael when he laid eyes on my even fuller "breasts." Men!

My next chemo is the 12th — assuming my counts are high enough. Please try to write to me before I get kiboshed. Thanks.

Lara, aka Laura (Ugh!)

Subj: Funny Story
Date: 06-10
From: Susan_P@aol.com
To: cre8f1@mindspring.com

Lara,

Hope you're in a lousy mood, 'cause if you're in a good mood, my funny story won't serve to cheer you up. (How's that for warped logic?)

I'm at my support group meeting, and Sue (you remember my namesake?) is telling us about a fender bender she was involved in this week. (No, that's not the funny part. I'm not about to find an accident funny — I'm not *that* warped!)

Anyway, Sue had just picked up a friend of hers for a lunch date. (Both women had mastectomies many years ago with no reconstruction, and both wear breast forms in their bras.) According to Sue, the two of them are stopped at a red light yapping about this, that and the other when someone rear-ends them. Sue's OK and immediately asks her friend if she's hurt. Fortunately, she's fine, too. But she's hysterically screaming, "Oh, no, Sue, my booby's gone. I can't believe this — Where's my booby?" Turns out the impact of the accident caused her breast to go flying. The two women are on their hands and knees looking everywhere for this woman's breast. It ends up on the floor under the backseat. Can you stand it? Sometimes you just gotta laugh, you know?

Subj: Flying Boob
Date: 06-12
From: cre8f1@mindspring.com
To: Susan_P@aol.com

That *was* funny. Steph will be here any minute to drive me to chemo. Can't wait, she said, running her fingers through her now short (but still thinning) hair. She could already feel the nausea rising.

Guess Who

Subj: Summer break
Date: 06-15
From: Susan_P@aol.com
To: cre8f1@mindspring.com

School's out, and potty training has officially begun. He's ready. At least in the world according to Gabby. I'll let you know what happens.

I look forward to hearing from you. Five down. Only three more to go.

Subj: I quit
Date: 06-19
From: cre8f1@mindspring.com
To: Susan_P@aol.com

Dear Susan,

I called Dr. Berns. I reminded him that he told me that my chemo treatments were somewhat optional. I reminded him that he told me that after four treatments, if I thought it was god-awful, I could stop. I told him that I've suffered through five treatments and I'm stopping. He told me to slow down.

He told me that I would hate myself a year from now if I stopped. I'm not sure I agree, but I'm willing to concede that I'm awfully deep into this and may be having a wee bit of difficulty seeing the forest — you know, all those damned trees in the way!

308

Anyway, for my last three treatments Bern said he's going to eliminate the cytoxin. So I'll only have the M and the F in my CMF cocktail, making it an MF cocktail — in more ways than one! He says it's the cytoxin that's causing me such discomfort. (Discomfort? Did I mention burning in my esophagus that lasted 7 days? Nausea that's unrelenting? And I can't smoke pot. Just the thought of smoke makes me heave.) No, I think it's safe to say that I've had it. And just in case you were wondering, so have my kids. Do you have any idea how it broke my heart when little Gregory walked into my room two days after this treatment and asked, "Is this a chemo day, Mommy?" God, my 6-year-old even knows the drill. A 6-year-old shouldn't even know the word "chemo," let alone have to witness what it does to his mommy every three weeks. (Yes, Gregory's now 6. His birthday was the 17th. He and John can go celebrate. They both survived birthdays without their mommies. I know just how Lisa feels. OK, so I don't. I've got Michael and she doesn't have Paul, but you *know* what I mean. You do, don't you?)

Subj: Glad You're Back
Date: 06-19
From: Susan_P@aol.com
To: cre8f1@mindspring.com

Welcome back, Lara. I see that, as usual,

you've rejoined the living with a vengeance. I just love how you spring out of your chemo stupor in such a rage.

I think the compromise of eliminating the C is a great idea. I hope it works and you sail through your last three MF-ing treatments ;-) Look at the bright side: It couldn't make you feel any worse.

Gabby's been toilet-training John; he just doesn't know it yet. I give her absolutely no chance and have told her so. He's not ready. But Gabby wants to try. And you know Gabby.

What's with your kids? When does Wendy leave for camp?

Subj: Busy
Date: 06-22
From: cre8f1@mindspring.com
To: Susan_P@aol.com

Sorry that it took so long to get back to you, but they pick up Wendy's trunk in two days, and with the last-minute shopping, labeling and packing . . . well, I've been busy. No, I've been swamped. Besides camp stuff I also had to write two press releases. I swear, if my temple sends me info about one more event they want me to publicize, I'm gonna convert.

This treatment had me down and out for more than a week, and I was really counting on some of that time to get Wendy organized. Best-laid plans. But we're ready now. Well, I'm ready. Wendy's not so sure.

Wendy first went off to camp the summer before third grade. She was itching to water-ski, go horseback riding and play tennis — three things she could not do at day camp. (They let you play tennis, but not until 4th grade.) Anyway, call me weak, but she talked me into letting her go at the ripe old age of 7 ½. But she loved camp and has never been homesick. In fact, she keeps a calendar in her room that's numbered backward until the first day of camp. That way she can know, at a glance, exactly how many more days are left before camp starts. Now, all of a sudden, she doesn't want to go. Three guesses why (and the first two don't count).

I've reassured Wendy that I'll be fine and that I will write to her every day, just as I have every summer since she first went to camp. (Yes, I always write *every single day*. What can I say? I'm simply desperate to win that Mother of the Year award.) I told Wendy that I would even write to her on my chemo days, although it might only be a few lines. I also got the director of the camp to agree to let Wendy call home whenever she feels the need to check on me. (Yes, this requires special permission. Unlimited calling is a definite no-no at camp. The kids usually only call once during the first four weeks and once during the second four weeks. But when you have cancer, you get special dispensation, I guess.)

The bottom line? I win. She's going to camp, but she's not feeling good about it. Still, Michael and I agree that camp really is the best place for her. It's been a rotten year, and if she doesn't have to watch me go through the last three treatments . . . well then, that's the best part about the rotten year, as far as I'm concerned. I also told Wendy that the doctor is changing my chemo so I won't be as sick. And I explained that by the time she comes back, I'll be ready for my brand-new boobies. She laughed and finally gave in. (Man, she's tough.)

Gregory's going to day camp. He'll be gone from 9:00 A.M. to 5:00 P.M. I'll be a Lady of Leisure. On chemo.

Subj: Tough-Stuff
Date: 06-23
From: Susan_P@aol.com
To: cre8f1@mindspring.com

On 06-22 cre8f1@mindspring.com wrote:
>*And I explained that by the time she comes back, I'll*
>*be ready for my brand-new boobies. She laughed*
>*and finally gave in.*
>*(Man, she's tough.)*

Yes, she is. She may *look* just like her father, but she's definitely got the strength of her mother. That's important, especially for a girl. At least that's what I tell myself whenever the

Giant Mouth starts attacking. It will serve her well, I say to myself. The world can be a dangerous place for a girl who's a dishrag. :-)

Subj: Boy Joys
Date: 06-24
From: cre8f1@mindspring.com
To: Susan_P@aol.com

They picked up her trunk this morning, but Wendy doesn't leave for camp until the 27th. (Poor thing. She'll miss my treatment on July 3.) I think it's safe to say that I won't be with Michael and Gregory when they attend fireworks, which Gregory happens to love. It only took him three years to get used to the noise, but being a real boy's boy, he now thrives on everything that's loud. Fire-engine sirens are a particular favorite. Speaking of favorites, he's discovered bathroom humor. He's recently begun making "fart noises" by slipping his hand under his shirt and into his bare armpit. By flapping his arm up and down, he compresses his hand and the escaping air makes a noise — or, according to Gregory, a fart. BOYS!

Subj: Re: Boy Joys
Date: 06-25
From: Susan_P@aol.com
To: cre8f1@mindspring.com

I look at John and he's still so sweet, I just can't imagine he'll ever fart with his armpit! (I knew *just* what you were talking about, though, because one of my nephews does the same thing. Must be a boy thing, because Gabby never had the inclination. Neither did any of her friends. Wendy?)

While you're getting chemo'd on the 3rd, Lisa's scheduled to leave the rehab hospital. (Another one of life's ironies that we could do without, I suppose.) Since Lisa will certainly need some help with the kids, as well as someone to help her at home and drive her to PT three times a week, Artie and his other brothers and sisters have all chipped in and hired a woman who will live with Lisa and the kids for a month. Once the month ends, we'll reevaluate how everyone's doing and take it from there.

I'm going to miss the kids. A lot. They've been a lot of work, and the circumstances that caused them to be here have brought me no joy — trust me on that. But just having two little ones around has been wonderful. They brought such life and excitement into our home. And laughter. A *lot* of laughter. It's been great for Gabby, too. She loves being a role model to someone who hangs on her every word. In fact, Gabby came to me last week and told me that she was glad we hadn't become a foster family to that 7-year-old. She started talking about how hard it's going to be to lose Jenny and John, and *they've only been here for two months*. She said she couldn't imagine forming a loving relationship with a little girl for *two years,* saying goodbye and (probably) never seeing her again. She said she doesn't know how people do it. (FINALLY! Something we agree on.)

I reminded Gabby that while we're sure to miss Jenny and John, we're family, so they will always be a part of our lives. In fact, I've already gotten Lisa to agree to let me pick up the kids every Friday afternoon on my way home from work. We'll keep them on Saturday and drop them back off with Lisa on Sunday, after church. But the "visitation schedule" isn't entirely selfish. By having the kids stay with us over part of the weekend, Lisa will have some time to herself, and the mother's helper can take a day off. Besides, it will also be good for Jenny and John. They've formed quite an attachment to us, and the continuity of seeing us regularly is important. (So say the grief counselors, and hey, who am I to argue with the professionals?)

Subj: Wendy's Gone
Date: 06-27
From: cre8f1@mindspring.com
To: Susan_P@aol.com

We took Wendy to the camp bus today. Every year it's the same routine: As the bus pulls out of the parking lot, all the parents start clapping. (This includes Michael, who always delays going to work until he puts his darling daughter on the bus.) I'm the only one standing there waving good-bye and biting my lower lip. Every year I wear my sunglasses and hope that no one notices the tears that trickle down from behind my tinted shades. But I don't fool Wendy. Even though today was overcast, before we left the house this morning Wendy says, "Oh, *Mo-om,* don't forget your sunglasses so I won't see you crying." Smarty-pants! After five years of seeing her off, you'd think I'd get used to it. But it's still tough, knowing my little girl will be gone for *8 weeks.*

Gregory was so cute. The bus was barely out of the parking lot when he says, "Our family doesn't feel like a family now that Wendy's gone." Please. The two of them are so close, and he really misses her when she's gone. But it's good for him to be the be-all and end-all of my parental attentions for the summer. And the older he gets, the more he seems to enjoy all that undivided attention.

Later. Lara

Subj: Quiet?
Date: 06-30
From: Susan_P@aol.com
To: cre8f1@mindspring.com

With Wendy gone and Gregory at camp all day, your house must be quiet. Mine's going to be. Four days and counting — till your chemo

and till the kids leave. I'm already in a bad mood.
  Susan

Subj: Writer's Cramp
Date: 07-02
From: cre8f1@mindspring.com
To: Susan_P@aol.com

My fingers are killing me, and I can barely manage to type. For the last two hours I've been writing Wendy a week's worth of letters. I figured that even if the chemo isn't as bad as it's been, I may not feel like writing her the promised letters. So I'm stockpiling. I now have letters written, sealed and addressed, just waiting to go out. I left yellow stickies on each one, so Michael knows which one to mail on Wednesday, Thursday and so on. If I'm incapacitated from my next treatment, Wendy will never know it from my letters. Brilliant, no?

  Good luck with the kids on Monday. I know that saying good-bye is not your specialty, but like you said, Jenny and John are family — and will be a part of your lives forever.
  Lara

Subj: Saying Good-bye
Date: 07-03
From: Susan_P@aol.com
To: cre8f1@mindspring.com

We just said good-bye to the kids. And I'm sitting at my keyboard trying to keep it dry. Wouldn't that just be the perfect ending to an already miserable day? "Gee, I don't know why my computer crashed. Do you think it had anything to do with the buckets of tears it was immersed in?"

I joke, but I don't feel like laughing. I can barely even manage a smile.

Gabby is in an equally bad mood, which is why she's trying to pick a fight with me. No takers. I just walked away and sat down at the computer.

The kids were really excited to be back in their own home, though. John went waddling off to the toy room. He waddles because he still has all the bulk from the diaper between his legs. Sadly, John does not return home toilet-trained, but it is not due to a lack of effort on Gabby's part, I assure you. Still, John does go home a *bigger* boy. Once Gabby realized that toilet-training him required active participation from the little pisher (pun intended), she decided to shift her goals. She used money from her allowance to buy guardrails for the bed. Yes, John is now a little man who sleeps in a big-boy bed (with guardrails) instead of in a crib. When Gabby told Lisa, she expected her to be thrilled. But Lisa cried. Mourning another milestone she missed, I guess. But there's nothing we can do about it now.

I've got to make dinner. Write to me as soon as you're up to it.

Susan

10

Subj: Better
Date: 07-09
From: cre8f1@mindspring.com
To: Susan_P@aol.com

Hello Susan,

Six down. Two more to go. This is assuming that my veins hold up. They're irritated, scarred and in crummy shape from all the chemo, and Berns had to stick me *three times* before he found one that worked. Overall this treatment was better, but not good. The side effects were just as severe, but they didn't last as long. I can make it through two more. I think.

Actually, I was lying in bed thinking that I couldn't make it through two more. In fact, in my mind I'd already decided that I was done. (NOTE: At the time I didn't know that in two more days I'd feel better. I expected another five or more days of misery.)

Anyway, *at the exact moment* I decided to call it quits, all of a sudden the picture of the kids that I keep on the dresser started to glow. I'm not kidding. The miniblinds in my room were shut, but somehow a single ray of sunlight had managed to sneak through the slats. It illuminated the picture of the kids. Nothing else glowed — only the picture. It lasted less than a minute, and then the glowing stopped. I'm not saying that it was a sign from God or anything; you know I'm not the type. And it's not like I believe in omens either. I'm not sure what I believe in, actually. But after the glowing picture, I believe that I'll finish my treatments. I can suffer a while longer for my kids. For those kids there's very little I won't do.

Subj: Heavenly Signs?
Date: 07-10
From: Susan_P@aol.com
To: cre8f1@mindspring.com

I will not comment on your glowing photo. I don't know what I'd say. However, I must say that it sounds like it was a very good move to prewrite your daily letters to Wendy. Being compulsive does have its advantages, doesn't it? (I ask because I, of course, wouldn't know.)

Knowing that you emerge from your chemo fog in a foul mood (although this time you don't seem to be as combative as usual), I've been saving a cute little tidbit for you. I heard it where I hear all my best breast cancer stories — at my support group.

A new woman joined the group. She had a single mastectomy and reconstruction, using a tissue expander. She's the first one to join the group who used that type of reconstruction, and I was so glad you've been sharing your details with me, as it helped us "connect." (That's one of the dumbest things I've ever written. Like it's not enough that we all have breast cancer in common? That's not enough of a connection? But what I mean is, *within the group* we all look for someone whose experience mirrors our own. Or at least is knowledgeable about what we're going through, or have been through.) I'm off track. Sorry.

This woman (Nancy) just had the exchange surgery where her surgeon removed the expander and replaced it with an implant. She tells us that before the surgery she writes, "STOP! Doctor, did you remember to wash your hands?" on one of those yellow sticky notes. Before she puts on the gown she has to wear in the operating room, she sticks the sticky note onto her navel. In the operating room she's anesthetized before they take off her gown. (These men are so considerate of our modesty, aren't they?)

Anyway, Nancy wakes up from the surgery pretty groggy and in a lot of pain. After she's vomited for a few hours in recovery (love the aftereffects of anesthesia, don't you?), they move her to her (private) room. She and her hubby decided that after a mastectomy, six months of CMF (which she sailed through) and six months of saline injections, she was finally at the end of the road. They decided to celebrate the achievement by blowing big bucks on a private room. I'm off track again. Sorry.

So Nancy's husband is already in her private room when they wheel her in. They move her from the recovery-room stretcher into her hospital bed. Finally Nancy and her husband are alone. He asks her if she wants to take a peek at her new breasts. She's all wrapped in gauze and bandages, but she agrees. He opens her gown. There, stuck to her stomach, is a sticky note that reads, "Hands Washed. Nose Picked. Ready to Go."

Subj: Jealousy
Date: 07-12
From: cre8f1@mindspring.com
To: Susan_P@aol.com

I'm still roaring. Thanks for the story. I have three things to tell you:

1. I'm jealous that Donahue doesn't have a sense of humor like Nancy's doctor.

2. I'm jealous that Nancy sailed through chemo while I have to vomit my way though mine.

3. I'm jealous that she got a private room.

Number three I can do something about, and I already got Michael to agree. Still, I've noticed that I suddenly have a green cast to my eyes.

Lara

Subj: Gabby
Date: 07-14
From: Susan_P@aol.com
To: cre8f1@mindspring.com

The Giant Mouth has been in a lousy mood ever since the kids left. I'm really trying to be understanding and cut her some slack, but it's hard. I walk away and she follows behind me, haranguing on about something or another. That's how bad it's gotten. I don't even know what we're disagreeing about anymore. That's not entirely true. The latest tirade came because I refused her permission to see an R-rated movie. This led to a heated (but one-sided) debate about how mature she is, how there's nothing that could happen in an R-rated movie that she doesn't already know about (hmm?) and how provincial I am. (I was impressed. I didn't know she even knew the meaning of the word.) It's the same-old, same-old here, I guess. Maybe she'll feel better after the weekend. I pick up Jenny and John after work this Friday, remember?

Subj: A Fill-up
Date: 07-17
From: cre8f1@mindspring.com
To: Susan_P@aol.com

Hi Sue,
Laura here. You know, the one who's *not* having chemo?

As I'm sure you've already figured out, I just got back from Dr. Donahue's. You are absolutely not going to believe this one.

I'm sitting waiting for Dr. God to see me. The

waiting room is packed, and he's running late. (Something new and different, no?) Anyway, there's this girl sitting across from me in the waiting room. She's probably in her late teens. When I tell you she's gorgeous, I am not exaggerating. In fact, I don't know if I've ever seen a more beautiful woman. (Does she qualify as a woman at 18 years old?) Doesn't matter. She's wearing this leotard thing that fits her like a second skin, leaving nothing to the imagination. I'm sitting and staring, trying to imagine why she's there. (Remember, Donahue does reconstructive and *cosmetic* surgery.) Anyway, I start at the top of her head and go down each body part, silently ruling out things. I decide she couldn't possibly be there for a nose job; hers is perfect. Her breasts are also perfect — well shaped, proportioned and perky. I decide she must be there for lipo, but there's nothing extra on her tummy, thighs or tush. Then I notice she has a notebook with her. Closer inspection (which required that I put on my glasses, since I *was* sitting across the waiting room) reveals that I'm wrong. It's not a notebook — it's a *portfolio,* and it's got the imprint of a modeling agency on it. (A famous one, too. I recognized the name at the time, but thanks to chemo-brain, I can't come up with it right now.) Anyway, this girl gets called in to see Donahue. When she comes out, she goes right in to talk with his nurse. (The one who handles all of his billing and hospital bookings.) No chance of eavesdropping since they closed the door.

Clearly they didn't understand that inquisitive minds would want a full report.

While Sandy is inflating me with still more saline (I swear, one day I'm just gonna pop), I try to sound casual as I pry.

ME: Sandy, that girl who came in here before me was so beautiful, I just have to ask: What could she possibly want Dr. Donahue to fix?

S: What do you think?

ME: I really don't know. I assume it's lipo, but there wasn't an ounce of fat on her. That's why I'm asking you.

S: Breasts.

ME: WHAT! (Susan, I swear, I was in shock. I thought if it wasn't lipo, it just had to be her nose — like maybe it casts a weird shadow at photo shoots or something.) But her breasts looked perfect.

S: They are. But the modeling agency wants them bigger.

ME: The modeling agency?

S: Yeah, they send Dr. Donahue a lot of their models. The agents think that the girls will get more work with bigger breasts. And so they send them here. And they pay for it, too.

ME: What do they pay for? The office visit?

S: No, the surgery.

Sue, it was the saddest thing. You know that I've always enjoyed Sandy, and the monologues she provides at my fill-ups, but I've always thought of her as a bit of a ditz. Today changed all that. She just looked at me and at my so-called breasts and said, "They should only know."

I'm not even sure what she meant by that. But it made me sad. This whole thing makes me sad. No wonder women are freaking out when they're diagnosed with breast cancer. Look at the messages girls are getting about their breasts from the time they're teens. I can't believe that agents are sending girls out for implants so they'll have bigger boobs. No, I can believe it, but why does it have to be flaunted in front of my face? *My* face, of all people's. It makes me so angry. I mean, women are always gonna be freaked out by breast cancer, but I have to believe that if, God forbid, that beautiful young girl ever gets diagnosed, she's *really* gonna freak. Look how they've conditioned her — already.

Excuse my ranting, as you can tell, I'm PPO (pretty pissed off. Like that? I'm inventing my own Netspeak.) Thanks for listening. I feel better now that I've gotten that off my chest — or should I say off my tissue expanders? :-)

How was the weekend with Jenny and John?

Subj: Weekend
Date: 07-20
From: Susan_P@aol.com
To: cre8f1@mindspring.com

The kids are great. Jenny is starting to read. She's very bright, and she and Gabby must have spent an hour together looking at books.

Gabby's back to toilet-training John. This time she *might* stand a shot at it, too. You know how they say you have to wait until they're ready? Well, he's getting there. She showed him the little potty (which was still in our bathroom). Instead of lifting up the potty and putting it on his head like a hat (which he used to do), he sat on it. He didn't pull down his pants, and he wouldn't let Gabby remove his pants either. But he sat down. A beginning. Gabby was thrilled and is convinced his days in diapers are numbered. I wouldn't go that far, but I know better than to correct Gabby. (That's one argument avoided.)

Subj: Good Intentions
Date: 07-22
From: cre8f1@mindspring.com
To: Susan_P@aol.com

I'd like to take all of my well-meaning friends, line them up and just shoot 'em. All of them. Let me explain:

I was complaining about my upcoming treatment (the 24th) to my friend Jill. She asks which treatment it is, and I tell her that it's going to be my seventh. She says, "Seven? There's only one more to go after that. That's not so bad!"

That's not so bad? Easy for her to say. Hey. I've got an idea: If it's not so bad, then why doesn't *she* take it for me?

Subj: A List
Date: 07-23
From: Susan_P@aol.com
To: cre8f1@mindspring.com

People are well intentioned, but that doesn't mean that they don't say stupid things. In fact, my support group came up with a list of things that people say or do that we really hate. (Don't pout, but your complaint of "That's not so bad," as it applies to the number of treatments yet to go, already made our list.) Here are some others that I think will get your goat:

1. "Why do you think you got breast cancer? Are you under a lot of stress?" OR "Why do you think you got breast cancer? Do you think that eating (INSERT FOOD) had anything to do with it?"

2. Any statement that begins, "If you just think positive thoughts . . ."

3. "With reconstruction, no one will ever know."

4. All of the "Just thinks," as in: "Just think, you'll never have to worry about saggy breasts." OR "Just think, now you can become any size you want." ETC.

5. Most statements that begin with the phrase "I knew this woman . . ." and include the word "miracle" in them.

6. "Do you like your hair short?" OR "I like your hair *better* short."

7. "Some good will come of this. Things always happen for a reason."

We also hate:

8. Everyone who tries to converse with us and refuses to use the C word.

9. Doctors who insist that the side effects from chemo are not cumulative. (We all know better, don't we?)

10. Books about breast cancer with some variation of the word "prevent" in the title. (What? Breast cancer can be *prevented?* Well, then, *you* obviously did something wrong. Otherwise you never would have developed the disease. You have only yourself to blame.)

Good luck tomorrow. And just think, after this you'll only have one more to go. THAT'S NOT SO BAD!

Subj: I'm Laughing
Date: 07-24
From: cre8f1@mindspring.com
To: Susan_P@aol.com

On 07-23 Susan_P@aol.com wrote:
> *3. "With reconstruction, no one will ever know."*

That's a personal favorite. When friends say that to me, I'm always tempted to ask, "Does that include me? How 'bout Michael?"

I'm off to get chemo'd. Toodles.

Subj: Hello?
Date: 08-01
From: Susan_P@aol.com
To: cre8f1@mindspring.com

You should be back by now. Where are you? If you don't feel like a long letter, that's OK. Just let me know you're all right.

Subj: Oops
Date: 08-02
From: cre8f1@mindspring.com
To: Susan_P@aol.com

I'm sorry if you were worried. But we've been away. (I could have sworn that I told you about camp visiting weekend. Obviously not. Sorry, but blame it on chemo-head.)

I no sooner emerged from chemo-hell than we hopped into the car and drove a million hours to beautiful, sunny New Hampshire. Then, as we usually do after visiting day, we stuck around for a few days to see the sights. Just got back.

Wendy's doing great. Most of her bunkmates came back this summer, so she's surrounded by girls she knows and likes. That's good, particularly this summer. Her head counselor says that sometimes Wendy's a little weepy (mostly at night), but for the most part she's fine.

As much as she enjoys camp, on visiting day Wendy always spends most of the day in tears.

Like you, she has trouble saying good-bye, and I guess the tension of knowing that's exactly what she's going to have to do causes the waterworks. We'll be in the midst of a conversation about something or another, and she'll be laughing. Then she'll glance at her brother and burst into tears. And this is her *normal* visiting day behavior. Can you imagine what *this year's* visiting day was like? Don't. You'll only feel depressed.

Every year I write a letter to Wendy before we go up to visit her. I write things like "Daddy and I are so proud of you. You've made so many great friends at camp who obviously care a lot about you. Have you gotten taller? You look like it. In fact, you look wonderful." I try to make the letter sound like I snuck off during visiting day and composed it on the spot. Sometime during our visit I slip the letter under her pillow. I'll never forget her very first summer at camp. I was hugging her good-bye, and Wendy was crying on my shoulder. I whispered in her ear, "After I leave, go inside your bunk. I've left you a surprise under your pillow." Suddenly her focus was shifted (or her curiosity was piqued), and she was willing to let me out of her clutches. Anyway, I've been writing her letters that I leave under her pillow every summer since.

This year as we're standing on the porch of her bunk saying good-bye, she's sobbing. And this year, as you might expect, the tears are gushing uncontrollably. She's struggling to get her breathing steady, because it's obvious that she wants to say something. As she gasps for air between every word her speech is distorted. Finally, however, she is able to get it out: "Did — you — re — member — to — leave — some — thing — under my pillow?"

I immediately have second thoughts about sending her to camp. I was only trying to give her an opportunity to get away from all the illness and suffering. I wanted her to have a carefree summer, filled with only good things. I just wanted to protect her. So why do I feel like I've done something so bad?

Subj: Doing our best
Date: 08-04
From: Susan_P@aol.com
To: cre8f1@mindspring.com

On 08-02 cre8f1@mindspring.com wrote:
>*I just wanted to protect her. So why do I feel like*
>*I've done something so bad?*

We can only do our best, Lara. We can only do what we think is right. Call the camp and see how she's doing now that you've been away for a while and she's had a chance to get back into the swing of things. If they tell you she's miserable, can you bring her home? *Would* you bring her home?

I picked up Jenny and John today. He walked into our house and headed directly for the bathroom, where, without hesitation, he sat his (clothed) little bottom down on the little potty. Poor kid. He clearly knows it's something that makes Gabby happy, but there's no doubt in my mind he has no clue about why. Still, it's *fun-ny*.

Jenny has turned into a walking, breathing stereotype of the girlie-girl. No more shorts for her. Dresses only. I don't know what Lisa will do when the cold weather arrives, because there's no way that Jenny's putting on a pair of pants. I know this from experience, having raised a stubborn little girl of my own.

And that brings us to Gabby. What can I say that I haven't already said? Except that she made me so angry last night that I said to Artie, "You know, it's too bad I don't believe in hitting her, because right now I'd really love to give her a good smack across that fresh mouth of hers." And do you know what my darling husband said?

"Ah, go ahead. It'll make you feel better, and if they arrest you, I'll tell them it was the first time. You'll get by with a slap on the wrist." Gosh, it's so comforting knowing I'm married to an attorney who will keep me out of jail but won't tell his loudmouthed daughter to knock it off. Daddies and their daughters. Do me a favor. Since I don't have a boy of my own to dote on, go coddle Gregory for me. Better yet, I'll go pamper John. But first I have to get him out of the bathroom. :-)

Subj: A step ahead
Date: 08-07
From: cre8f1@mindspring.com
To: Susan_P@aol.com

I may be suffering from chemo-brain, but do you honestly think that I haven't already called the camp? You should know me better than that. (I started calling two hours after we left to make sure Wendy had calmed down. I've called every day since.) They assure me she's fine and having a blast with her bunkmates. Color war begins soon, and she always loves that. So all in all, no permanent damage was done (I hope), and we made it through the summer. My next, last and forever final treatment is on August 14. Michael asked me what I'd like to do to celebrate. I told him that simply knowing it's the last treatment is celebration enough.

Gregory has strep. Go figure. It's not the season; none of his friends have it; nonetheless, he's got it. This is a potential problem because: (A) Gregory sometimes gets very sick with strep, and (B) I can't get it. If I do, Berns says it will probably make me very sick, since my counts are low and my immune system is weak, thanks, of course, to the chemo. *If* I get it, I'll have to delay my final treatment, so Berns's best advice to me is to stay the hell away from Gregory. That should be no trouble at all, since Michael is at a seminar (i.e., boondoggle) in California until the end of the week. Nothing, absolutely nothing, is easy.

Oh, no. Gregory's vomiting.

Subj: Continued
Date: 08-07
From: cre8f1@mindspring.com
To: Susan_P@aol.com

I'm back. The last five hours have been a nightmare. I told you that Gregory sometimes gets really sick from strep. This, naturally, would be one of those times. Besides giving him a sore throat and a headache, strep sometimes makes him throw up. And this (of course) would be one of those times. This is especially bad because he's vomiting the liquid antibiotic he's taking to fight the strep infection. So I have to take him back to the pediatrician's office for a shot of a single-dose antibiotic that they can inject into his butt. (Let me tell you how much Gregory enjoys those. But it's not like we have options, you know?)

Just walking into the pediatrician's germ-infested waiting room, I hold my breath. Runny noses and coughing kids (who do *not* cover their mouths) are everywhere. I peruse the waiting room before picking out two seats that are as far away from these human germ factories as possible. We aren't sitting for two minutes before Gregory begins to vomit. Fortunately, he's got a

335

mom who travels with her own private stash of plastic Baggies. His vomiting finally stops just as my tears begin. Not the silent, trickle-down variety either. Crying tears. Noisy, look-at-me-sobbing-uncontrollably tears. I feel all eyes on me when the nurse takes us next (and out of turn). Gregory's doctor seems genuinely concerned and asks me what's wrong. I'm tempted to answer him, but where would I begin?

1. I'm run-down from chemo. Physically and emotionally. I look and feel disgusting, and I don't care that I've only lost half of my hair and that it's not noticeable to the rest of the world. It's noticeable to *me*. And I count.

2. I'm angry with my helpless son, whom I now view as the enemy, because there's no doubt in my mind that his illness will become *my* illness. It will be *his* fault that I'll have to postpone my last chemo treatment, and I was really looking forward to being done!

3. Michael is useless. I phone him for moral support. I reach him on his cell phone, *on the golf course,* ready to tee off from the 7th hole. Forget it. I truly hate him.

4. I hate Wendy, too. She's having a ball at camp, and I could really use a little help here, you know?

In fact, Susan, I think it's safe to say that as of this moment *you* are probably the only person in this world that I don't hate. But I warn you. Tread lightly. I'm on a roll.

Subj: I'm crying
Date: 08-08
From: Susan_P@aol.com
To: cre8f1@mindspring.com

I'm crying for you, Lara. But I'd be a liar if I didn't tell you that I'm laughing, too. One day you'll also look back at this and laugh. I promise. But I agree, you've given new meaning to the phrase "having a bad day." Have you thought about calling Look Good . . . Feel Better? It's a makeover program for cancer patients. And it's free. The theory is if you look better, you'll feel better. I'm quoting now from one of my support group handouts: "Volunteer cosmetologists can teach you makeup tips, either in a group or in one-on-one workshops. You'll get hands-on techniques and pointers to help minimize the skin, nail and hair problems that can go along with cancer drugs and treatments." LG . . . FB also provides free wigs, not that I'm suggesting you need a wig. Half of your hair is like a full head on anyone else. But I know that's not the point. Let's just not lose sight of what's really important here, though. Your other "half" will grow back. Promise.

Hey, if it makes you feel any better, Gregory's not the only one with an off-season ailment. I've got this cough that must be the start of a summer cold. I hate those. They take *forever* to go away. But I know better than to complain about my cough to you — of all people. I hope Gregory's feeling better. My best advice to you is to wash your hands as often as possible, and just to be on the safe side, wash them with your fingers crossed. :-)

Subj: An all-niter
Date: 08-09
From: cre8f1@mindspring.com
To: Susan_P@aol.com

On 08-08 Susan_P@aol.com wrote:
>*One day you'll also look back at this and laugh. I*
>*promise.*

Could we just add that to the list of things that people say that pisses us off?

I was up every couple of hours with Gregory. He's no longer vomiting, because he's got nothing left to come up. He's got the dry heaves, though, and screamed for me all night long. I'm exhausted.

I phoned the pediatrician's office to tell him that Gregory's still sick. The nurse said I should give him nothing for two hours, then give him a sip of clear liquid. Wait a half hour. If it stays down, give him another sip. Wait 20 minutes. If it stays down, give him another sip. Wait 10 minutes. If at any point he starts to vomit, I'm to stop, wait 2 hours and start again from the beginning of the liquid litany. So far he sips and vomits. And we return to jail.

Subj: Infestation
Date: 08-10
From: cre8f1@mindspring.com
To: Susan_P@aol.com

Gregory and I just returned from that den of infestation they call a waiting room. The pediatrician says I'm to give Gregory nothing until 2:00. Then a sip of ginger ale. Then back to that cockamamie schedule of a sip every so many minutes. I'm to call him at 4:00 and tell him how Gregory's doing. Gregory? What about *me?* I haven't slept in days, and I'm wasted.

Subj: An update
Date: 08-10
From: cre8f1@mindspring.com
To: Susan_P@aol.com

It's 4:00, and I told the nurse that Gregory's no better. She asked me if I could hold for a couple of minutes while she speaks to the doctor. When she returned to the phone, she told me that the doctor will call me back within the half hour, so I'm taking the time to squeeze in a note to you. Poor Gregory. He's so weak that he just lies on the couch. His lips are all cracked and dry, and he's still got dry heaves. It's really . . .

I'm back. The doctor just called. He says that he wants to admit Gregory to the hospital, hook him up to an IV, give him some high-dose antibiotics and hydrate him. The doc's going to meet us there in half an hour, so I'm going to pack up a few things. Can I get hysterical yet?

Subj: Poor Guy
Date: 08-10
From: Susan_P@aol.com
To: cre8f1@mindspring.com

Lara,
   I can't believe this. But I'm sure that once they get the appropriate medicine into Gregory, along with some saline, he'll be good as new. But putting an IV into that little guy . . . man, that's tough. Please give me an update ASAP. When's Michael coming home?
   Susan

Subj: Hospital?
Date: 08-11
From: Susan_P@aol.com
To: cre8f1@mindspring.com

Dear Lara,
   I'm going to assume that since you haven't written, you're staying with Gregory at the hospital. (At least I hope that they're allowing you to stay with him. It would be awfully scary for him otherwise.) Based on that assumption, by the

time you read this letter, he'll be home. And that's good.

Nothing's doing here. We're boring, which probably sounds mighty appealing to you right now. My cough never developed into a full-blown cold (yeah!), but I'm still hacking away.

Lisa's doing really well and no longer needs full-time care. She's driving again and has a baby-sitter coming in to help her out three days a week. And best of all, she has us to take the kids on the weekends. :-) Slowly but surely, normal life returns. Speaking of normal life — I'm off to work.

Sue

Subj: MIA no longer
Date: 08-12
From: cre8f1@mindspring.com
To: Susan_P@aol.com

Michael's back. He flew in on the red-eye and went directly from the airport to the hospital. He's staying with Gregory now, so I came home to toss in my laundry and get some rest. (I knew that you were concerned about my little guy, though, so I wanted to give you a quick update before I shower and snooze.)

Gregory's doing much better. In fact, he may be discharged this afternoon. Tomorrow morning, at the latest. They ran lots of tests (mostly blood) and have decided that he indeed had strep, but he also had a bad virus that was making him vomit. By the time we reached the hospital, he was so dehydrated that even his tongue was cracked. But after less than 24 hours on the saline (lots of Cohens getting lots of saline these days!), Gregory perked up considerably. I wish I could say the same for me. I slept in a chair that opened into a cot. (I'm using the term oh, so loosely.) My back is killing me, but aside from that I did OK. I told the nurses I was on chemo, which turned out to be a smart move. They were wonderful. And so accommodating. They even let me use the microwave in the nurses' station. (My friends came by with food for me and toys for Gregory.) Aside from having developed a fear of anyone who wears a white lab coat or tries to tie a tourniquet around his arm, Gregory has come through all of this like a trooper. I wish I could say the same for Gregory's mommy.

Subj: Good News
Date: 08-13
From: Susan_P@aol.com
To: cre8f1@mindspring.com

Thanks for the update about Gregory. I'm glad everything turned out to be OK. Are you still going for your treatment tomorrow?

Subj: The good ol' college try
Date: 08-14
From: cre8f1@mindspring.com
To: Susan_P@aol.com

I'm waiting for Emmy. She should be here any minute to take me for my last treatment. I hope. Actually, I'm trying not to get my hopes up. After the week I've just had (and the sleep I haven't had), I figure there's a pretty good chance that my counts will not be high enough for me to get chemo'd today. I'm prepared for the worst. And if it turns out that I'm wrong and I *do* get my last treatment . . . well, then I guess you could say that I lucked out. (There's something definitely wrong with that last sentence. Did I say that I'm lucky to be getting chemo?)

If I don't pass inspection, I'll write to you when I get back from the city. Otherwise, assume I got poisoned and I'll write when I can.

Lara

11

Subj: No Mail
Date: 08-15
From: Susan_P@aol.com
To: cre8f1@mindspring.com

Well, no news is good news. When I didn't get any mail from you, I knew that you were being chemo'd *for the very last time.* Congratulations, my friend. This is no small victory, and I hope you reconsider and take Michael up on his offer to celebrate. May I be so bold as to also suggest that a nice little piece of jewelry might also be called for (perhaps inscribed with the date of your last chemo treatment)?

Lara, think of what you've just accomplished. You have stared some of your greatest fears right in the face and you have walked away. And you walk away not only victorious but knowing that you have done everything humanly possible to give you and your family the kind of future you want. And deserve. One filled with happiness and good health.

My very best to you now and in the many, many years ahead.

You go girl,
Susan

Subj: My Future
Date: 08-16
From: cre8f1@mindspring.com
To: Susan_P@aol.com

On 08-15 Susan_P@aol.com wrote:
>*One filled with happiness and good health.*

Amen.

I'm still sick, so this will be brief, but I wanted to thank you for the beautiful wall hanging. It arrived yesterday. It's *wonderful,* and when I feel better, I'm going to hang it up in my office. (That way, whenever I'm sitting at my computer, I'll be able to look across the room and see your lovely sentiment plastered on my wall.)

I've decided that you're not a Sue *or* a Susan. You're a Suzy. As in Homemaker. I joke, but it came as such a surprise. You never told me that you did *needlepoint!* Anyway, I'm truly touched that you would take the time to make me such a special gift. When Wendy saw it, she immediately wanted to know, "What does that mean, Mommy? 'A Dishrag Nevermore.' " I told her that it was a long story. One that she won't fully appreciate until she's much older. :-)

Thank you again. You're a gem.

Love,

Lara

Subj: You're welcome
Date: 08-17
From: Susan_P@aol.com
To: cre8f1@mindspring.com

Dear Lara,

I wish I could take credit for the idea to send you a final chemo gift, but it's a rip-off. (My in-laws sent me roses when I had my last treatment.)

From the moment of my diagnosis it seemed that the entire world was involved in my life. Something was always ringing — when it wasn't the phone, it was the doorbell. In fact, there were so many deliveries of flowers and plants that we kept a stack of dollar bills by the front door so we never had to go looking for a tip for the delivery guy. But as the radiation and chemo treatments wore on, public interest waned. Our closest friends and family members remained up to the minute of course, but the more peripheral friends dropped out of the picture. (I'm not complaining. It would have been more of an intrusion than a help if they had continued with all that attention.) Anyway, by the time I had my last treatment, all the plants, flowers and phone calls had become a distant memory. And then the roses from my in-laws arrived. The flowers reminded me of how I'd felt only a few months earlier, when I was first diagnosed. I remembered how resentful and full of anger I was at being thrown into the cancer arena. But the flowers also served as a reminder of how far I'd come. I'd walked into the valley of the shadow of death. And I'd walked away. My roses lasted for a little longer than a week, but I still remember that every time I looked at them I was reminded of all I'd left behind. And all I had to look forward to. I thought about sending you flowers, too. But I wanted you to have a more permanent reminder of your walk into that same valley. And I also wanted you to have a permanent reminder of me.

Look to the future, Lara. Take this experience, along with all its pain and sickness, and don't forget it. It will make you appreciate all the things you once took for granted in this thing we call life.

I'm getting preachy. I'd better go. Write when you're feeling better.

With love from Susan

Subj: Not better yet
Date: 08-19
From: cre8f1@mindspring.com
To: Susan_P@aol.com

Still queasy, but knowing it's for the last time has helped give me the energy to get out of bed. (At least for short periods of time.)

Thanks for your letter. Preachy is fine — as long as you don't make a habit of it. :-) Actually, I've also been feeling retrospective and trying to put the last few months in a "place" I will understand, but I think I'm still too close to everything to be able to do that.

Wendy comes home on the 26th. I always do something new to her bedroom while she's away. This year I wasn't up to any big projects, so I took Gregory to one of the local arts-and-crafts stores. He painted a plaster mold of a car (such a boy!), and I painted a plaster mold of a W. I did it in red-and-white stripes, since everything in Wendy's room, from her jewelry box to her desk accessories, is either red and/or white. I've got a week to get the W hung. I think I can manage that. Just not now. I'm going back to bed; my office is spinning.

Subj: Floating away
Date: 08-21
From: Susan_P@aol.com
To: cre8f1@mindspring.com

On 08-19 cre8f1@mindspring.com wrote:
>*my office is spinning.*

Point made. (I think you meant that your "head" was spinning.)

I'm getting ready for my biannual ovarian sonogram, which is in one hour. I can't believe it's already been 6 months; didn't I just have one?

Be sure to talk to Dr. Berns about how he intends to screen you for ovarian cancer. Some oncologists only do the CA-125 blood test every 6 months/year. But I figure if the sonogram can also be used, I'm better off doing both.

The sonogram is painless but uncomfortable, because you've got to drink tons of liquid beforehand. With your teeny-tiny bladder I don't know how you'd hold everything that I've already had to drink. I'm ready to float away and still have another quart to go! And just to make matters a little interesting, I still have my cough, and every time I hack I feel like I'm going to wet my pants. This appointment could prove to be downright embarrassing.

Subj: Dry pants?
Date: 08-22
From: cre8f1@mindspring.com
To: Susan_P@aol.com

So, Susan, were you able to make it though your test yesterday with dry pants? (If not, I'm sure Gabby would allow you to sit in on little John's potty-training sessions.)

Thanks for the info about the sonogram. When Berns was giving me my last chemo, he told me that at my next appointment (which won't be until after my implants are inserted) he'll explain my follow-up exam schedule. He did say that he'll be seeing me regularly for the rest of my life (as will Dr. Goldberg). But Berns was rushed and told me not to worry about anything now; we'll discuss everything the next time he sees me.

I see Donahue tomorrow and hopefully will leave there knowing when my implant surgery will be. Till then.

Subj: All Dry
Date: 08-21
From: Susan_P@aol.com
To: cre8f1@mindspring.com

I did not wet my pants, although with every cough I was afraid that I would. Thank you so very much for your genuine concern, Lara. (And you call yourself my friend!)

My ovaries are fine (although they don't function, since, as I think I may have mentioned once or twice, chemo put me into menopause). How about you? Are you *still* menstruating, or is that a joy that only Wendy has to look forward to?

The radiologist doing the sonogram asked about my cough. (It was sort of hard to ignore. It's always worse when I lie down, and most of the test is done in that position we all know and love: flat on your back, knees in the air.) When I told her that I've had it for a month, give or take, she made me promise to see my doctor. She doesn't know that coughs that linger are the only kind of coughs I get.

So when are you getting your boobies, Lara?

Subj: Boobs
Date: 08-23
From: cre8f1@mindspring.com
To: Susan_P@aol.com

Donahue likes to wait one month after chemo ends to do the exchange. I can't wait to be finished, but Dr. God says that the results are better and my recovery will be easier if I give my body some time to bounce back a bit first. It makes sense, even though I wish we could just do it tomorrow. My last chemo was August 14, so I'm gettin' my new knockers on September 14. Or should I say that "Laura" is getting them. Remember that story you told me about the woman who put the sticky note under her gown that asked the doctor if he'd washed his hands? Well, I'm going to rip off her idea. (Hey, if you can do it with a final-chemo gift, I can do it with this.) Anyway, over my right expander/breast I'm going to put a note that says "My name is Lara." And over my left expander/breast I'm going to put a note that says "Rhymes with Sarah." If you think I'm joking, I'm not. I already told Michael about it, and he thinks I'm crazy but agrees it's funny. I figure, why not finish this thing with a good chuckle? Besides, it'll make a good story for your support group (although I'm sure that Donahue will *not* write a note back to me)!

Right after my bilateral my friend Carol came over to visit and brought me a gift. It was one of those silky two-piece numbers from Victoria's Secret. At the time I thought it was a little inappropriate, but then I figured, well, sometimes Carol is a little inappropriate. (It's why I love her.) Still, I was baffled by her choice of gifts and couldn't help but wonder if it was her idea of a joke. I certainly wasn't feeling sexy, and I didn't think I ever would again. I shoved the gift into my bottom drawer. But last night I wore it. When Michael saw me, he was salivating. I felt . . . well, I felt sexy. And I don't even have the real McCoys yet. Speaking of the real thing . . .

Donahue had Sandy give me a little more saline. (Now you know why my husband was foaming at the mouth.) Once I was fully loaded, Donahue came back into the examining room and explained the upcoming surgery. He needs to build internal "pockets" under my skin to hold the implants in place. He says there'll be lots of stitches and he'll probably do a lot of liposuction, too. (Hey, Doc, give me a break. How much liposuction can you do? I weigh 105 pounds. I somehow managed to gain weight during chemo!) I told him that it sounds pretty painful, and he said to expect "discomfort" for a few days. He said that once I'm fully healed from the surgery, he'll do my nipples. He gave me two options:

Option One: He pinches up a bit of skin from the center of each "breast" and sews around it, making a "nub." This means I'll have three-dimensional nipples that stick out just like real ones. Once the stitches are removed, the nipples and the areola (the darker, flat area around the nipple) are *tattooed.*

Option Two: Flat nipples. He just tattoos the entire thing right onto the center of the breast mound. Nothing sticks out.

I'm currently leaning toward option three. No nipples. I can't seem to get the image of a tattoo parlor, complete with beaded curtains, and a tattoo artist with a gold front tooth out of my mind. If I can ever get past such visual imagery, *maybe* I'll reconsider. But for now it looks like I'll remain a nippleless wonder. (Whenever Gregory walks into my room/bathroom and I'm naked, I wonder if I should alert him to the fact that most women don't look like this. They *don't* have scars and they *do* have nipples. But then I figure, why bother? If I say nothing, by the time he's a hormonally driven adolescent, he'll be pleasantly surprised.)

Subj: Gabby
Date: 08-24
From: Susan_P@aol.com
To: cre8f1@mindspring.com

Speaking of 'hormonally driven adolescents,' mine has a boyfriend. It's her first, so it's a very big deal. I'm trying to act like it doesn't faze me in the least, but I think I'm just as excited about it as she is. Maybe more. I know nothing about him, but I figure it doesn't matter; it's not like she's getting married. But still, *a first boyfriend.* Remember yours? I certainly remember mine. The best kisser. Ever.

Subj: Wendy Returns
Date: 08-26
From: cre8f1@mindspring.com
To: Susan_P@aol.com

I could tell you that Wendy's home, but that wouldn't be true. "Wendy's back" is more accurate. We picked her up from the bus, and she took advantage of the half-hour drive home to recap her entire summer. We walked into the house, and she ran upstairs to her bedroom. (She was obviously eager to see what I'd done to her room this summer.) She loved her striped W. I'd also hung up some shelves and picked up a new CD tower (that I spray-painted red, of course). She was thrilled. Kissed me and reached for the phone, all in the same motion. Before I knew it, I was agreeing to drive her over to her best friend's house. That's where she is now. Michael keeps giving me the hairy eyeball, because I wouldn't allow him to play golf today. "Your daughter's been away eight weeks," I said. "You should be home with her." Gregory keeps asking when he's going to see his sister, and I'm in a state of shock. Kids!

Subj: Life
Date: 08-27
From: Susan_P@aol.com
To: cre8f1@mindspring.com

LOL over Wendy's homecoming. Lara, she has a life. Get used to it, since it gets much worse. (I almost added "before it gets better." But we haven't arrived at the "better" part just yet, so I have no way of knowing if the expression is actually true.)

We took Jenny and John back home this morning — right after he peed into the potty! Gabby's walking around gloating, "See, I told you he was ready."

School starts tomorrow. Thank goodness.

Subj: School
Date: 08-29
From: cre8f1@mindspring.com
To: Susan_P@aol.com

I can't believe that school starts so early for you. It doesn't start here until after Labor Day. It's a good thing, too. We're not even close to ready. We're still in the haircut and shopping stages. Gregory has outgrown everything (again!), and Wendy's begging me to replace most of last year's wardrobe. The only thing she really needs, though, is shoes. As usual, she ruined her sneakers at camp. (Every year I tell her not to bother to bring her sneakers home, but she does, and every year I take them directly from her trunk to the trash.)

I love the fall. It's the Jewish New Year, and let me tell you, the timing couldn't be better. I'm really ready for a fresh start. And then we've got Israel coming up. (I'm giving Wendy another day or two before I start nagging her to practice the Torah portion she'll be doing in Israel.) The time is just flying by, now that I'm off of chemo and on to living my life. Speaking of . . .

I played tennis today. It felt so great just to be out there. And I didn't mind losing. Well, not as much as I used to mind losing, B.C. (That's *Before* Cancer, not *Breast* Cancer.) Something tells me that I'll be measuring a lot of my experiences B.C. How about you?

Subj: My Cough
Date: 08-30
From: Susan_P@aol.com
To: cre8f1@mindspring.com

There's no easy way to say this, so I'm not going to try to be diplomatic.

I went to see my doctor about my cough. He gave me a chest X-ray, and there's a spot. It doesn't look good. I need more tests, but he says he's pretty sure it's cancer. (At least he was honest.) I'm having a bone scan tomorrow to see if it's anywhere else. I haven't stopping crying. In fact, you'll have to excuse any typos, because

I'm crying so hard right now that I can't see the screen. Artie's on his way home from work. Then Gabby comes home. What do I say?

Subj: No
Date: 08-31
From: cre8f1@mindspring.com
To: Susan_P@aol.com

Oh, my God, Susan, I don't know what to say. You know that I'm here for you, and anything that I can do, I will. You know that. I just can't believe it. This is so unfair. I'm almost done . . . and now this. I know it's hard to be optimistic, but try. Remember, you've made it through this once before. And you can make it through again. {{{{{{ }}}}}}

Subj: Help
Date: 09-01
From: Susan_P@aol.com
To: cre8f1@mindspring.com

Lara, you once offered to do some research for me on the Internet. Could you do me a favor, please, and start reading about recurrences, new treatments, new medicines, whatever? E-mail me with anything you find that you think I can use or discuss with my doctor. I know that you're busy with school around the corner and the holidays and everything, but I really need as much information as soon as possible. I know you'll say yes because I know you. So thank you. I'm scheduled for surgery to try to remove the tumor in my lung the middle of next week. I'll try to be in touch before then, but if you don't hear from me, I know you'll understand.

Gabby's having a bad time of it. She refuses to go to school. Hopefully, after the surgery we'll get some good news and be able to have a plan of attack that we can all live with. (Pun intended.)

Subj: Research
Date: 09-03
From: cre8f1@mindspring.com
To: Susan_P@aol.com

Dear Susan,

This letter has an attached file. In it you'll find anything and everything you ever wanted to know about breast cancer recurrences, including some trials going on around the country. I will continue to research and send along anything I think you can use. Is there anything else that I can do for you? Anything?

Subj: re: Research
Date: 09-03
From: Susan_P@aol.com
To: cre8f1@mindspring.com

Lara, I knew I could count on you. But we've got miles to go before we're done, you know? So get some sleep. (I noticed that some of those files you sent me were transferred to your computer as late as 2:00 A.M.) I want your help, but I want you to get your beauty rest, too. I'm going to need you, and your e-mail. Tell me something funny. I need to laugh.

Susan

P.S. Thank you for the roses. And the card. Even though you made me cry.

Subj: A Visitor
Date: 09-03
From: cre8f1@mindspring.com
To: Susan_P@aol.com

Dearest Friend,

By the time you get this letter, I will be on a plane on my way to see you in the middle of your cornfield in Canton, Ohio. (That's my attempt to make you smile. I figure if you're smiling, you won't be mad at me for landing on your doorstep without an invitation.)

Artie knows I'm coming. Don't be mad at him for not telling you; I begged him not to. I was afraid you'd ask me not to come — and you know how I have trouble disobeying your wishes. You may not need me with you now — in fact, you probably don't — you're such a strong, courageous woman. The bravest woman I've ever *not* met. But it's time to change all that. I think we need to meet, face-to-face. You may not agree, but it's too late. I'm already en route. It's probably very selfish of me, but *I* need to be with you during this time. I know you think there's nothing that anyone can do for you now, but you're wrong. There's something you don't know about your friend Lara: I give a great foot massage!

I can't wait to see you. And all I have to say is that I sincerely hope you do *not* sound like Mickey Mouse!

I love you, my friend. And I can't wait to meet you.

With love,
Lara

EPILOGUE

Three Years Later

Subj: re: Inquisitive Minds
Date: 09-14
From: cre8f1@mindspring.com
To: theGmouth@aol.com

Dear Gabby,

Thank you so much for your letter. I was surprised to hear from you, but I'm so glad that you decided to write. I'd be happy to answer your questions, and don't worry — I won't be spilling any secrets I had with your mom. Our relationship was very open, and I don't think she ever asked me to keep anything from you or your father. Then again, we never anticipated an outcome that didn't include her.

It's nice to hear that you're getting along so well with your dad. I'm glad he was able to bring another partner into the practice so he could spend more time at home with you. Your mom is smiling down on him for that, don't you think?

Gabby, your mother loved you dearly. In fact, I know for certain it was her love for you and your dad that kept her alive that last year, long past the months her doctors predicted she'd survive. But it was because of *you*, Gabby, that she battled all the way down to her last breath.

I understand why you're upset about all the fights. And you may think they were nothing but wasted time, but your mom valued *every single day with you*, honey. Even the stormy ones. (Yes, Gabby, I'm well aware of the fact that she sometimes called you the Giant Mouth.) But that's not something you should feel guilty about. Your mouth was part of your charm, and believe it or not, she got a kick out of it. Really. Unfortunately, she was afraid that if you knew she found it funny, you wouldn't take her seriously, and then all hell would break loose. See, your mom believed in control. I don't know if she was like that before her first battle with cancer, but by the time I met her, she was clearly someone who needed to feel like she was in charge. Perhaps she felt that by being in charge she could somehow control her cancer. I don't know, but that was always my take on it.

As far as the arguments between the two of you . . . well, that's just part of what teenage girls and their moms *do*. (It's what Wendy and I do now, too — just as your mom predicted.) It's part of growing up, I guess. But my best advice to you is to try not to dwell so much on the negative things that were said and try instead (I know it's hard) to remember all the times your mom told you that she loved you. Better yet: Think of all the times that your mom said, "I love you,

Gabby," even *after* you said or did something that you're now having trouble forgiving yourself for. Because you can't go back and start over, even though I understand why you wish you could.

But you're right — you *can* go back and finish the needlepoint your mom was working on when she passed away. But only if it's something you *want* to do. If it's something that brings you comfort and makes you feel closer to your mom, then do it. If not, then don't. Only you know what makes you happy, and you shouldn't worry if I or anyone else thinks it's "morbid."

Your idea to finish your mom's needlepoint reminds me of one of her e-mails. (I wish I'd saved them all, but I didn't think of it until it was too late.) It's dated July of her last year, so it must have been about six months after your grandpa passed away. (Oh, Gabby, how is it possible that someone your age has already had so many painful losses?) In her letter your mom described how she found you one afternoon: lying on your bed, a pillow completely covering your face. You were spread-eagled on top of your comforter, *with your shoes on.* She admitted that it was unusual to see you stretched out like that (and she was about to chew you out for having your shoes on the bed), but she stopped when she realized your radio was on — and turned to a *Spanish* station. She told me that when she asked you about it, you said that you'd been upset because you were having trouble remembering

363

what your grandpa looked like. "But when she listens to Spanish music," your mom wrote, "she says that she has no trouble remembering. She can see her grandpa's face clearly. I should have told Gabby right then and there how touched I was. But I knew I'd dissolve into a puddle of tears. (She *hates* when I get all emotional.) So I just nodded and left her to listen — shoes and all. But my little señorita-in-training proved to me once again that the only thing bigger than her giant mouth is her kind and loving heart. What an unbelievably great kid!"

Gabby, your mom loved you (and your kind heart) so much, and she knew that you loved her, too. Just not always. See, your mom understood that sometimes girls really do hate their moms, because she was also a teenage girl who sometimes hated her mom. And I can confidently predict that if you're fortunate enough to have a daughter someday, she will also hate you. *Sometimes.* (Just for the record, boys are great too, but they don't fight with their moms with the same passion as teenage girls.)

And that's what it's really about, Gabby. Passion. Your mom had a great passion for life. She passed that on to you. And while she was never *happy* to have run-ins with you, on one particular occasion (when she knew she didn't have much longer) she confessed to me that she *was* glad. She said that if she had to leave her little girl in this world without her mother, she was thrilled and relieved that the girl was strong, capable and intelligent — *with a really giant mouth.*

Yes, sweetheart, in the end you provided your mom with what she truly needed: the reassurance to believe that you'd be OK. *Your mouth* gave your mom the permission she needed to let go; she didn't have to suffer anymore. But you don't have to take my word for it. In her last letter to me your mom wrote, "I couldn't have asked for a greater blessing. And if I have to leave my little girl in this world without her mother — and damn it, it looks like that's the case — I really do find comfort in knowing that Gabby knows how to speak up for herself. (See, I always said that giant mouth of hers would come in handy!) And not to pat myself on the back too hard (Better not. I'm too weak; I'd fall over), but I'm awfully proud of the job I've done raising her — and I really do find some solace in the fact that I'm leaving her at an age when she's old enough to remember me. (Poor John doesn't remember his daddy. Even Jenny has trouble.) I worry, though, that too many of Gabby's memories will be of the bad times between us and not enough of the good. Artie has promised to constantly remind her of how very much I loved her."

See, Gabby, your mom also worried that this day would come. But I think she believed that you'd look back on your relationship and blame *her* — not yourself — for the harsh words you sometimes exchanged. She was worried that you'd think she didn't love *you* enough.

I've attached a separate file that contains

copies of some of the letters your mom sent me. Maybe her words will make you feel better. (As I said, I don't have them all, but I have most of them from her last year.) I hope they help. But if you'd rather not read them, that's OK, too. If you think they'd be too painful — just delete them. (I have my own copies on disk.)

Gabby, if you'd like to write to me again, I'd *love* to hear from you. In the meantime, try not to be so hard on yourself. And oh, yes. Use that giant mouth of yours to do great things. It would make your mom so proud.

With love,
Lara

P.S. One last thing: No, absolutely not. I do not think you're strange *at all* for humming "I'm Gonna Wash That Man Right Outa My Hair" when you shower. However, if it makes you think of your mom, I don't think you should be humming it at all. I think you should be *belting* it out at the top of your lungs! That your mom would really love.

Subj: A Promise Kept
Date: 09-14
From: cre8f1@mindspring.com
To: mega10Sfan@msn.com

Dear mega10Sfan (Is that "Mega Tennis Fan?"):
I hope you don't mind that I'm answering you

directly, but since I don't read the breast cancer bulletin board on a regular basis, this is really the best way for me to communicate with you.

Every fall I skim through the postings on the board until I find someone I feel I can connect with. (Isn't that silly? We all have — or had — breast cancer. You'd think that would be enough of a connection, wouldn't you?) But I guess when I scroll through the messages, I look for someone I think I can help through her struggle with this dreadful disease, *and* I look for someone I think I can relate to. And let me tell you — *you* I can relate to! In fact, when I read your post, it reminded me so much of myself that I laughed. Don't be mad. It's just that when I first found *my* lump, I put on my *underwear* inside out. (At least you were only walking around in an inside-out *T-shirt.*)

All joking aside.

I was very sorry to read about your diagnosis. I was thrilled, however, to learn that your cancer was discovered in its early stages. That's great news, because it means that your chances of surviving this disease are *greater than 90%*. (I didn't used to like statistics, but those are the kinds of statistics that should give you great comfort.)

I also found my cancer early. I had a bilateral (double) mastectomy with reconstruction (tissue expanders/saline implants), followed by six months of chemo (CMF). That was about 3 ½ years ago. I've been healthy ever since. (Feel free to knock wood for me.)

Anyway, mega10Sfan, do you have a name? I'm Lara. (Rhymes with Sarah.) And I love to play tennis. In fact, I'm late for my doubles game. Feel free to e-mail me directly with any questions you may have. Be well.

Subj: re: A Promise Kept
Date: 09-15
From: mega10Sfan@msn.com
To: cre8f1@mindspring.com

Dear Lara,

Thank you for your letter. Yes, I have a name — I'm Bonnie. Do you mind if I ask you some questions? I've got tons, but I promise I'll keep this brief. (After all, I don't expect you to spend all day typing answers to some stranger in Iowa.) Anyway, I was wondering . . .

AFTERWORD

Peter I. Pressman, M.D.;
Surgical oncologist;
coauthor of
*Breast Cancer:
The Complete Guide*

Concern about breast cancer is high on any woman's private list of fears, even if ultimately heart disease becomes a more frequent problem and lung cancer the major cause of mortality. Yet it wasn't so long ago that breast cancer wasn't talked about in public and information was not so easily available or shared.

We have traveled far in the past three decades. Individuals have made a genuine impact on accelerating the change from radical to more conservative approaches to treatment. Duplicating the role model of AIDS activists, women have organized, enlisting corporate sponsors in walks and marches, to raise funds and awareness about the disease. The tremendous amount of medical progress in detection, treatment and prevention keeps breast cancer in the news, and by speaking out, the survivors have helped to make visible what was once a private disease.

Dear Stranger, Dearest Friend shines a light on these private matters.

The American Cancer Society estimates that one in eight women will develop a breast cancer sometime during her lifetime, but this is a *cumulative* risk, assuming all women will live into their ninth decade. So although the concern about developing cancer is generally perceived as higher than it actually is, when it does occur, it is always a terrible surprise. This book, which could only have been written by a woman who has "been there," takes you on a fact-based journey of that surprise. In this fictionalized memoir of her breast cancer experience, Laney Katz Becker literally bares all. It is a tough and realistic account, but ultimately it is a celebration of life. It is the story of how she emerges intact, spiritually, mentally and physically, having experienced a woman's worst fear.

Every woman is unique and will have her own personal response to the diagnosis and treatment of breast cancer. But "personal" does not have to mean "private." By sharing what she has learned, Laney Katz Becker provides valuable insight for *any* woman who has ever wondered how she would react to the diagnosis of a breast tumor. She covers how women deal with their husbands, partners, mothers, children, friends, the workplace — as well as the trivia of everyday life.

As a doctor whose practice is devoted to treating women with breast cancer and promoting early detection, I know that nothing is more important than communication and dialogue. These are the only ways a woman can effectively and properly monitor her diagnosis, her treatment and her lifelong care. *Dear Stranger, Dearest Friend* contains valuable information and messages about these issues. It is up-to-date, recognizing the important and visible role that the computer and e-mail technology now play in providing women with the facts they need to make informed decisions. It contains information I would encourage all women to discuss with their physicians.

ACKNOWLEDGMENTS

This is a work of fiction; however, it is based very closely on my own experience with breast cancer. Although there was no single "Susan" in my life, I met many courageous women through the Internet bulletin boards. They helped inspire this character and this story.

A first novel requires special handling, so I want to thank my editor, Carrie Feron, for her kid gloves. Thank you also to my agent, Anne Hawkins, of John Hawkins and Associates. We've taken our own journey from stranger to dearest friend and I want you to know that I've enjoyed every step. I especially value your insight and experience, and I always look forward to your (funny) e-mails.

I owe a huge thank-you to my internist and oncologist, Dr. Bernard M. Kruger, Lenox Hill Hospital, who first saved my life and years later read through this manuscript to ensure its medical accuracy. I now know that his thoroughness and meticulous attention to detail are not limited to the exceptional care he gives his patients.

I am blessed to have many friends with kind hearts and compassionate souls. My personal struggle with breast cancer would have been a much more difficult battle if not for the support of my dedicated friends, who doubled as my designated drivers. They include Stephanie Garry, Lucia Roberta, Randi Kapelman, Wendy Ganz, Robin Elkin, Charlie Elkin, Emily Gilbert, Caren Raylesberg, Bonnie Loewenstein, Adrienne Simpson, Toby Miller, Deenie Ruzow, Jill Thau, Susan Weiss, Wendy Sklar and Barbara Goodman. Other dedicated drivers who deserve thanks for carting my kids include Nan Mason, Dona Schaitkin, Gayle Balsky, Nancy Bayer, Monica Powtan and Caryn Tanner. To the many other friends and acquaintances who visited, supplied us with meals, ran errands, watched the kids, sent beautiful notes and flowers and kept our phone ringing, what can I say except thank you for your outpouring of kindness. The journey traveled was easier because of you. Rabbi David E. Greenberg was also a strong supporter, providing his spiritual and personal guidance (and phone calls that always seemed to come at just the right time). Beth Breakstone was patient and helped me decipher the medical jargon in my pathology reports. She also gave me permission to whine. Thanks, Beth. My sister Sheila Rothstein deserves a separate thank-you. She was my own personal Flo, and her selflessness brought us closer together.

My parents, Jan and Art Katz, and grandparents, Ruth and George Walker, have always been among my biggest fans, but it was my youngest sister, Marci Ungar, and my husband, Harold, who gave me the gentle nudge — what the heck, it was a shove — that I needed to pursue this novel. Harold's "push" was nothing new to me. He almost single-handedly propelled me through one chemo treatment after another, assuring me that I could do it, even when I began to believe otherwise. All of life's challenges are made easier because he is my partner.

My thank-you list would not be complete without naming my children, Whitney and Mitchell. They kept me going then; they keep me going today. And Whitney, thank you for allowing me to use your poem, "I Remember." I've always told you that I love your poetry, and now maybe you'll believe that I wasn't "just saying that."

BREAST CANCER RESOURCES

Bulletin/Message Boards

America Online: Enter keyword: *healthtalk.* Also on AOL: Enter keyword: *thrivemedical* (click *breast cancer,* then click *post).*
Compuserve: In the Health Professional Section, select *Cancer Forum* or *GO CANCER* (type *CANCER,* click *Go).*
Prodigy: Go to *help.prodigy.net.* In the search box, type *Bulletin Cancer.*

On-Line Breast Cancer Centers
(Most also include message boards.)

SusanLoveMD.com
www.susanlovemd.com
Avon Breast Cancer Crusade
www.avoncrusade.com
Gillette Women's Cancer Connection
www.gillettecancerconnect.org
Lifetime Online
www.lifetimetv.com/health/breast cancer
Be sure to sign up for a free monthly e-mail reminder to perform breast self-exams.
allHealth.com
Www.allhealth.com/bcc

Just Us
members.aol.com/gmcmullen/justhome.htm
Thriveonline
www.thriveonline.com/health/herhealth/med-ical/breastcenter. index.html
Women.com
www.women.com/health/breastcancer
WebMD
my.webmd.com/condition_center/brc
drkoop.com
www.drkoop.com/conditions/breast_cancer

On-Line Support

Cancer Care Online Support Group
www.cancercare.org/services/online3.htm
LISZT, the mailing list directory
liszt.liszt.com/select/Health/Cancer
Select *subcategories: Breast Cancer* for Internet discussion groups, mailing lists, newgroups and IRC chats.
Breast Cancer Newsgroup (on AOL only)
Enter keyword: *newsgroups,* select *Search All Newsgroups,* type alt.support.cancer.breast

On-Line Information

Breast Cancer Newsletter
www.breastcancer.net
Get the latest news delivered directly to your computer. Subscriptions are free and sent to over

5,000 breast cancer survivors, health professionals and legislators.

Association of Cancer Online Resources (ACOR)
www.acor.org

CancerLinks
www.cancerlinks.org/breast.html

FDA-Certified Mammography Facilities
(in your area)
www.fda.gov/cdrh/mammography/fda_certified_mammography_faci.html

Nancy Oster's Sample of Breast Cancer Resources on the Net
www.silcom.com/~noster/bcinfo.html

Oncolink
www.oncolink.upenn.edu

Medscape
www.medscape.com

Mayo Clinic Health Oasis
www.mayohealth.org

MAMM Magazine
www.mamm.com

Internet Shopping

Becoming, Inc.
www.becoming.com/home.asp
A catalog of lingerie, clothing and headwear for breast cancer patients.

Wear It Now
www.pinkribbonjewelry.com

Jewelry and accessories. Part of each purchase is donated to research.

Breast Cancer Organizations

American Cancer Society
1599 Clifton Road N.E.
Atlanta, GA 30329-4251
800-ACS-2345
www.cancer.org
Its Cancer Resource Center can be found at:
www3.cancer.org/cancerinfo/load_cont.asp?ct-5

The Breast Cancer Research Foundation
654 Madison Avenue, Suite 1209
New York, NY 10021
646-497-2600
www.bcrfcure.org

Look Good . . . Feel Better
CTFA Foundation
1101 17th Street, NW, Suite 300
Washington, D.C. 20036-4702
800-395-LOOK
www.lookgoodfeelbetter.org
A national partnership of the Cosmetic, Toiletry and Fragrance Assocation, the American Cancer Society and the National Cosmetology Association that provides free makeovers to cancer patients.

National Alliance of Breast Cancer Organizations (NABCO)
9 East 37th Street, 10th floor
New York, NY 10016
888-80-NABCO
www.nabco.org

National Breast Cancer Coalition
1707 L Street, NW, Suite 1060
Washington, D.C. 20036
800-622-2838
www.natlbcc.org

National Cancer Institute
Office of Cancer Communications
NCI/Building 31, Room 10 A 18
Bethesda, MD 20205
800-4-CANCER
www.nci.nih.gov

SHARE
1501 Broadway, Suite 1720
New York, NY 10036
212-382-2111
www.sharecancersupport.org

Susan G. Komen Breast Cancer Foundation
5005 LBJ Freeway, Suite 250
Dallas, TX 75244
800-IM-AWARE (Helpline)
www.komen.org
Information about the foundation's Race for the

Cure: 888-603-RACE

Y-Me
212 West Van Buren Street, 5th floor
Chicago, IL 60607-3908
800-221-2141
www.y-me.org

Williston Park Public Library

LARGE TYPE

FIC
BECKER, LANEY KATZ
DEAR STRANGER, DEAREST FRIEND

07/04   P26.95

WITHDRAWN